Ethel Carnie Holdsworth

General Belinda

The Ethel Carnie Holdsworth Series

General Editor: Nicola Wilson

Roger Smalley is a retired teacher whose publications include Breaking the Bonds of Capitalism: the political vision of a Lancashire mill girl (Lancaster University, 2014). He is currently working on a history of the Clitheroe parliamentary constituency which relates Ethel Carnie Holdsworth's activities to the wider tradition of dissent in north Lancashire.

Nicola Wilson is a lecturer in English at the University of Reading. She is the author of *Home in British Working-Class Fiction* (Ashgate, 2015) and has published on working-class writing in *Key Words; The Oxford History of the Novel in English, vol. 7* (2015); and *A History of British Working Class Literature* (2016). In 2011 she introduced and edited Ethel Carnie Holdsworth's 1925 novel, *This Slavery* (Trent).

Ethel Carnie Holdsworth

General Belinda

WITH AN INTRODUCTION BY ROGER SMALLEY

Edited by Nicola Wilson

Kennedy & Boyd

2019

Kennedy & Boyd
an imprint of
Zeticula Ltd
Unit 13,
196 Rose Street,
Edinburgh,
EH2 4AT

http://www.kennedyandboyd.co.uk
admin@kennedyandboyd.co.uk

First published in 1924 by Herbert Jenkins.

First published in this edition 2019

Note on the text

The copy-text for this new edition is Herbert Jenkins' Popular Edition, sold at two shillings. The text of the current edition, set in Bookman, follows that of the original text as closely as possible, retaining older forms of English usage and grammar.

Ethel Carnie Holdsworth published under her maiden name (Ethel Carnie) and with various versions of her married name.

General Belinda was originally published as by Ethel Holdsworth.

Front cover image: Ethel Carnie Holdsworth.
Reproduced with kind permission from Helen Brown.

ISBN 978-1-84921-136-9

Acknowledgements

Nicola Wilson: I would like to thank Roger Smalley for the continued generosity he has shown me in sharing his knowledge on Ethel Carnie Holdsworth. I would also like to acknowledge my 'Class Matters' students for the enthusiasm with which they have approached Ethel's writing, and to thank in particular Ffion Evans for her careful copy-editing on this new edition.

Contents

Acknowledgements v
Contents vii
Introduction *by Roger Smalley* ix
Suggestions for Further Reading xxxiv

General Belinda 1

INTRODUCTION

by

Roger Smalley

By 1924, the year in which *General Belinda* was published, Ethel Carnie Holdsworth had established her propaganda style. An important part of it was the use of fiction as a vehicle for her revolutionary political vision. She believed that by presenting her views on the evils of capitalism within the structure of popular romances she could make her readers think about the causes of their social and economic distress, and create activists in the class struggle.

There was nothing new in this. William Godwin, for example, had sought a wider audience for his *Enquiry Concerning Political Justice* (1793) by working his radical philosophy into a novel, *Caleb Williams*, which was published the following year. George Bernard Shaw and William Morris, with whose work Ethel was familiar, promoted socialism through a similar covert literary strategy, and a near contemporary, Phyllis Bottome (1882-1963), made a critical fictional response to the Great War in *A Servant of Reality* (1919). But these were writers in easy circumstances with establishment links; Ethel Carnie was from a family of Lancashire factory workers with a formal education that ended when she entered the mill at the age of 13 in 1899. How did she transcend these disadvantages and become a pioneer of the use of fiction in the cause of women and the working class?

She was born in Oswaldtwistle, one of the smaller east Lancashire mill towns, on New Year's Day 1886, but by 1892 the Carnie family had settled in Great Harwood. It was a move of some significance, for it gave Ethel access not only to thriving branches of emerging political parties of the Left – the Social Democratic Federation in Burnley and the Independent Labour Party in Blackburn – but to the local Co-operative Society Library. It opened three evenings a week for book loans, and four for the use of a newsroom that carried newspapers and periodicals, and had an impressive reference collection. Here Ethel found standard works of literature, history, politics, trade unionism and co-operation, reading whenever she could in the autodidact tradition at home and in the mill.[1] The Great Harwood Co-operative Society Library played a crucial role in her intellectual development and shaped the concerns that dominated her life subsequently.

Ethel's writing had been praised at school and she wrote poetry as a teenager that was stimulated, she claimed, by the rhythmic sounds made by weaving machines.[2] It came to the attention of the Blackburn Author's Society which sponsored the publication of her first collection, *Rhymes from the Factory*, in 1907. Two editions soon sold out and earned Ethel consideration as a distinctive new voice amongst working-class poets, one which avoided stereotyped forms of thought and showed warm sympathy for the suffering of the poor.[3] Further volumes of verse followed – *Songs of a Factory Girl* (1911) and *Voices of Womanhood* (1914) – but poetry was gradually superseded as her preferred medium of expression by journalism and prose fiction.

Clarion was the most successful of the new papers created to promote the political Left. It was started in Manchester by Robert Blatchford in 1891, with sales in excess of 95,000 by 1908, the year he offered Ethel Carnie a job. He asked her to move to London to write for *The Woman Worker*, which he had recently launched to campaign specifically for the social and political equality of women. For 25 weekly issues she wrote about the hypocrisy of the ruling class, women's rights, universal brotherhood, and socialist unity, and commented on major issues of the day such as Lloyd George's 'People's Budget' and suffragette agitation for the vote. But Ethel's strident tone shocked Blatchford and he soon sacked her. By 1910 he was suffering from ptomaine poisoning, had lost much of his radical zeal, and resented Ethel's criticism of his call for a robust response to German militarism.[4]

Although it ended acrimoniously, Ethel valued her experience as a Blatchford journalist, for it had given her the belief that she could improve the lives of the oppressed through writing. Her essays and shorter prose had been accepted by co-operative or socialist magazines since 1906, and in 1913 Methuen published her novel *Miss Nobody*, recently re-issued by Kennedy and Boyd to mark its centenary. It was the first of ten,[5] which together represent a major aspect of her attack on capitalism in its various forms. *General Belinda*, the sixth in the sequence, focuses on the exploitation of domestic servants, but several of its chapters deal with war.

Ethel Carnie married Alfred Holdsworth in April 1915. The following month the *Blackburn Weekly Telegraph* published a letter in which Ethel complained that her name was being fraudulently used as the author of pro-war material. She made it clear that she was opposed unequivocally to both the war and the prospect of conscription. Her critical campaign against government policy was continued with great vigour through the British Citizen Party, an organisation which played a major role in the peace movement in 1915 and 1916, holding anti-conscription rallies in many Lancashire towns. The one held at Salem School Hall in Nelson attracted an audience of over a thousand, and Ethel took the chair. When a pro-war contingent stormed the platform she jumped on to the piano, appealed for calm, and led the singing of 'The Red Flag'. Nevertheless it was an hour before the stewards restored order and the meeting could continue. Even in a town as sympathetic to dissent as Nelson, the British Citizen Party faced hostility from the authorities, for it received a bill from the Salem School trustees for the damage caused and some municipal councillors called for it to be denied the use of public venues in future.

The incident was raised in the House of Commons by Philip Snowden, the MP for Blackburn, but the government dismissed it as a minor disturbance. Such an attitude was likely to provoke further intimidation, and when a military band prevented some of those trying to get in to its next meeting the British Citizen Party cancelled the rest of its schedule.[6]

Alfred Holdsworth was a conscientious objector. His application for exemption from military service after the introduction of conscription in March 1916 was turned down by his local tribunal, but he accepted a non-combatant role as a teacher of typing and was sent to the Western Front in 1917. Ethel turned her husband's departure into a propaganda opportunity by walking to the railway station with him waving a red flag, but Alfred's enlistment caused Ethel considerable hardship, for their daughter Margaret had been born in the spring of 1916 and the serviceman's wife's allowance was all she had to live on. She tried to supplement it by writing. *Iron Horses*, a story about the dreadful working conditions in Lancashire cotton mills, was serialised in *The Co-operative News*, and the *Weekly Dispatch* commissioned an article on 'Women and the War'. Ethel used it to challenge the glorification of war peddled by many papers, and to reject the role of patient acceptance recommended by the government. She demanded recognition of the suffering that separation from loved ones caused, and gave vivid examples of it from what she saw around her: women who took on extra work so that they could send food parcels to under-fed soldiers; women who had received no army pay for six weeks despite soaring prices; women who were psychologically damaged by fear of invasion or the taunts of neighbours if their men had not joined up; and women with revolution in their eyes queuing to buy fish tails while duchesses urged them to economise.[7]

The article provides an intriguing glimpse into the effects of war but it generated little income, and when Alfred left for France Ethel took cheap lodgings with the Simm family in Blackburn. Her second novel, *Helen of Four Gates*, was completed there. It was published in 1917 but she can have received little for it at the time, as Arthur Simm considered her to have been destitute in 1918 when she was informed that her husband had been killed. For over a year Ethel thought she was a widow, but when the war ended Alfred was discovered alive in a British hospital having been transferred there from a German prison, and he was reunited with his family in 1919. Ethel fictionalised these experiences in the last chapters of *General Belinda*, with Alfred re-cast as Belinda's nephew Reggie. She represents him, along with the conscripts of all contending armies, as the victim of a capitalist inspired conflict which pitted worker against worker for private profit. She mourned for them all – 'They're all somebody's lads', as Belinda says in this novel (182).

However the principal target of *General Belinda* is domestic service. In 1911 eleven per cent of the female population of England and Wales was 'in service'. The figure was not so high in Lancashire where factory owners depended heavily on women workers, but the return of soldiers after 1918 and the slump in the cotton industry after 1920 changed that. It is not known whether Ethel Carnie was ever a domestic servant, but another Oswaldtwistle mill girl, Margaret McCarthy, was. She became a Young Communist League activist, and accused the municipal authorities of trying to solve the problem of unemployment amongst women by forcing them into service. The motive, she claimed, was not concern for the welfare of redundant weavers but a desire to get them off the register so that they could not claim the 'out of work donation'.[8]

The Women's Industrial Council, an independent philanthropic organisation founded in 1894 to try to improve working conditions for women, investigated domestic service in 1916. Its report suggests that there was widespread resentment amongst those so employed because of the long hours, cramped accommodation, limited access to bathrooms, loss of control over how free time could be used, and in the case of 'generals' – that is maids-of-all-work who were usually the only servants in their employers' households – loneliness. The Council recommended that better accommodation be provided, set hours with some free time off each day established, the maid's cap abolished because it was seen as a badge of slavery, and a system of instruction set up to create greater efficiency and enhance the status of the job.[9]

The Women's Industrial Council's report was among the documents relevant to the condition of the working class which were held in the Great Harwood Co-operative Society Library, and Ethel studied them closely. The plot of *The Taming of Nan* (1920), for example, turns on the application of the Workmen's Compensation Acts of 1897 and 1906 to the industrial injury which incapacitates one of the main characters. But if Ethel was familiar with the findings of the Women's Industrial Council, her interest in domestic servants was differently motivated. The Council was dominated by middle-class women anxious to maintain a source of labour on which they relied, whereas Ethel was concerned about the servants themselves. She had been writing about their difficulties since the late 1910s, and by 1922 three stories featuring Belinda Higgins, an unemployed weaver driven by necessity to accept work as a 'general', had appeared in *The Wheatsheaf.*[10] Belinda is a most appealing heroine. Her competence, generosity, honesty and reliability gives authority to the proletarian voice, and conviction to the Marxist analysis it offers.

In the novel Belinda is placed in a variety of situations from which she can criticise capitalist values. She wonders 'that people could for shame spend so much on robes and furs when so many poor creatures were up and down the world half naked' (101). It is an instance of selfish and unnecessary consumerism that she calls 'pots and pans worship' (148), symptomatic of the greed capitalism encourages, and morally bankrupt in her view because it makes drones of the rich. However the author's main purpose is to expose a system which her contemporaries commonly justified by representing the master as a benevolent parent and the servant as a fortunate child in receipt of useful training. Ethel characterises domestic service, rather, as the legalised exploitation of vulnerable girls, often involving sexual harassment. It represents an outmoded and oppressive class structure which she seeks to dismantle. She accepts that voluntary abolition, or the extension of union protection, are unlikely, so she proposes a radical interim alternative – let masters and servants eat together in symbolic recognition of their equality.

Readers may smile at the impracticality of such a contract. It might work in fiction when a spirited Belinda Higgins is the protagonist, but in real life, where the struggle is between tyrannical employers and timid employees, it will not. Nevertheless Ethel stuck to her belief that literature had the potential to create change. Great emphasis is placed on it in *General Belinda.* A fortune teller asks for payment not in cash but with a poem that might touch the hearts of her uncaring children, and it does:

'After a week she received a card. The old woman's message was brief. It merely said, "It has worked", as if Belinda's song was a new purgative'.(131)

And when Belinda reads in Plato's *Republic* that 'there can be no mediocrity with sincerity... But the recan be no greatness without it', she believes she has discovered a rare truth.

The writers Ethel valued for their fictional support of her political vision are most readily identified from *General Belinda.* The text includes reference to Shakespeare, Blake, Burns, Coleridge, Lamb, Ruskin, Hugo, Longfellow, Twain, Maeterlink, Hardy and Wells. Although it is known that she read the Brontës,[10] and that the novels of Jane Austen, Elizabeth Gaskell and George Eliot were in the Great Harwood Co-operative Society Library, women do not feature in the list. They were not included either when the Holdsworths advertised a plan for the distribution of books amongst the working class in *The Clear Light*, a monthly newspaper they had started in 1923. Readers were asked to donate their unwanted volumes, with striking agricultural workers in Norfolk earmarked as the first recipients. *The Clear Light* requested the same authors that *General Belinda* recommends, but with the addition of Crabbe, Shelley, Scott and Dickens. Meredith was excluded as too subtle, and Marx as too difficult. Classics of fiction which carried clear humanitarian messages were considered more stimulating and effective teachers than volumes of political theory. The absence of women from a list drawn up by a feminist may seem contradictory, but it reflects the dominant position held by men in the production of writing that Ethel Carnie Holdsworth thought capable of leading the oppressed out of domestic servitude and other forms of capitalist bondage. It was a dominance that she challenged not only in *General Belinda*, but in all of her novels.

The mid 1920s was Ethel's high water mark, the period when her activism seemed boundless. It was stimulated by events which suggested that capitalism was in its death throes – the collapse of Tsarism in Russia, the advance of socialism throughout Europe, and the election of the first Labour government in Britain in the year *General Belinda* was published. Ethel had declared her support for the Communist Party of Great Britain when it was established in 1920, and gave leading roles to communists in her next novel, *This Slavery* (1925). The Holdsworths were amongst the first to recognise the danger posed by the growing admiration for Mussolini in Britain, and in 1924 *The Clear Light* became the mouthpiece of the National Union for combating Fascism. That year Ethel also joined the anarchists Charlotte Wilson and Emma Goldman in a campaign to free the Bolshevik dissidents who had been imprisoned in Arctic gulags after the Kronstadt rising was suppressed by the Red Army.

But that was as near as she got to a New Dawn, for by 1926 her dream of a socialist utopia had evaporated. *The Clear Light* had consumed all she had earned as a writer, and had to close, the Labour government had fallen, and her marriage had broken down. Her wish to change the world remained strong however, and she continued the fight against capitalism for another decade. Further novels, journalism and poetry were written, and she joined the Labour Party and the committee of the Workers' Theatre, but no evidence of composition or other forms of political involvement after 1936 have been discovered.

The Kennedy and Boyd reissues of Ethel Carnie Holdsworth's fiction will help to re-establish her reputation and give her a proper place in the literary protest tradition to which she made such an important and distinctive contribution. A growing awareness of her writing has led to her recent identification as the early twentieth century's only working-class woman poet, and *Miss Nobody* is now considered to be the earliest published novel written by a working-class woman. [12] But accurate as these judgements may be, they tend to represent the author as a curiosity worth remembering mainly because she was first in the field. Ethel's achievement was far greater than this, for her novels circulated widely and both carrier-story and covert message were effective. *General Belinda* was dedicated to Percy Redfern because he had convinced Ethel that her work was helping the reading public to cope with the problems of the times. It was encouragement like this that sustained her effort over 30 years, during which her propaganda style was deployed in the service of the oppressed.

Like Percy, today's readers should value *General Belinda* not only for its splendid central character, but for its passionate call for a more humane society which excludes war and empowers women. These are noble objectives which should still resonate in a world where international conflict, misogyny and irresponsible capitalism are common.

REFERENCES

1 *Women's Outlook*, Sept. 1920, 295.
2 Ethel Carnie, *Rhymes from the Factory* (Denham and Co., Blackburn, 1907) pp. vii–viii.
3 *Blackburn Times*, 20 Feb. 1909, 7.

4 Albert Lyons, *Robert Blatchford. The Sketch of a Personality* (1910; London: Clarendon, 1951), p. 174.
5 The 'ten' excludes *Iron Horses* (1915) and *All On Her Own* (1929) which are better described as novellas; *Down Poverty Street* (1922) which has been lost; and *The Woman in the Red Shroud* (1925) which was not completed.
6 *Colne and Nelson Times*, 3 Dec. 1915, 4.
7 *The Straits Times* (Singapore), 28 Sept. 1917, 12.
8 Margaret McCarthy, *Generation in Revolt* (London: Heinemann, 1953), p. 151.
9 Christina Violet Butler, *Domestic Service: An Enquiry by The Women's Industrial Council* (London: Bell and Sons, 1916), *passim.*
10 *The Wheatsheaf*, July 1920, 101-2; September 1921, 133-34; April 1922, 53-4.
11 *Woman Worker*, 20 Oct. 1909, 367.
12 Jane Dowson and Alice Entwistle (eds), *A History of Twentieth-Century British Women's Poetry* (Cambridge: CUP, 2005), p. 57. Florence Boos (ed.), *Working-Class Women Poets in Victorian Britain* (Toronto: Broadway Press, 2008), p. 42.

Suggestions for General Reading

Ashraf, Phyllis Mary, *Introduction to Working Class Literature in Great Britain. Part II: Prose* (Berlin: Ministerium, 1979).

Black, Clementina (ed.), *Married Women's Work* (1915; London: Virago, 1983).

Bruley, Sue, 'Women and Communism: A Case Study of the Lancashire Weavers in the Depression', in *Opening the Books: Essays on the Cultural History of British Communism*, eds. Geoff Andrews, Nina Fishman and Kevin Morgan (London: Pluto, 1995), pp. 64-82.

Caedel, Martin, *Semi-Detached Idealists. The British Peace Movement and International Relations 1854-1945* (Oxford: OUP, 2000).

Carnie, Ethel, *Miss Nobody* (Kilkerran: Kennedy and Boyd, 2013).

Holdsworth, Ethel Carnie, *Helen of Four Gates* (Edinburgh, Kennedy & Boyd, 2016).

Holdsworth, Ethel Carnie, *This Slavery* (Nottingham: Trent Editions, 2011).

Frow, Eddie and Ruth Frow, 'Ethel Carnie: Writer, Feminist and Socialist', in *The Rise of Socialist Fiction 1880-1914*, ed. by H. Gustav Klaus (Brighton: Harvester, 1987), pp. 251-65.

Hannam, June, and Karen Hunt, *Socialist Women: Britain 1880s to 1920s* (London: Routledge, 2002).

Hilliard, Christopher, *To Exercise Our Talents. The Democratisation of Writing in Britain* (London: Harvard UP, 2006).

Liddington, Jill, *The Long Road to Greenham: Feminism and Anti-Militarism in Britain since 1820* (London: Virago, 1989).

Martin, Jane, *Making Socialists. Mary Bridges Adams and the fight for knowledge and power, 1855-1939* (Manchester: MUP, 2010).
Martin, Jane and Joyce Goodman, *Women and Education 1800-1980* (Basingstoke: Palgrave Macmillan, 2004).
McCarthy, Margaret, *Generation in Revolt* (London: Heinemann, 1953).
Pearce, Cyril, *Comrades in Conscience. The story of an English community's opposition to the Great War* (London: Francis Boutle, 2014).
Roberts, Elizabeth, *A Woman's Place: An Oral History of Working-Class Women 1890-1940* (Oxford: Blackwell, 1984).
Rose, Jonathan, *The Intellectual Life of the British Working Classes* (New Haven and London: Yale UP, 2001).
Schwartz, Laura, "What We Feel is Needed is a Union for Domestics Such as the Miners Have": The Domestic Workers' Union of Great Britain and Ireland 1908-1914', *Twentieth-Century British History* 25:2 (2014): 173-192.
Smalley, Roger, *Breaking the Bonds of Capitalism: the political vision of a Lancashire mill girl. The life and work of Ethel Carnie Holdsworth 1886-1962* (Lancaster: Lancaster UP, 2014).
Summers, Anne, 'Public Functions, Private Premises: Female Professional Identity and the Domestic Service Paradigm in Britain, c. 1850 – 1930', in *Borderlines: Genders and Identities in War and Peace, 1870-1930*, ed. by Billie Melman (London: Routledge, 1998). pp. 353-76.
Tebbutt, Melanie, *Women's Talk: A social history of 'gossip' in working-class neighbourhoods 1880-1960* (Aldershot: Scolar, 1995).
Todd, Selina, *Young Women, Work, and Family in England, 1918-1950* (Oxford: OUP, 2005).
Wiltshire, Anne, *Most Dangerous Women: Feminist Peace Campaigners of the Great War* (London: Pandora, 1985).
Zurbrugg, A. W. (ed.), *Not Our War. Writings against the First World War* (London: Merlin, 2014).

General Belinda

TO
PERCY REDFERN
I DEDICATE THIS BOOK
WITH SINCERE APPRECIATION
since he first saw in "General Belinda" a character worthy of presenting to the public—and kept faith in her, and the book, through all their fellow-wanderings, vicissitudes, repulsions and indignities—knowing that, at last, they would find their place.

CONTENTS

CHAPTER I	A Little Home Breaks Up	5
CHAPTER II	Belinda Casts Her Anchor	18
CHAPTER III	Belinda Learns to Lie.	32
CHAPTER IV	The Crash	46
CHAPTER V	Belinda Aids a Poet	59
CHAPTER VI	Belinda Stays—and Goes	71
CHAPTER VII	In the House of a Literary Man	86
CHAPTER VIII	Belinda Protects Her Character	99
CHAPTER IX	In Search of an Antidote	107
CHAPTER X	The Muses Call to Belinda	118
CHAPTER XI	A Wedding—Conflicting Auras—and Tragedy	130
CHAPTER XII	Belinda Strikes a Smashing Blow Against Pan and Pot Worship	144
CHAPTER XIII	Belinda Refuses to be a Burnt Offering on the Shrine of Mammon	158
CHAPTER XIV	A Doll's House	164
CHAPTER XV	Poets—Burglars—and Belinda	169
CHAPTER XVI	Great War Shadows Belinda	182
CHAPTER XVII	A Draft Goes Out	189
CHAPTER XVIII	The House of Shirts	198
CHAPTER XIX	"Peace"	208

CHAPTER I

A Little Home Breaks Up

"DAD'S late, Belinda," asserted Mrs. Higgins.

"Nay," said Belinda. She was stirring something in a pan over the fire. The little clock on the fire-shelf was half an hour fast, a custom handed down from Belinda's maternal grandmother, who had held it as a maxim that it was better to be half an hour in front than half an hour behind.

"He'll die a drunkard yet," complained the woman on the bed in the corner of the kitchen. "Oh, the terrible misery drink has caused! And I gave him that tale Mr. Senior lent me, about the man who pawned his child's coffin for drink. He laughed, Belinda!"

"It made me laugh, too," confessed Belinda, smiling. The smile revealed large white teeth, and Belinda ceased to be plain, even though her nose was semi-flattened and her mouth large.

Mrs. Higgins was evidently nonplussed by her daughter's statement that the book she had wept over gave only food for amusement to both father and daughter.

"In the first place," said Belinda, scattering salt into the pan, "I didn't believe that story."

"A minister wrote it," affirmed her mother. "I don't see what good it would do him to tell a lie."

"Some folk don't bother so much about doing good as making folk miserable," said Belinda, stirring the salt well in. "And, in the second place, the kid got a coffin after all, and it was only the pawnbroker lost on it. Then it brought about their repentance, so what was there to cry over?"

"Ey, Belinda, I don't know what tha'll come to," said her mother, dropping into the dialect. "I really don't."

Belinda's expression said that she had full faith in coming out as well as the average human.

Mrs. Higgins was watching the clock again.

"Well, he is going to be drunk this time," she moaned.

Belinda set the pan on the hob. She was used to this type of dialogue, for it happened every Friday night, when Samuel Higgins received his wages, and called for a pint of beer on the way home from work. Belinda spread the cloth, eyeing it a little critically, and turning it inside out, though that did not quite satisfy her either.

"Don't set me a cup. I'm too upset to enjoy anything," said Mrs. Higgins, tearfully. Chronic rheumatism does not tend to cheerfulness of temperament.

Belinda set the cup just the same. To do otherwise, she knew, would have hurt her mother's feelings. It was always at this time, too, that Mrs. Higgins' forebodings that her husband would die a drunkard ended, and she began to cheer up, knowing quite well that Sam at that very moment was coming up the little street.

"Happen the clock is a bit too fast," said Mrs. Higgins.

"I shouldn't wonder," agreed Belinda.

"I wonder if he'll have brought any kippers," said Mrs. Higgins.

"He said he would," answered Belinda. The usual brightness of Belinda was becoming super-brightness. She pulled a big chair up to the table, set a pair of tattered slippers inside the fender, gave the glorious fire another stirring, then stood, quietly waiting, hands on her big hips.

The door opened.

"Ey, you don't need to wipe your feet, dad, I've not cleaned the passage," shouted easy Belinda.

Steps came up the flagged passage towards the lamp-lit kitchen.

The door of the room opened, and, looking smilingly in on the two women, was a medium-sized man with ruddy cheeks and black eyes. He was carrying a string bag full of provisions. He handed Belinda the bag and sat down, drawing a deep breath.

"You've walked too fast, dad," Belinda told him.

There was a slightly anxious look in her eyes. Higgins gave his daughter a look that told her to say no more, lest his wife should suspect that he was ailing. It was usual to shield Sarah Higgins from all worries.

Belinda emptied the bag on the bed for the inspection of Mrs. Higgins, who occasionally said, "How much was this?" or "These apples aren't so good," or "I wish I could shop myself." Pa Higgins took out of his pocket a little bottle of tablets.

"Cured a man who'd been a cripple thirty years," he affirmed. "One after every meal. From now to Christmas—that's three months—take 'em regular."

"It's waste o' money," protested Sarah Higgins. But she got Belinda to reach her glasses, so that she could read the testimonials.

The cheerful meal began, Mr. Higgins retailing all the news he had gathered during the day, less for personal satisfaction than for the benefit of his wife, who had been a bedridden woman for fifteen years.

"This is good, Belinda," praised Samuel Higgins. "She'll be a cook yet, mother. If aught happened to me, our Belinda could find a place in the world." He appeared to check himself from saying more, at sight of his wife's look.

"If aught happened thee, Sam," said Mrs. Higgins, "I shouldn't live to need aught long."

The Friday evening passed in the usual manner. When Belinda had cleared the table, washed the pots, and mended the fire, the clock struck eight. The rentman arrived, and some bandying of words took place between Higgins and their landlord, in which Higgins hinted that it was well to be some folk, though he looked quite content to be himself. The "burying brass" man came, and was paid his one shilling, a sum which insured that none of the family of three would be left unburied in case of death. Samuel Higgins was in great good humour this evening.

"It's a pity we've to wait till we snuff it for that money," he said, meditatively.

"It is," agreed the insurance man. "Best take out a *life* policy."

Higgins grinned.

"It takes us all our time to live," he said, cheerfully. "Anyhow, you wouldn't take me in a life-club. I've only one lung, and my liver won't work, and my heart goes pit-a-pat whenever I see a nice young lass." He looked slyly at his wife with this last sentence.

"Get out with thee!" she rapped out.

The burying-brass man departed.

Then the young man came with the weekly packet of tea, and Higgins must tease, and draw him out at the same time.

He was the last comer. Higgins heard the door close behind him with satisfaction, which expressed itself in his getting closer to the fire.

"Now, when you two women have done talking," he began.

Which made Belinda laugh outright, for Higgins had been talking ever since he came in. She walked over to the corner shelf and reached down his concertina.

"Music hath power to soothe the savage beast," said Higgins, humorously, with a twinkle in his eye. "But it didn't soothe the folk next door, did it, Belinda? What did they say, Belinda?"

Belinda made her face look very serious.

"They said, 'We hear strange noises quite late at night. The place must be haunted.'"

"That's it," grinned Higgins. "Now, Belinda, get thy fiddle, and we'll do some more strange noises."

For two solid hours did Mr. Higgins, Belinda, and Mrs. Higgins take part in the evening concert. Belinda could play only first and second shifts, but made up for it by plucking the strings, and Mr. Higgins swayed to and fro with his concertina, whilst Mrs. Higgins sang, trying to keep up with them. The music varied from "Could I but stand where Moses stood" to "Maid of Athens," and if Higgins sang "jelly-fringe" for "jetty-fringe," what matters it?

"They can say what they like," affirmed Mr. Higgins. "There's nothing like a bit of music for keeping the heart up. If I had anything to do with heddication I'd see that every child could play some instrument—if it was only a mouth-organ or a Jew's harp. Well, Belinda, it's getting bedtime."

Belinda made cocoa, and cut bread. Mr. Higgins fetched in a bucket of coals.

"I'm taking our Belinda to Belle Vue to-morrow," said Higgins.

Belinda looked all the flushed surprise he had expected. Her black eyes sparkled. She looked handsome with that joy upon her.

"Anybody born on Guy Fawkes' Day deserves takin' to the fireworks," said Higgins. "But we'll not wait till her birthday. Never leave till to-morrow what you can do to-day."

Belinda took her candlestick. She kissed her mother.

"Tha can give me one, Belinda," said Higgins.

Belinda was a little surprised.

"Just here, where the flies skate," her father told her, and bent his head, showing the baldness of it.

Belinda gave him a hearty kiss on the spot that Mr. Higgins called his desert of Sahara.

"We'll have a good day to-morrow," asserted Higgins. "We've ten shillings to spend between us, Belinda."

"So that's why you've not been smoking," guessed Belinda. Her eyes were a little misty.

"Good-night," said Higgins.

Belinda went. She entered her bedroom and shut the door softly, setting the candlestick down, and sitting on the chair by the bed.

It was a room with the walls full of pictures cut out of magazines and journals. They were mostly fastened with drawing-pins. Belinda sat with clasped hands, staring before her. She was wondering why dad had asked for that kiss on his desert of Sahara. It was an unusual thing for him to be demonstrative with her, his unsentimental offspring, though quite common for him to show tenderness to his ailing wife.

"I expect it was just his fun," said Belinda to herself. She undressed and crept into bed, blowing out the candle. She woke out of what seemed a long sleep.

"Belinda!" came her mother's voice. There was the sound of a fall afterwards.

When Belinda got downstairs she found her father in a heap by the bedside. Belinda lifted him in her arms, quite unconscious of her mother's shrill outcries. She knew as she saw his face that the end had come.

"Dad! Speak if you can!" she begged.

There was a slight flutter of Higgins' eyelids. He was trying to open his eyes.

"Ta-ta, Sal," he managed to say.

Mrs. Higgins burst out again.

"Hush!" commanded Belinda, almost sternly. Then: "Dad, can't you speak to *me*? It's Belinda, dad!"

Higgins made a superhuman struggle. His eyes opened. Belinda saw that he could not see her. Her great hand gripped his.

"It's all right, dad," she said, clearly. "You've naught to fear. You've done what's right. I'll look after mother, dad."

A faint smile passed over Higgins' face. Belinda was studying it intensely. Her big black eyes were drinking in every fading expression.

"I'll always look after mother, dad," she repeated, slowly, clearly. "Can you hear?"

She fancied that her father tried to nod his head.

"Ta-ta, General," he managed at last. It was the name he had given her as a child, because of her spirit.

He became a dead weight.

The clock ticked louder than ever Belinda had heard it in her life.

"Belinda?" Her mother's tones were an agonizing question.

"Lie down, mother," begged Belinda. Her face was very pale, her look dazed.

"Belinda!" wailed Mrs. Higgins.

Belinda laid her father down by the bed and closed his eyes.

"Don't leave me," moaned Mrs. Higgins.

Fear and grief equally swayed the feeble heart of the invalid to whom Sam Higgins had stood for everything—from daily bread to consolation. It was useless to entreat Mrs. Higgins to be left alone with the dead whilst Belinda called someone in. So Belinda was forced to knock on the wall to summon the people who had objected to their musical evenings. The blows she gave on the back of the chimney with the brass candlestick seemed to strike her own heart.

"Halloa!" sounded a voice outside the street-door five minutes later.

"Come in!" said Belinda.

Bill Greenwood entered the kitchen. Belinda looked at the young man who had proposed to her thirteen times, and been calmly refused every time.

"He's gone," said Belinda.

Bill Greenwood took in the scene.

"What can I do?" he asked.

"Fetch the doctor," Belinda told him.

Bill went. When the doctor came, he said it was no surprise to him. Higgins had been to see him only that night. He always called on Friday nights.

They laid Sam Higgins out in the kitchen, the place that he loved.

"Stick to me," pleaded Mrs. Higgins. "Stick to me, Belinda."

"Ay, I'll stick to you, mother," promised Belinda.

The eternal night passed like a terrible nightmare. Mrs. Higgins was asleep—asleep from sheer exhaustion of grief. Belinda was wide awake—quiveringly awake from intensity of sorrow. She was pondering the problem of life, too, though death lay only an arm's length away, cold, tranquil, done with the hurly-burly of poverty. Belinda had never been taught to earn her living, and now upon her shoulders was thrust the burden her father had broken under. Belinda was too short-sighted to go into the factories.

"I shall have to go out to service," she decided. "I can do that."

Next day Belinda got a girl-friend to stay with her mother whilst she went to see her brother Jonathan, who lived five miles away, at Syke Gate, a small industrial village. She walked in the grey drizzle, through which the hills magnified by mist stood like giant Sorrows. The bird-notes wounded Belinda. At last the church-spire appeared. Belinda hurried on to the middle house in a tiny row. A woman in a printed cap and printed apron, over a brown dress Belinda would have worn for Sundays and been proud of, was cleaning the brass door-knocker. There were still yellow and bronze chrysanthemums in the little garden, and a tall pink hollyhock dripping rain.

"Halloa!" said the woman, turning.

The word was a query rather than a welcome.

"Dad's dead," said Belinda.

"Never!" said the woman in the cap, in a shocked voice.

"Yea, it's true," said Belinda.

"Jonathan'll be in soon," said Jonathan's wife, "go in, I'll be in in a minute."

Belinda went into the spick-and-span little house, where she always felt so uncomfortable. She was vaguely sarcastic that Annie was finishing cleaning the door-knocker.

"She'd finish cleaning the door-knocker if all the world were dead!" thought Belinda, trying to arrange herself so that no rain-drippings went from her skirt upon the carpet.

Annie came in two minutes later. She put her polishing rag and the polish away in the tidy box, closed the cupboard door, took off her apron, and put the question that had disturbed her so soon as the shock of Sam Higgins' death had subsided and she had realized it as a fact.

"You'll not be able to keep the house on, Belinda," she said.

Belinda shook her head. The motion shook little drops of rain from her hat upon the freshness of the sofa chintz. Belinda knew it worried Annie.

"I came to see if our Jonathan would have mother," said Belinda, plainly, though it was the most difficult thing she had said in her life, not excepting the thirteen times she had said "No" to Bill Greenwood. "I shall have to go out to work, and will support her. But her place is here—with our Jonathan. They spent all they had saved to give him a good trade. My mother's not going to strangers."

It was the gauntlet. General Belinda threw it down boldly. The two women eyed each other.

"We shall have to see what Jonathan says," said Annie, suavely. Belinda knew that her sister-in-law was going to work against indirectly, hypocritically, her good plan for her mother.

"Ay, we'll see," said Belinda, taking the pins out of her hat.

She knew that Jonathan had degenerated since he married this proud young woman, who was ashamed of the humble parents who had pinched to give him his chance—the chance that allowed her to be proud. But Belinda knew also that Jonathan had looked miserable through not visiting his parents more often. She counted on the force of filial love against a love that had resulted in meanness—Belinda had a great deal of faith in human nature—also in her own powers.

"Here's Reggie," said Annie, as the door opened.

Jonathan's nine-year-old son was home from school.

"Halloa!" he said to Aunt Belinda.

There was a casualness that was almost insulting in his tone. He was being brought up to be a snob. Belinda did not appear to notice it. She fumbled in her pocket for something.

"Here's a little book, Reggie," said Belinda.

Reggie took it with an air that said he knew it would be rubbish. Then he gave an exclamation of delight. Belinda had brought him a book of sea yarns by a famous writer of boys' stories.

"I knew he'd like it," beamed Belinda.

Reggie looked at her. Under the artificialities he was being bred amongst some dormant good feeling yet survived. He forgot Aunt Belinda's old clothes. He threw himself on the sofa by her side and squeezed her arm.

"But how did you know I'd like that?" he asked.

"Because I bought it for myself, and read it," said Belinda.

Reggie gave her a keen look, as though he had only just discovered her.

"You've jolly good taste—for a woman," he admitted.

Belinda smiled at him.

"I think you'd be better sitting here, Belinda," said Annie. "It's more out of the draught."

Belinda knew the reason of this solicitude. Annie was wanting to put a spoke between Reggie and his shabby aunt.

"What made you come?" asked Reggie, candidly, after a while.

"Grandad Higgins is dead," said Belinda.

"I say!" said Reggie.

He stared at Belinda. Her air of quiet cheerfulness was bewildering. But he noticed now that she had not laughed since he came in, and her face looked tired and white.

"I'm sorry," said Reggie.

His mother crossed the room and began to pull down the blinds. Reggie stared at Aunt Belinda, her black eyes shining through the gloom. He had not seen much of his grandfather.

"I'm awfully sorry," he said. As he looked at Belinda in that boyish way, a Higgins look, more of spirit than body, flashed out in him. Turning, his mother saw it.

"Your Grandma Higgins may come to live here," said Belinda, boldly. "If she does, be good to her. That would please Grandad Higgins better than pulling down the blinds, or flowers, or anything."

Annie Higgins looked furious.

"Halloa! That's dad," cried Reggie, as the bell rang.

Mrs. Higgins went down the passage.

"Belinda's here," said Belinda's sister-in-law.

Jonathan came into the kitchen, smiling a welcome. Belinda knew that she was welcome to her brother, but that he was afraid to be too affectionate.

"What's brought thee?" he asked, using the vernacular as in the days of their childhood.

"Jonathan!" said Annie. "The boy'll pick those words up."

Belinda saw her brother wince. The dialect had dropped from his lips naturally.

"I forgot," he said, humbly.

"Jonathan," said Belinda. "I've brought bad news. Dad's terribly ill, Jonathan. In fact—I don't think he'll get better."

"Dad!" gasped Jonathan. He went ashen. "I'll—I'll be ready in two ticks," he said hurriedly. "What's to do with him? Why didn't you let me know? I know we haven't come a lot, but it's been more carelessness nor aught else."

Belinda saw his inner conscience, its agony, its remorse.

"It's too late!" she said, sadly.

"But—" said Jonathan.

He stared into Belinda's face.

"Linda!" he cried, and shrank back as though he had received a blow.

"He died last night, as he was pulling his socks off, at eleven o'clock," said Belinda.

"Did he—did he mention me?" queried Jonathan.

His eyes were almost closed, as though he suffered physical pain.

"He hadn't time," said Belinda. "But I know what he'd have liked thee to do, Jonathan. He'd have liked thee to take care o' mother, so that I can go out to work for her. Can she come, Jonathan?"

She ignored Annie utterly. It was the sister asking the brother to take care of their mother, who had only him.

"Come? Ay," said Jonathan, in a firm voice.

Then he saw his wife's face. She was trying to smile, but—her look was daggers.

"My mother can't go to the Bastille," said Jonathan.

He was opposing his wife's will. It was difficult to him—his eyes apologized, but his jaw was set squarely. Reggie was observing both his parents, also Belinda. A curious penetration was dawning in his black eyes—the Higgins eyes. He crept near to Belinda.

"You've won," he whispered.

Belinda started, then looked at him. Her eyes had a hurt look, rather than a triumphant one, which puzzled Reggie.

"I'm on your side," he whispered.

"Well, let's have our tea," said Annie. "I'm quite agreeable for Jonathan's mother to come."

She was going to fight indirectly. Strategy was going to be her weapon. Belinda knew it. Temporarily, she had won, as Reggie said. For the rest—she would have to wait and see.

CHAPTER II

Belinda Casts Her Anchor

EVERYTHING happened so rapidly afterwards, that whenever Belinda looked back on it it was like a series of cinematograph pictures. First, there were the preparations for the funeral, and the visits of the local firemen to see their dead colleague. Mrs. Higgins never lost her terror at the presence of death, even though her reason knew, as Belinda said, "that those who loved us in life would not hurt us in death—if they could." Belinda bought a couple of ham-shanks, and boiled them, ready for the funeral tea; and Mrs. Greenwood, next door, made tarts, and was sorry for having complained of the musical entertainment of the Higgins. Belinda told Mrs. Greenwood that they were giving up the house, and would have to sell the furniture.

It was a rainy day when Sam Higgins was carried out of the little house where he had been so adored. Mrs. Greenwood was staying with Mrs. Higgins, and preparing tea ready for the return of the funeral guests. Belinda, her brother and his wife, and little Reggie were in the first cab following the hearse. In the next were the firemen, and they were telling tales of how Sam had been the most dauntless of them all.

In the first cab utter stillness reigned, until Annie said, pettishly, "Sit still, Reggie!"

Through the grey streets, that looked more grey with the rain, they proceeded. The cab windows were mud-splashed. There was the sickly scent of lilies warring with the sweet perfume of roses Belinda held on her lap—red roses, the favourite flowers of Sam Higgins. Belinda knew and loved Omar Khayyam. Amongst her dad's favourite flowers was a little card, on which she had written these words:

> Lo! some we loved, the loveliest and the best,
> That Time and Fate of all their Vintage prest,
> Have drunk their Cup a Round or two before,
> And, one by one, crept silently to Rest.

It was when the cab was ascending the road to the big hill-cemetery, and the monumental stones struck her sight through the mud splashes, that the most terrible desolation fell upon Belinda.

"It's raining again," complained Annie, who was thinking of her hat." Belinda had no need to worry about hers. It was an old one dodged up. The jacket she had on was borrowed from Bill Greenwood's sister for the day.

Whenever Belinda looked back on that putting of her father in the ground, she remembered only rain—rain dripping from the thin, wind-swaying trees, new earth piled up, the minister's monotonous voice, and, at the end, Jonathan saying, "Come away, Belinda." His face was wet with more than rain. Belinda had shed no tears. Then there was the journey back, the sense of leaving a precious something behind, and Annie's saying that her feather was quite ruined, and Reggie asking questions about heaven which his mother told him were rude.

They reached the little house, where tea was ready. Mrs. Higgins was sitting in a chair by the hearth, having refused to be in bed on this day. It was as Belinda heard the firemen talking of her dad's calmness when a fire was raging that she lost the sense of having left her dad in the wet, cold ground of the hill-cemetery, bleak and wind-swept. She was seized by a dull realization that the fearless memory they were talking of was Sam Higgins himself—that the thing which had been in the house three days, cold and silent, was not he.

At last they departed, Jonathan saying he would arrange for the ambulance van to take his mother to Syke Gate, as soon as Belinda dropped a postcard.

Belinda poked up the fire and got her mother back into bed. She had been wondering, during these days, if it had been kind to her mother to shield her from all the worries; whether it would not have distracted her mind from her own aches and pains to have shared them. She decided to test this theory now.

"If I'd only known he were ailing!" moaned the invalid. "To think—I were shut out o' knowing, Belinda!"

"We did it for the best," said Belinda. "Well, mother, you shan't be shut out o' things any more."

So Belinda told her of the necessity to sell the furniture in order to pay off the doctor's bill, as they were leaving the district. It was a severe blow to Mrs. Higgins. Perhaps she had until then harboured a hope that the goods could be stored—that some time, somehow, they would have a home again.

"It's hard on you, mother," said Belinda.

Mrs. Higgins rallied.

"No harder than on thee, Belinda," she said.

Tears were dripping as she spoke. She was wondering if she had not been growing rather selfish through being shielded. Belinda smiled a difficult smile.

"I shall meet folk—see fresh things. Happen I'll learn a lot," she said. "I think I was meant to go out into the world. Anyhow, I'll have to go now."

"Annie doesn't want me," said Mrs. Higgins, in a trembling voice.

"She doesn't," agreed Belinda, candidly.

"I don't like going where I'm not wanted," sobbed Mrs. Higgins.

Belinda took her hand.

"Look here, mother," she said, steadily. "*Our Jonathan wants you.* He's been wanting you and dad, the sight of you, all these years, and she's been starving him of you. Never think of her not wanting you. Think of him wanting you. There'll be some fun yonder, mother—and it's jolly good for 'em. Our Jonathan were getting rickets, mother."

"Rickets?" queried Mrs. Higgins, who had only heard of rickets as a child-ailment.

"Soft boned," said Belinda, smiling. "Soft boned in the mind, through giving way. You're going to see our Jonathan fight for you, mother, and it'll make him a man."

"Tha'll allus tell me thy troubles, Belinda?" asked her mother. "At least, if I can't work, I can share thy troubles."

Belinda promised.

It was borne in on her that she and her father had deeply wronged the ailing woman.

Next day the broker came. The way in which he handled the furniture, pictures, and crockery made Belinda want to hit him on the head.

"These are out of date. We can't get much for these," he would say, and then offer a price that absolutely staggered Belinda.

At six o'clock next morning the broker's cart came.

"Sixteen pounds for a home!" lamented Mrs. Higgins. "Oh, Belinda!"

Belinda squeezed her hand.

"Happen it's all for the best," she said. But her heart was breaking afresh to see every loved piece of furniture go out and on that cart. When her dad's chair went she gulped hard.

"We might ha' kept that," moaned Mrs. Higgins. "But Annie wouldn't have had it. It's not fine enough."

"If we started keeping things, we'd want to keep the lot," said Belinda, outwardly stoical.

The walls began to grow bare around them. At last there was nothing left but the chair on which Mrs. Higgins was sitting. The ambulance for which they waited appeared in the nick of time. Bill Greenwood was off work with a boil. He came at sight of the van and helped Mrs. Higgins into it. Belinda paid the fee for loan of the van to Syke Gate and back, and clasped the rest of the money inside her mother's hand.

"Keep your heart up, mother," she shouted, cheerily. "*I shall.* I'll write twice a week."

"Ay," came in muffled tones from the van. A door closed, and Belinda watched the vehicle go.

Belinda had answered an advertisement for a servant in the Heathill paper, and was going after the place that afternoon.

Bill Greenwood was staring at Belinda. She looked more worn than ever he had seen her.

"If you married me, Belinda, you'd have a home for your mother," he said.

Belinda came out of a brown study, and looked at him. She put the question that had haunted her often.

"I wonder why you want *me*?" she asked.

"Because," said Bill, "you're the bravest woman I've struck. Now, Belinda, why don't you want me? Come, it's only fair."

"Because," said unique Belinda, "you're only a working chap, and I've read somewhere that what he earns isn't enough to keep two—or it might be more," she said, unblushingly. "It's a question o' figures, Bill. Just figures. But figures is bad things to get over."

She went to have a meal with the Greenwoods, after locking up the house and taking the key to the landlord. It was now ten o'clock. Mrs. Greenwood, as the appointment was not till three, persuaded her to stay until one o'clock.

The time drifted on.

At ten to one, Bill Greenwood set out walking to the car with Belinda.

"It's a big change, Belinda, going out to work for a living at thirty years old," said Bill. "But I think you'll come through."

Belinda was pleased.

"What does it feel like?" he asked. He had witnessed Belinda's courage in a compressed space. She was going out into the big world.

"A bit fluttery like," confessed Belinda. "Like being on the scenic railway—an' not knowing an' not caring—only a bit. But as near as I can tell— a bit fluttery."

"I know," said Bill, nodding. Then: "Here it is."

The car swung along towards them.

Belinda waved her shabby, gampish umbrella to signal the driver. She got on the car. Bill Greenwood watched to see if she was looking back, but she never looked back. After all, he had almost known that she would not. She was no waverer.

"Heathill," said Belinda, when the conductor came.

It was two hours before she reached her journey's end, having to change cars several times. Then she walked through Heathill streets. She was feeling worn out, for all the excitement of the past days. Sam Higgins' advice came into her mind:

"If ever you feel peckish, Belinda, get a beef-steak pudding. There's a lot of courage can come out of a beef-steak pudding."

"A beef-steak pudding," ordered Belinda, in the poorest chop-house she could see. It was a tiny place, partitioned, a trestle-table, oil-cloth covered, behind each division, and a form on each side of it. Belinda's dad had called these *feeding places*, as distinct from cafés, where folk ate.

Whilst she was not troubled with shyness, she had a feeling of newness upon her, the result of being on her own in the big world.

"Peas?" inquired the tubby man in the white apron, who looked as round as though he devoured all the beef-steak puddings himself. There was a sleek, greasy look about him, and he had a beaming eye.

Belinda was going to say "No" to the question as to whether she would take peas, when she saw an ill-looking youth staring at her, a piece of pudding suspended on its way to his mouth.

"Fine peas, these," he informed her, with the familiarity of one poor traveller greeting another. There was no rudeness in it. Had there been, it is quite possible Belinda would not have noticed it.

"I'll take peas," said Belinda, smiling at the youth.

She noticed that his shirt-sleeves needed mending.

"Pepper?" he inquired.

Belinda nodded, and he pushed it across the narrow table to her.

"Jolly good sixpennyworth, this!" he said.

Belinda nodded assent.

"Stranger in Heathill?" asked the youth.

"Going after a place in service," Belinda informed him.

"Oh! that advert, in the *Express*?" he said, as though there had been only one.

"That," said Belinda, taking it out of her bag and pushing it across the table.

He grunted, looking at it.

"Rotten shop," he said. "What they want is someone with the strength of a horse, the two-facedness of a crocodile, and no backbone."

These requirements rather took Belinda's breath away.

"I mean," explained the young man, "it's a right slave-hole. They live beyond their means, so they only have one servant, though there's work for two and a help. Folks are always coming for money, and the servant has to lie like ——"

He stopped himself just in time.

"Go on," said Belinda. "And no backbone?"

"No backbone—because the missus is a regular Turk, and if anyone has a temper there, it's her that has to have it."

"Sounds pretty bad," said Belinda.

"Won't suit you at all," observed the youth. "You're too honest. Sal stuck it two years, but it's nigh killed her."

Belinda looked at him questioningly.

"My wife," he explained. "She had to go out to work—for I've got consumption. I'm going off. Want to buy some views of Heathill?"

With a sudden change of manner, a brisk, businesslike air that was tragic, and made Belinda's throat hurt, he produced a paper parcel of highly-coloured photographs, with the sky bluer than ever Heathill's smoke allowed, and its buildings apparently in new stone.

Belinda chose six very carefully. She chose one of the Park, so that she could send it to her mother telling her she often sat there—that is, if she got the place. The others she chose to suit Mrs. Greenwood, Jonathan and Reggie.

"How much?" she asked.

"Twopence each," he said, apologetically.

Belinda put down half a crown.

"No change," she said.

He flushed—a flush that covered up the sickly pallor

of his face, with its bony structure showing almost terribly.

"But I didn't mean to –" he began.

"No change," said Belinda, firmly. "And, I say, if I get that place, I might drop in to see you on my nights out."

The youth grinned as he wrapped up his postcards.

"You won't get none," he said.

"But you always get nights out," said Belinda.

"There was always something—the kid sick, or someone coming to supper, or something," said the youth. "They did her out of it almost every time." He gave Belinda their address.

"I shall want something definite," said Belinda, referring to nights out.

She went out, leaving the youth smoking a cigarette.

What she had heard was not very good. But it was Belinda's philosophy that it was best to know the worst. Take this place she must. She could not afford to play even a week.

She hurried on to Lilac Grove and found it on the very edge of Heathill. Number ninety-six was her number. "Browning House" was the title of the villa where domestics were treated so badly. The lawn was very trim and green, and in the centre stood a tiny figure of Mercury, set round with scarlet geraniums. A couple of stone vases, one on each side the steps, were also full of geraniums. Belinda walked up the steps and rang the bell. She tried to make sure her hat was on straight before the door opened, for it had an odd way of toppling. A tired-looking woman in a coarse apron opened the door. Belinda guessed that this was a day woman, in until the maid was engaged.

"I've come about that place," said Belinda.

"Round to the back door," said the charwoman, wearily. This was the seventeenth, and Mrs. Riddings was not suited yet.

"Anyhow, she'll be plain enough," thought the charwoman, sarcastically, of Belinda.

Belinda went down the little path, under an arbour where a rose or two yet lingered, and saw a door at the head of six stone steps. She went up these, and tapped at the door. No one heard her. She tapped a long time, then stood waiting. Steps sounded. Belinda decided to wait until they came near enough, then to knock again. Even as she waited, a startled exclamation of "Oh, don't, sir!" came to her ears.

"A kiss," said a man's whispered voice.

"Oh, no!" protested a woman's voice, a pretty, soft voice.

"But I shall," said the man's voice.

"I shall scream," proclaimed the woman. Belinda knew intuitively that she would do nothing of the kind, from the sort of voice that she had.

Belinda opened the door, walked into what turned out to be a sort of pantry, and found herself face to face with a tall, grey-haired man, who was just releasing a young woman, who had let fall a millinery-box. Mr. Riddings staggered against the shelves, and touched a gravy tureen, which upset, and let the gravy trickle down his grey broadcloth. He gave a masculine ejaculation and stared at the apparition in shabby black, the black eyes regarding him with an almost malicious twinkle of fun.

"What are you doing here?" he asked.

"I knocked and knocked," explained Belinda, meekly, "and that woman told me to come to the back door. I'm after that place."

The young woman with the millinery-box was looking gratefully at Belinda. She seized her opportunity and darted away.

"You're rubbing it in," said Belinda, alluding to the gravy. For Mr. Riddings was using a towel. "You'd best press it out with a flat-iron, between brown paper. It'll take it out like magic."

Mr. Riddings stared haughtily at Belinda. Then, the spectacle of himself pressing gravy out on to brown paper with hot flat-irons was too much for him. He smiled.

"But you really oughtn't to do it," said Belinda, seriously.

"Do what?" asked Mr. Riddings, though he knew quite well.

"Kiss folk," said Belinda.

"Shouldn't I?" queried Mr. Riddings.

He was a connoisseur in women, and saw any charm at once. Belinda's was a unique one, springing from character. Moreover, her eyes, her wonderful eyes, and those white teeth, and her bearing, uncringing, comradely.

"Let me try," said Mr. Riddings, quite in jest.

Belinda snatched a carving knife from a platter, and he let go suddenly.

"You've backed the wrong horse this time, mister," said Belinda.

She marched out of the pantry, found herself in what was evidently the servants' kitchen, entered a passage, collided with an umbrella stand, and found herself staring down a red-carpeted hall, with doors opening on each side.

Voices sounded in one of the rooms.

Belinda stood hesitatingly, gazing about her. There were many pictures in the hall. It was a beautiful place. Their own old house seemed dark by contrast. And yet—they had always paid their way, whilst here was debt and lack of principle, and a grub of ugliness eating away inside all this exterior beauty.

"I'm so sorry, but I couldn't give so much," said an exquisitely modulated voice.

A young woman came out, looking rather vexed. Then a grand personage appeared in a loose gown, which Belinda afterwards learned was an afternoon gown, worn at the wrong time.

"In fact, I'm quite sure you wouldn't suit me," said Mrs. Riddings.

Belinda caught a glimpse of the girl's face as she passed the chair on which she had placed herself to wait. She smiled an inward smile. The girl was too beautiful for the jealous wife.

"I thought it was as cheap sitting as standing," apologized Belinda, catching her eye. Mrs. Riddings stared, then seeing no rudeness in Belinda's demeanour smiled a little stiffly.

There was an interview which Sam Higgins would have described as "short and sweet, like a donkey's trot," and Belinda found herself engaged at the salary of twenty-four pounds a year, as general, and her own caps and aprons to buy and pay for laundering. She had two hours off on a Monday evening, and every alternate Sunday evening to go to church. Belinda had said she was religious, when Mrs. Riddings asked her, but did not say what church she attended, and was not asked.

"Let her try to do me out of going to listen to the band on a Sunday!" thought Belinda. "I've got to have a bit of music."

Mrs. Riddings showed her over the house, where everything was kept, and said that it did not matter about Belinda not being highly trained so long as she was willing.

Belinda said a very characteristic thing, just as they were turning from the linen cupboard.

"I'm like an ass," said Belinda, "the better you treat me, the better I shall work. That's fair, isn't it?"

"I'm sure we shall get on well together," said Mrs. Riddings. She believed the raw northern woman had the makings of a good slave, on her own confession.

She forgot that what Belinda had in mind might not be what she had in hers.

"She looks strong, too," she said to Mr. Riddings over the supper table, where Belinda had placed a very fine potato pie.

"But—how beastly ugly," lamented Mr. Riddings.

"I'm sure the girl is not bad-looking," said Mrs. Riddings—the opposite to what she usually said.

After washing all up, Belinda crept upstairs to the room that Mrs. Riddings had told her was her bedroom. It was so damp that the paper was coming loose, had a tiny round window, like a porthole, and just one chair and a small table. Tired as she was, Belinda wrote in pencil a postcard to her mother. It just said, "I have got that there place," and had four kisses on the card, presumably one for Annie, too. Then Belinda wound up the alarm clock to go off at six-thirty, crept into bed, and fell asleep, to dream that she was at home, and that her father came in and shook hands with her—that he was alive. The surprise was so great that she sat up in bed, tears of joy on her face. Then she saw the moon through the round window—the strange room, full of shadows—and heard the hall clock strike. She remembered. She was not at home. She had begun life in the big world.

"I wonder when this bed was slept in last?" thought Belinda, shiveringly. She made herself sleep again.

The alarm clock seemed to go off before its time, but when Belinda looked, she saw there was no deceit about it. It was really six-thirty. She dressed by candlelight, criticizing the dampness of the room, the ugly stains on the paper.

"I shall want something different to this," decided Belinda, the bold. "I wouldn't put a tomcat in a hole like that."

"Higgins!" called Mrs. Riddings' voice.

"I'm up," said Belinda, reassuringly.

"It's seven o'clock, Higgins," said Mrs. Riddings.

"The alarm clock must be wrong then," said Belinda.

"Don't argue, girl! Hurry. Mr. Riddings has to get to the city by ten-thirty. Take his shaving water up as soon as you can."

Belinda bobbed out at her room door in time to see a pink dressing gown flying along the landing and the red slippers of Mrs. Riddings.

Belinda had been used to wake up gradually.

She felt a little cross, until she remembered it was her father's burden she had taken up where he had laid it down. She ran downstairs, lit the gas-jet, set on the little, kettle, and soon had Mr. Riddings' shaving water boiling. Belinda did not know where he kept his shaving pot, so she put it in an empty jam-jar, just as she had used to do for her dad.

"Higgins—my shaving water!" yelled Mr. Riddings.

"Coming," said Belinda, bluntly.

CHAPTER III

Belinda Learns to Lie.

WHEN Belinda arrived on the landing with Mr. Riddings' shaving water, she was confused by the number of doors she saw. Out of which room had issued that yell for shaving-water? One door was slightly ajar. Belinda could not forbear a modest peep through the door aperture. She beheld a perfectly angelic-looking boy of about seven, in pink and blue pyjamas, dancing up and down on the bed.

"Which is Mr. Riddings' room?" inquired Belinda.

"Come in!" invited the hope of the Riddings.

Belinda entered a jolly room, bedight with animal pictures, a tiny bookcase, over which hung a fishing-rod. A small table stood near the bed, and upon it were spread some foreign coins, ranged in a circle round a bowl of goldfish.

"You're the new slavey," Jerry informed the lady with the jam jar.

"Nothing of the kind," said Belinda. "I'm nobody's slave. Well—not if I know it."

Jerry grinned.

"You'll see!" said the precocious and sophisticated imp. "Oh, I say, that's not dad's shaving jar! My eye! Won't he like the gollywog on the side!"

"Which door?" asked Belinda.

The small boy regarded her with a friendly look.

"Did she get you for twenty pounds?" he inquired, confidentially.

"No, twenty-four," said Belinda, smiling. "Here—stop jumping on that bed. You'll have the mattress through."

"My eye! So you beat mother!" exclaimed Jerry. "I heard her tell dad she wouldn't give a penny over twenty a year. I wonder why you got it."

Belinda knew. She knew that Mrs. Riddings had engaged her because she was so plain, and also because the jealously suspicious and hypocritical woman had gauged the fact that, in big things, at least, Belinda was to be trusted.

"You mind your own business!" said Belinda. "You ought to speak more respectfully of your parents. When I was your age I thought they could catch sparrows by putting a bit of salt on their tails."

Jerry Riddings had never been addressed so by a domestic in the whole, brief course of his existence, and, as Mrs. Riddings had never kept a servant as long as the last, Jerry had seen a few.

"You mind how you speak to me," he said, pouting, "or I'll report you to mother for insolence," he said. It was so funny that Belinda laughed.

Jerry stared at Belinda's twinkling eyes and the white teeth—at the whole laughing face. Gradually his face relaxed. He came to the foot of the bed.

"I say, what's your name?" he asked.

"Belinda," said she.

"Oh, we never give slaveys their Christian names," he said. "What's your last?"

Belinda stifled an un-Christian thought.

"Higgins," she said.

"Now, look here, Higgins—" said the boy.

"If you call me Higgins I shall call you Riddings," said Belinda. "But, look here, I've no time to waste—where's your dad's room?"

"Number four," said Jerry. "I say, Higgins—"

Belinda was going out of the room. She turned and looked back. Two chubby hands were grasping the bed-rail.

"I like you," said Jerry, thoughtfully.

Belinda paused.

"I don't like you," she said (a cloud spread over the boy's face) "—when you're cheeky," amended Belinda.

He brightened. Belinda went out.

"At least there's one honest person in the establishment," she thought, "though they've almost ruined him."

During the next three days Belinda experienced the bitter shattering of all her dreams about domestic service. From earliest morning until late at night she was having her vitality used up to its fullest possibility. She was not regarded as a human being, nor ever approached on the level, but always from a pedestal that made her appear small, and which, as she looked up to it in turn, made the directing figure upon it appear small and mean in its tyrannies.

Whilst she cooked a three-course dinner and Mrs. Riddings ate cream in abundance, Belinda was stinted of tea—mere common tea—so that she had either to have it look like washing-up water or deny herself of it excepting for one meal a day.

In a house which required at least two strong maids, Belinda was expected to do all—with the exception of arranging the flowers and opening the door to visitors, though Mrs. Riddings spent many hours a day reading third-rate novels and playing the piano. In the solitude of that damp room where even light was limited to her, Belinda wept once—wept in burning indignation that one human being should be allowed to buy another for twenty-four pounds a year and subject her to such treatment. Sometimes, from the little scullery window at home, Belinda had admired sunsets as she washed up the tea-things. Belinda was too tired, now. Only the feeling that she had taken up the burden her dad had laid down kept her from running away, after giving Mrs. Riddings a piece of her mind.

Perhaps, amongst all the lesser indignities that came to hand, to a mind naturally independent and sensitive, was the fact that she must take her meals alone, in the place where she cooked, pots and pans about her, and never even able to ask little Jerry to have his tea with her. Mrs. Riddings had plainly shown that "her boy" must not be too friendly with a menial.

On the fourth day Belinda wrote to her mother. Having finally decided to make of her mother a real friend to tell her troubles to, Belinda did the thing thoroughly. She gave a picture of the whole situation, and herself on the rack, winding up with the Belinda-like piece of philosophy:

"But I would not have missed it for worlds. And, after all, if somebody did not look after the poor things, they'd be in a bad way—so it's really a work of charity.

"P.S.—I hope to come home on the second Saturday."

Belinda little dreamed of what would happen on that eventful Saturday. Two days after sending her epistle, Belinda received an answer from her mother. It was not long, but Belinda knew that every word of it had cost physical pain in those swollen wrists, and was deeply touched. It was the first letter her mother had written to her, for the simple reason that, though she was thirty years old, Belinda had never been away for longer than half a day in her life. She read that letter in a corner of the morning-room, before the venetian blinds were lifted, and the sunlight and shade made a curious barred pattern on it as she read, the sweeping-brush, wrong end up, used to rest on whilst she read:

"dear b,

"i am sorry u ave such a hard plase but u must be brave i now u are and i will be if i can but it his a very hard plase here as A wud like to be shut of me ure father wud tern in is grave but i am glad e his at reste were the wiked ceace from trubling i am sorry for our Jonathan as e was alwis a good boy and it is a pity but it cant be elpt good nite an bless u and keep u all rite his the prair of ure lovin mother,

"Sarah Higgins."

Mr. Riddings came into the room as Belinda was reading this letter, between the lines rather than on them. Belinda's eyes were wet.

"Halloa! Love-letters!" he said, briskly.

He was getting to respect Belinda, though his wife said the girl was very amateurish, and pigheaded on some points, in the bargain.

"From my mother," said Belinda.

Never by a look had she ever shown that she had remembered the incident in the pantry.

"Ah, these mothers!" said Mr. Riddings.

Belinda pushed into her pocket the letter that had been a new revelation of her mother's character, showing her both courageous and sympathetic.

There was something queer in Mr. Riddings' tone.

"My mother is eighty," said he.

"The *Sporting Times* is in the rack," Belinda informed him, for he appeared to be seeking it.

"Ah, yes, Higgins, so it is," he said. Belinda did not wince as much as when they called her "Higgins" first time.

Mr. Riddings seemed to forget the *Sporting Times*.

He was standing, back to the fireless grate, tipping up and down on his toes, watching Belinda brush the carpet, on her hands and knees—scratch, scratch, as if she dare not stop.

"Eighty on Tuesday, Higgins," he said.

"I hope she's well and happy," said Belinda.

She looked up. Mr. Riddings looked a little uncomfortable under the glance of those black eyes.

It was curious how solemnly splendid they could look sometimes, as well as laughing.

"She has excellent health for such an old dame, Higgins," said Mr. Riddings. "A little deaf, but that is nothing. A very wonderful old person, nevertheless."

Belinda went on brushing. It was a respectful and monotonous sound, with the chirp of the sparrows on the eaves outside as an accompaniment.

"This is herself, Higgins," said Mr. Riddings, failing to speak lightly.

He opened a pocket-book, and took out an unmounted photograph. Belinda laid her brush down and came over to look at it. She saw an old lady in a dolman—an old lady with Mr. Riddings' features, but not his bored expression, and upon her was unmistakably the working-class stamp. It was in her bonnet, her boots, and her pose of body.

"Where does she live?" inquired Belinda.

"In the Heathill almshouses," confessed Mr. Riddings.

He confessed it with a sense of getting rid of a guilt that had weighed heavily on him.

"Do you mean?" asked Belinda.

"Mrs. Riddings could not do with her here," said Mr. Riddings. "So—we send her a postal order now and then. You see, the people we meet—"

"Eighty," commented Belinda. "She'll be meeting the saints in their glory before long, and they won't care about her old dolman and her elastic-sided boots and—her poverty."

"So you are religious?" smiled Mr. Riddings.

"Who said so?" scoffed Belinda. "Can't a body have a bit o' human feeling for another poor body without being religious?"

She spoke warmly and her eye flashed.

"I'll tell you what I'd like you to do for me, Higgins," said Mr. Riddings, like a man making up his mind. "I'll get Mrs. Riddings to give you a day off on Tuesday, and you must run round to see my mother. I believe she would like to have you on her birthday."

"Why not go yourself, sir?" inquired Belinda.

Mr. Riddings noticed that she spoke more respectfully than she had done since she came into the house. He knew that it had something to do with his having descended from the superior air of master.

"No, that is impossible. Cora will be home on Tuesday," said Mr. Riddings, as much to himself as Belinda. "Carl Rosa's are here, and I promised her and Jerry the treat."

They heard Mrs. Riddings descending the stairs. Belinda half expected Mr. Riddings to flee. He was in no little terror of his wife's jealous tantrums, one of which had taken place since Belinda came, but not on her account.

"Higgins!" she called.

"In the morning room, ma'am," answered Belinda.

Mrs. Riddings entered. She seemed surprised to find her husband in the room, and gave Belinda a look which that person felt through her back hair. But when Belinda looked up from the dustpan to take instructions, Mrs. Riddings' suspicions faded.

"Whatever else she is, she is trustworthy," was the feminine verdict.

Belinda finished the room.

Mr. Riddings surprised his wife by lighting the fire.

"The girl has a lot to do," he said, frankly.

Mrs. Riddings was puzzled.

"Oh, yes. But she's healthy and strong. They are built for it," she said, languidly. "And I don't think the nervous organisms of these roughly-brought-up people suffer from the wear and tear as do the more highly developed. It's the same in the animal kingdom."

Something like a laugh sounded from behind Mr. Riddings' newspaper. Then he laid it on his knees and looked at his wife over it.

"You're getting twice as much out of Belinda as you did out of Sal," he said, almost brutally. "But you wouldn't say that Belinda isn't a thousand years ahead of Sal."

It was an unanswerable argument.

Belinda waited on them, after serving breakfast.

"Cora will get here by the 9.30 train on Tuesday," said Mr. Riddings. Whatever he was as a husband, Belinda had discovered that he was a good father, and this morning had shown himself at least a little conscience-stricken regarding his mother.

"Mr. Denvers is coming again," said Mrs. Riddings. Mr. Riddings frowned.

"It's a miserable way out of our difficulties," he said, in a suppressed tone of irritability.

"She couldn't do better," asserted Mrs. Riddings.

Belinda had, on the second day of her arrival, seen old Mr. Denvers: a white-haired, sickly gentleman, who lived at Myrtleside, at No. 99. Belinda had a quick brain. Could it be that they were about to try to match their daughter with that old, sickly man, or was it some relative of his? She had heard of it in story books—but surely, in real life—

"You can go, Higgins. I'll ring if we want you," said Mrs. Riddings, suddenly aware of Belinda and Belinda's ears. Perhaps it was Belinda's eyes that had made her feel ashamed of a transaction of which she was equally ashamed and equally determined.

Belinda found herself looking forward with great interest to the arrival of Cora Riddings, who had just graduated brilliantly at Newnham. She had seen a photograph of her, and she did not think her very attractive, save for a certain charm of expression, a soft fineness about the mouth. Jerry was counting the days off between now and Tuesday. Evidently his sister had a warm place in his heart.

On Tuesday, just as Belinda was making cakes for tea, the bell rang.

Belinda opened the door after a little delay, during which it had not rung again.

"Mother in?" queried a tall girl, smiling warmheartedly.

"Oh, you're Miss—"

"I'm Cora," said she, marching in and taking off her furs. "I've heard about you, Belinda. Dad has told me how you will put coals on the fire without tongs." She laughed merrily, taking off her hat.

"She's busy with the dressmaker, miss," said Belinda.

"Who? Mother?" said Cora. "I left her six months ago with the dressmaker—she must have been with her all the time. Oh, don't worry calling her, Belinda. I'll just have a tune." She darted off into the drawing-room and, opening the piano, was soon singing in a fresh clear voice, "Caller Herrin'."

"Cora!" exclaimed her father, running downstairs.

Jerry came sliding down the banister.

It seemed to Belinda that the house grew brighter, better and less tyrannical with the coming of this young person, even though she added to the work and wanted so many things doing for her. Sometimes she came into the kitchen and dried whilst Belinda washed, and she helped Belinda to make apricot jam one afternoon, though her mother expostulated with her.

"I'm doing it because I want to," she said. "I don't believe we ought to be as helpless as we are, mother. It would be rather awful if we found ourselves on a desert island, wouldn't it?"

But one thing Belinda saw with growing horror, and that was that Cora Riddings, young and bright, was being enmeshed in a web of her mother's weaving, and that the innocent spider in the web was Mr. Denvers, the sixty-five-year-old man, who was really seventy-five in many ways. The culminating point was reached when Mr. Denvers, half-doting from ill-health, came to Browning House with the sheaf of parchments proving his shares in various factories and real estate.

"Don't leave the room, Higgins," said Mrs. Riddings.

They wanted her as a witness.

Poor old Denvers was proposing for the hand of Cora, and quite guilelessly bringing his parchments with him to prove his wealth. Belinda went hot and cold, for she had guessed that the letters Cora Riddings gave her to post, one per day, addressed to a certain Thomas Baines, were to a young man whom Cora liked, but to whom her parents had some objection.

Cora Riddings came into the room even whilst Belinda wondered as to what was going to happen.

"Cora, dear," said her mother, "Mr. Denvers has done you a very great honour. He has asked your father and myself for your hand in marriage —and we have given our consent."

Cora flashed a horrified look at her father. He sat biting his nails—a working-class habit he had not been able to lose. He always did it when he was worried.

"But, father!" protested Cora.

Poor Mr. Denvers could not hear all that was going on.

"I brought these to show that I'm *bona fide*," he said, beaming at Cora. "Now, don't you think she ought to marry me?"

He pushed his parchments across the table and addressed Belinda. He was only a poor, amiable, half-demented creature.

"I think," said Belinda, in a tone that would have startled any person not absolutely stone-deaf, "that if you married her grandmother, it'd be more like it."

Mr. Denvers stared at Belinda, shaking his head gently.

"No, no!" he protested feebly. "It's that girl I want, not her grandmother."

"Higgins, don't forget yourself!" said Mrs. Riddings, furiously.

Higgins had her own opinion on that point. She knew that Mr. Riddings would like her to forget herself, that Mrs. Riddings would like her to quite overlook herself, in fact. But she contented herself with saying, in a meek tone contradicted by her fine black eyes, "He asked my opinion, ma'am, and I gave it."

But Belinda's remark had lifted the scene from sordid tragedy into satirical farce.

"It's for Cora herself to decide," said Mr. Riddings, shouting at Mr. Denvers. "Good gracious!"—in an undertone—"Why doesn't he carry an ear-trumpet?"

"Cora knows her duty," said Mrs. Riddings.

Belinda saw that Cora had been made to feel that her parents' dilemma of debt was for her to solve. The girl had in her some of the stuff of which martyrs are made.

"I couldn't live with him, mother," said Cora.

"You'd get used to him. Age is nothing," said her mother. "There are disparities worse than the disparity of youth and age. And—he's almost seventy, now. He would not trouble you long."

Belinda was turning to leave the room.

"Oh, you needn't go, Higgins," said Mrs. Riddings.

"I couldn't bear him," said Cora Riddings, suddenly, a flush on her cheek, a flame in her eye. "And it isn't because he's old." She stopped herself from saying more.

"Why is it, then?" inquired Mr. Riddings. "I thought the chief objection was his age."

Cora was silent.

"I'm sure we should be happy," said the old man, feebly. "See—these are capital shares. Ten per cent., and safe as eggs." He chuckled. It was like the sound of dry peas rattling in a bag.

“I’m not a horse!” flashed Cora, in a towering rage. “How can you think I would marry the poor old man *so?*” She dashed past Mr. Denvers, saying, as she reached his chair, “ No, Mr. Denvers, no!”

“She won’t have me!” he said, smiling piteously. “It’s because I’m getting on in years a bit, isn’t it? Eh, but I’d have been good to her.” He fumbled after his stick, and Belinda helped him to the door, down the steps, and right to his own door.

It was late that night when Belinda heard a tap at her door. Belinda was buying her own candles, and reading ten minutes every night before going to sleep, as an antidote to all the grubby work she was doing.

“Come in,” said Belinda, putting down her book. She half suspected it was Mrs. Riddings come to “blow her up” for her interference.

“Sh-sh!” said Cora’s voice.

She entered the room, carrying a candle, whose light showed up a face swollen with honest tears.

“I have come to you in my dire need,” she said.

Belinda thrilled, because it was so absolutely like a book. Belinda had never realized just how romantic she was until that moment.

“Sh-sh!” said Cora, in a listening attitude. She went to the door of the room and looked along the passage. Apparently all was well. She re-entered the room. Belinda was sitting on the bedside in her homely nightdress that was made out of a couple of Sam Higgins’ old shirts.

“Have you ever been in love, Belinda?” inquired the girl, a little nervously.

Belinda was thinking.

“I don’t know,” she said, ponderingly. “What does it feel like? If you’ll tell me what it feels like, I’ll tell you if I’ve had it.”

Cora could not forbear a smile.

“Has your heart ever thumped hard when anyone came near you?” she asked, shyly.

“No,” said Belinda. “I can’t say it’s gone any faster. I did once have th’ palpitation, but the doctor said I should leave off having chips to my supper.”

Cora Riddings could not tell if Belinda was quite sincere.

“Well, it doesn’t really matter,” she said. “I want you to run an errand for me. Will you?”

“I’ll do anything for you,” said Belinda.

“There is a young man I am in love with,” said Cora, dreamily staring at the hole in the damp wall. “If I stay here I shall end by marrying Mr. Denvers. I know I shall. It isn’t that I’m weak. But I shan’t be able to bear to think of dad in the Bankruptcy Court. I’m fond of him. But I know it’s the right thing. They’re not living as they ought to here. It’s the thing that ought to happen, this smash. To go on will be worse tragedy. Do you know Ibsen?”

Belinda shook her head, looking a little pathetic in her ignorance.

“They’ll be driven into a smaller house,” said Cora, “in a strange place, and they’ll get out of the set they’re in. They’ll have a sporting chance of being more like human beings—and—it will be better for Grandma, too.”

“They do live a cat-and-dog life, here,” said Belinda.

“But if I stayed,” continued Cora, “they would break me down. I know they would. I should think of dad’s face in the court. No, I must go away. You poor thing! You’re shivering. Get into bed.”

Belinda got back into bed.

Cora Riddings frowned at the walls of the damp room.

“A rotten hole, this, to put anyone in,” she said, witheringly. “Yes, I shall go. They deserve it. They’ve no morals. They put you in here—and they’ll even sell me, their flesh and blood!”

Then she told Belinda her plans.

"You'll elope?" said Belinda.

Cora nodded.

"I'm afraid, though, you'll lose your place!" she said, regretfully.

Then a bright idea seized her.

"I say—come and keep house for Tom and me!" she said.

Belinda's face lit up. The brilliant girl-graduate and the drudge shook hands.

"You can have every night off," said Cora.

Belinda got an idea.

"It would be fine," she thought, "to get places with newly married couples, a year with each. They'd be so grateful, poor things!"

Cora, later, went softly out, leaving Belinda quite dazzled at the prospect of being fairy godmother in a real love tale.

CHAPTER IV

The Crash

NEXT day, Mrs. Riddings was out of one temper into another. Belinda guessed the reason, she had noticed two blue envelopes in the morning's post. Somebody demanding money, evidently.

If Mrs. Riddings had not looked ill, Belinda, after all that had passed, would have thought her a perfect monster. As it was, she did her level best to make everything go smoothly, though it was pretty much like trying to calm things down when everybody's nerves were shaken by the knowledge that wreck was imminent.

Jerry came in during the morning and said two queer-looking men were outside, looking at the house. Whereupon Belinda was sent to inspect them from the attic window, and to report. Hoping to cheer the family, she gave it as her opinion that they were only admiring the geraniums— which made a slight smile flicker over Cora Riddings' wan face. Bailiffs admiring the geraniums was such a unique idea that it could only have originated in Belinda.

"Stop that!" called Mrs. Riddings, when Jerry put on the musical box, midway during lunch. Jerry stopped the machine in the middle of the National Anthem.

"Don't you see I've a headache, boy!" said Mrs. Riddings, half apologizing for her sharpness. She was very fond of Jerry. Belinda liked her for it. She would always give even the devil his due.

It was when Belinda was washing up the crockery, in the little scullery, that the boy peeped in, and Belinda guessed that his mother had gone to lie down. Mrs. Riddings did not encourage familiarity with menials.

"What's the matter with everyone, General?" he asked.

Belinda started.

She had not heard that pet name since her dad lay dying in her arms.

"I say—" began Jerry.

He was surprised to see Belinda's eyes fill with tears so quickly.

"I've—I've a headache," explained Belinda.

"So's Cora, so's mother," said Jerry. He looked at her reproachfully.

"Are you getting middle-class?" asked the imp. "I say—don't wipe your eyes on the pot-towel, Higgins. It is not done."

Higgins laughed.

"It'd be as much as my place is worth," she said. "You won't tell?"

"Tell! My eye! I wouldn't have you leave us for the world, Belinda. I say—would you like to see me spin my new top? It's got red, white and blue paper on."

Belinda nodded.

"But why did you say you'd a headache?" queried the insistent one.

"Because lies is catching," said Belinda.

Jerry pondered.

"Then you've not a headache?" he said.

Belinda shook her head.

She told him how, when she was a tiny girl, half his age, she used to march about in a paper cap, beating a drum, and leading imaginary armies, and that she would be nothing less than a General, and how it had grown into a name of quite another meaning—a name not meaning battle, but love, though it was leading all the same. How only her father had called her that, and he was now dead.

"What made you say it?" asked Belinda.

"Because you stand like one. I once saw a real one. He stood like you, and he had the same sort of look."

There was a little pause.

"What *is* the matter with everyone?" asked Jerry again. "Why does mother jump when the bell rings?"

Belinda looked at him, and then made up her mind.

"Because you owe money for stuff you've had," she said, bluntly.

Jerry could not understand.

She explained. The shame that overspread his face was tragic to see.

"We can't help it, you and me," said Belinda. "But—when you grow up and have a house of your own—always cut your coat accordin' to your cloth, or a bit less, if aught."

Jerry was looking at his coat.

"If you've only a ha'penny and want a penny bun," went on Belinda, "wait till you've got the other ha'penny. For if it cost three farthings to make that bun, somebody's lost a farthing an' their wages for making it, if they get only a ha'penny. Though Robin Hood was a fine man," she said, irreverently. "But your father's not Robin Hood, an' your mother's not Maid Marion. They ought to stump up. *They* don't give it to the poor."

Jerry fetched out his top.

"What will they do, if they come for the money?" he asked, referring to the mystery-men.

"Take the furniture."

"I say," said Jerry, haltingly.

Belinda smiled.

"Can I put my fishing-rod in your box?"

Belinda said "Yes," and he ran off.

Cora Riddings peeped in.

"Shoo—" said Belinda gently to the half-blind tabby cat, sitting on the four-legged stool that was Belinda's dining-chair. Puss had been one of the items Mrs. Riddings had economized on, but Belinda had fattened her a little already, and her eyes looked less like gas-lamps.

"Oh, bother the hairs!" said Cora, and sat down, lifting the cat on her knee.

"You *are* going to help me, Belinda?" she asked, after Belinda had wiped the last of the dishes.

"I will," said Belinda, violently.

They both laughed.

"I shouldn't have felt so *shoormong* about it," began Belinda.

"What was that word?"

Belinda said she was studying French. "Just to keep my mental balance. Two inches of candle every night, and a French book," she beamed.

"I see," said Cora, repressing a smile.

"Well, I shouldn't have felt so (what is it?) of helping you, but I prayed for my dreams to be directed. You see, it's like this. Helping you, I'm going against the missis—and she pays me my wages. I was in a bit of a fog. But I've looked it all up in Napoleon's *Book of Fate*," she continued, contentedly, "and it says 'success is in store for you if you dream of a rainbow,' and, as I was sat on the rainbow, it should be twice as good."

"You were dreaming about sitting on a rainbow?" queried Cora.

"Fishing," said Belinda, earnestly. "And that's a good dream unless you catch naught. Success in love and marriage, so you'll be all right."

"I believe you're romantic, Belinda," said Cora, in surprise.

"I believe I should be—if I didn't sit on the tendency."

Belinda saw the jibe when Cora inquired, "Can you sit on a tendency?" Belinda was a strange mixture of intelligent acuteness and ignorance, bound together with quotations and misquotations, a pathetic reaching after culture that was almost a religion.

"Do you know where Jenny Lane is, Belinda?" asked Cora, watching her get out the baking-board and the flour dredger ready for making the patties.

"Where the Health Food place is," said Belinda.

Cora nodded.

She looked towards the open door and listened.

"I want you to go to the end of Jenny Lane," she said, flushing, "and at three o'clock you will see a young man in a brown suit, with a green leaf in his coat. You must wear a green leaf, so that he will know you. We must break away, now—or I shan't have the heart to do it when the crash comes. Give Tom this letter. It contains all arrangements."

Belinda was looking at Cora.

"But the missis told me to make patties for tea," she said, in a harassed way. Staving off irate butchers and helping in elopements, apparently were only incidents in this household, where she had not a moment's leisure during a sixteen-hour day, until she crept into bed in the dark room.

"Oh, I'll make the patties," said Cora, lightly. "H-m, what is there in them?"

"Potatoes, sliced thin," said Belinda, laughingly. "You'll find the tins on the first shelf there." She could not guess from the brilliant young college graduate's self-confident tone that Cora had never made a puff in her life.

"Mother won't be up for an hour and a half yet."

Belinda hurried, nevertheless.

She drew a breath of delight in getting into the open air. Her eye received delicate pleasure from the sight of the saplings covered with leaves turning brown, and she fell to wondering if, when she reached the "sere and yellow," she would be going from place to place, a domestic serf. She realized that it was quite possible, that it was, in fact, highly probable, and the thought made her ache a little.

"There's sure to be a place somewhere where I'd be appreciated," she thought, and wound up, "I must keep my eye skinned."

Several Heathill people turned to look at the quaint figure in the man's jacket, the black sailor hat, too small by a size, the rather long skirt, and the green leaf so prominent on her breast. Belinda's walk was certainly and definitely masculine, and she held her head up with a look that said she thought no small beer of herself. But if anyone smiled, the smile was immediately quenched when Belinda smiled back with those black, amiable, glancing eyes and their frank beauty, as if receiving a compliment or a friendliness. They were the eyes through which looked the soul of a woman, the clear vision of a little child, the bravery of a close fighter with poverty, and one as yet neither crushed nor embittered by it.

At the end of Jenny Lane was a young man in a brown suit, a green leaf in his buttonhole.

"Are you Mr. Baines?" inquired Belinda.

He touched the green leaf.

It was romantically thrilling to Belinda. He was not handsome, but there was a charm about him. Belinda was glad he was not good looking. She held it as a maxim that good looks were unnecessary in men.

"I'll look at the arum lilies whilst you read your letter."

Tom Baines saw Belinda's eyes, and took the familiarity in good part. He stood on the kerb, reading the letter. Belinda stared into the florist's window, her mind full of roses, carnations, camellias, and golden-hearted lilies against banks of moss. But there was a pot of pet roses that almost made Belinda butt into the shop and ask the price, though she knew that she could not buy them whatever the price was.

"Oh, I say—" said Tom.

Belinda started as though the voice had come out of the pot of pet roses.

"Higgins, my name is," said Belinda.

"Will you tell Cora, Miss Higgins," said Baines, respectfully, "that I will meet her on No. 3 Platform at 10.30 to-night. Don't bungle, for heaven's sake! Miss Riddings is a minor, you see."

Belinda looked puzzled.

"I don't mean a collier," he said, genially.

"Oh, I didn't think you did. I'm not so hignorant. But I always thought it was something to do with Irish music."

"Cora is not of age to marry without parental consent," explained Baines. "If—if we were overtaken—well, there'd be trouble. If we can manage to hide away for a month, they can't do anything."

Belinda said they would have to hope for the best. There was something irresistibly warmhearted, as well as comical, in the way she said "we" —linking herself up with the mad escapade of the two lovers. The young man in brown thanked Belinda, and she told him that he was welcome, and that she believed we were born into this world to do good turns for each other, and that, so far, it had cost her nothing.

He watched her disappear at the end of a long street, and his verdict was that she had too much originality to be a servant very long—at least, in one place.

When Belinda, heated and anxious, reached the gate of Browning House, she saw that Cora was looking for her through a window.

"Oh, blow it!" thought poor Belinda, who was feeling very tired, "the missis is getting up. I hope the patties are all right."

When she opened the back door, she knew that the patties were all wrong. Cora had also smelled them. Belinda and she rushed together to the rescue. Belinda arrived at the oven door first.

"Cinders," said Belinda, trying to smile.

She was swallowing hard. She could hear the missis turning on the bathroom tap, and felt like having a bath herself, instead of which she would be hauled over the coals.

"They were all right a moment since," said Cora, in surprise and regret.

"Higgins!" came Mrs. Riddings' voice. "Have you set the place on fire?"

Belinda went to the foot of the stairs.

"It's the patties, ma'am," she said, humbly.

Cora was going to chip in.

"Shut up," breathed Belinda, "or she'll know you sent me out."

"Do you mean to say you have allowed the patties to burn, Higgins?" almost shrieked Mrs. Riddings. "Good gracious! I can't take a needed rest but everything goes wrong. I suppose you were reading some trashy romance." Mrs. Riddings herself read every novel, in its expensive edition. It was too much for Belinda.

"If I like a bit o' luv," she said, indignantly, "I don't see that it matters to you."

"I shan't take any impertinence," cried Mrs. Riddings, authoritatively.

"Poor Belinda!" said Cora. "I'm awfully sorry about the patties."

They spread them out on the table ready for Mrs. Riddings to inspect. Belinda's indignation turned to a wry smile as she gazed at them.

"Fancy Mr. and Mrs. Symon Rhodes eating them," she said, and Cora exploded. They were her mother's best friends and were coming to tea that day. Mrs. Rhodes had said that she read nothing but Court news.

"How did he look?" asked Cora. "Did he look happy after he read my letter?"

"He did and he didn't. He looked more like he couldn't help it. And his hands shook, and I don't think he quite knew whether he stood on his head or his feet. It is No. 3 Platform, half-past nine, to-night."

"You're a darling!" said Cora. "Half-past nine?"

"No. 3, half-past nine," said Belinda, repeating her mistake, for the patties, despite her bravado, were worrying her.

Ten minutes later, Mrs. Riddings, looking as fresh as a daisy, came down and pitched into Belinda. Her great point was the fearful waste of material. There was a brief passage of arms between her and Belinda.

"You must have been brought up in a gutter, girl!" said Mrs. Riddings. That roused the Belinda who had been making only apologetic defences. To say that she, Belinda Higgins, had been brought up in a gutter, even if it were true, was an insult to those dear people at home. Belinda's hands went to her hips.

"I was born as good as you," she said. "An' I can look the whole world in the face, for I owe not any man, which is a jolly sight more than you can say. If you'd ha' bin born at one time you'd ha' bin put where folk could find you—in one o' them prison-houses for debt, an' you'd ha' happen bin fain o' even them patties, there." She pointed to the things with an eloquence that had passed into farce—save that Belinda's black eyes were yet full of tears, tears brought by insult to her people, the idea that they were gutter-folk.

"I burnt those patties, mother," said Cora, coolly.

"You!"

The word came swift as a bullet. Belinda was pulling faces and making signals to Cora to say what a fool she was, and to stop her if possible.

"Since I am going to marry a poor man," said Cora, "I thought I had best take lessons in cookery, so I got

Belinda to let me make the patties. *She* did not burn them at all."

"But—she was overlooking you, I suppose," said Mrs. Riddings.

She turned suddenly on Belinda.

"You have been out, Higgins?" she challenged.

"Me!" cried Belinda, trying to look innocent, and blushing frantically.

"You've been sending this girl as a go-between," said Mrs. Riddings. "Now, it's no good, Cora, you can't get off with Tom. You are watched —"

Ting-a-ting.

Mrs. Riddings lost her temper.

"You take a month's notice, Higgins," said she, and sailed off to open the door.

Cora was looking at Belinda in a troubled way.

"Don't worry," smiled Belinda. "I was going to leave. In fact, I've an idea where I'm going next. As one door shuts, another opens."

Belinda began to cut bread and butter for tea.

"It's no use, ma'am! We're coming in," said a rough voice.

"But I tell you, Mr. Riddings has already wired," protested Mrs. Riddings.

"We haven't got no wire, have we, Bill?" said the rough voice. "It's no good shuttin' the door, ma'am. The foot's in, an' we're within our rights. Bum in, Bill!"

"Higgins!" called Mrs. Riddings, hysterically.

Belinda came to the rescue.

"Make them go, the coarse brutes," appealed Mrs. Riddings to Belinda.

"What do you want?" inquired Belinda, looking a General indeed.

"The goods an' chattels," said the one addressed as Bill. He was a sandy-haired man with a cast in his eye, and there was a trace of embarrassment in his manner.

Mrs. Riddings was recovering. Belinda's rush to her assistance had given her courage, and the colour was coming back to her face. She had a dim sense of gratitude to Belinda, to whom she had said that she had been brought up in the gutter, not many minutes ago; and mentally cancelled the month's notice.

"You've to show your paper, haven't you?" said Belinda, though she knew nothing of such matters.

"The warrant's there," said Bill.

He had taken a fancy to the servant. Belinda's black eyes, as she had asked what they wanted, had been very splendid, and to Bill she quite overshadowed the lady of the house, despite her cap being all on one side.

"Let me see!" said Mrs. Riddings, sharply, haughtily.

Belinda's way of dealing with these men had inspired her. As yet, too, she could hardly realize that her furniture could be seized, that it was possible they would not go on just as they had done— for years.

She looked at the paper.

Then she gave an exclamation of horror.

Mr. and Mrs. Symon Rhodes were coming towards the house. Mrs. Riddings turned sick. Belinda always said, afterwards, when she told the tale, that Mrs. Riddings was green as grass, as she moaned: "Higgins! What shall we do?"

General Belinda took command.

"Come in," she said to the bailiff's men, "and wipe your feet, please." They followed her into the kitchen.

"What'll you have?" said Belinda, looking at Bill.

She set them a couple of stiff-backed chairs, and invited them to the table, her table, at which she had to dine, alone, "like a wild beast."

"What's the menoo?" asked Bill.

"Cold sausage, an' cheese, an' onions."

Bill would have the hot dish.

"Trot out the sausage," said his mate.

"Can't you come to-morrow instead?" asked Belinda.

Bill laughed.

"To-morrow! We're here—till the goods goes. Or—until the cash comes forth."

"Oh, yes," floated Mrs. Rhodes's high-pitched voice, from the drawing-room, "It is quite true. The blinds were down as we came by. After all, the poor old man has ailed a long time, and really —he is better off," piously. "And how fond he was of Cora! Syncope, Dr. Pate said. He must have a lot of money. A great pity Cora did not marry him."

Belinda was listening. She realized that they were referring to Mr. Denvers. It was scarcely credible.

She turned to the bailiff's men, who, also, had heard.

"The old chap the girl was engaged to has snuffed it," she explained. "He's as rich as a Jew. Ten to one he has left her a fortune. Now, don't go and bang into the drawing-room while those two folk are here. It's no good hurting folks' feelings on top of their pockets. So behave yourselves."

"You haven't a bottle of beer?" asked Bill.

"Happen I have, an' happen I haven't," said Belinda, coming as near coquetry as she could get, which was not very near. She got out a bottle from a cupboard.

"My! that's a top on it," said Bill, holding up the glass.

Cora was coming into the kitchen, sent by her mother for tea and cakes.

She stared at the two men.

"Who are you?" she asked.

Belinda had not known before how much she could look like her mother.

"Bums," said Bill, amiably. "You haven't any cigs on you, have you? Ladies do smoke, they say."

Cora went pale. She had known the crash would come. It was here. Could she calmly walk out of this wreck, to love—and leave her parents to face the music?

After all, they had educated her, clothed her, fed her. The bell rang. It was her father. No one but he rang like that—one long, echoing peal.

"I'll go, Belinda," she said, and went to break the news.

CHAPTER V

Belinda Aids a Poet

WHEN Cora Riddings opened the door, she saw that her father was not well. His face was a nasty grey colour and he appeared to breathe with difficulty.

"Ill, dad?" she asked, quickly. He nodded assent, murmuring something about a stitch in his side.

"The Symon Rhodes's are here," Cora told him in a low voice. He looked weary and irritated. "But I think they are getting ready to go," went on Cora. She would have told him of the other visitors, who certainly were not ready to go, but her courage failed her.

"Tell them I've gone up to my room. I must lie down," said Mr. Riddings.

"Dad's not well," said Cora, going into the drawing-room, where Mrs. Symon Rhodes was slowly drawing on her yellow gloves.

"I sent him to lie down," Cora informed them.

They departed five minutes later, expressing the hope that poor Mr. Riddings would be all right in the morning. Never had Mrs. Riddings seen them depart with such delight in her heart.

"Those awful men, Cora!"

"I've seen them. But I don't see anything awful about them. I think it is we who are awful."

"You've had your share in the prosperity," said Mrs. Riddings. "And—you could have saved us. Perhaps if you had said 'Yes' the other night the poor old man would have made you his heiress. I suppose you still mean to stick to that shipping clerk?"

"I intend to marry Tom, mother."

Belinda, who was carrying away a tray, overheard that.

"Oh, Higgins, take Mr. Riddings something hot. He's a cold," said Mrs. Riddings, casually.

Higgins thought of her father's loving care of her mother all those weary years. Whilst Mrs. Riddings was still arguing with Cora, prophesying dreadful things that would happen if she married Tom Baines, Belinda was mixing a hot drink. She took it up to Mr. Riddings, "There's something hot here, sir," she said. "It'll do your cold good."

"Set it on the mat," said Mr. Riddings.

"Are you in bed?"

"Yes."

"Then I'll bring it in. You might make yourself worse," said Belinda, and, turning the knob, she walked into the room.

Never had Mr. Riddings been so surprised. "Set it on the table there, Higgins," he told her.

She stood looking at him in a sympathetic way that was embarrassing to a man who did not know how he was going to pay her her month's wages.

"I'd drink it hot," she advised. "It's good stuff—so father always said."

"Does it do your father good?"

"It *did.*"

"Did!" said Mr. Riddings, taking a gentle sip.

"He died," said Belinda. The tears she had been unable to shed at the funeral came easily now. A drop splashed on Mr. Riddings' hand as he was setting the cup back on the table.

"I beg your pardon," said Belinda. She was apologizing for the tear that had dropped on his hand.

"How old was your father?" asked Mr. Riddings.

Belinda told him.

"My age," he said. "H'm!" He stared at the window-curtain, then observed, without looking at her: "You're a good girl, Belinda. You may go," and there was something like human kindness in his voice, restrained though it was by custom.

"I'll wait for the cup," said Belinda.

She waited, sitting on a little chair near the open door.

"I'm sorry the bailiffs are in," she said, after a while. She thought that he knew, that Cora had told him on opening the door for him.

"The—the what?"

"The bailiff's men, sir," replied poor Belinda, noting the terrible change that had passed over Mr. Riddings.

"Do you mean to say—?" he began. "There, get out, Belinda, and take the cup. I'm getting up. I'll throw the fellows out."

"They've a warrant, sir."

The crash he had been steering against had at last come.

Belinda went downstairs with the empty cup, very sorry, and yet very glad—sorry for the Riddings, glad for her own financial soundness. Only a pound stood between herself and penury, nevertheless she had that superior feeling of financial soundness, as she went up and down amidst the falling splendours of the house of Riddings. She wrote a letter to her mother. The bailiff's men were playing dominoes in the kitchen, Bill throwing out hints about "love-letters" and wishing he were the "chap that was goin' to get that letter" Belinda was writing. To all of which Belinda made no answer, but scratched away on the thin poor notepaper—eight sheets a penny, with a free blotter advertising pills:

"Dear Mother,

"I do not think I shall reign here long as they are going broke, in fact, the bums are in, and I don't know if I'm watching them or they're watching me. Anyhow we're all in the same kitchen. Of course I feel a bit anxious about my wages, but so far they have not borrowed off me and I still have the pound. I hope A. is treating you pretty decent. She would like this street. But give me our own old house and the old friendly street. I wonder how much old Rednose made out of our furniture. Well, we'll try not to mind. Hello! there's the missis calling—you'd think me very precious if you heard the number of times they call me to the rescue. But I broke the boss in on the boot-cleaning question. He isn't a bad sort when you get to know him, and maybe I'll clean his boots while he's not so grand like I used to do dad's, though he did kick, didn't he? I *must* go. She's coming. God bless you—good-night—keep your end up,

"Ever your loving Belinda."

She thrust this into an envelope as Mrs. Riddings bounced into the kitchen with: "Higgins, didn't you hear me?"—whilst Bill grinned behind his hand.

"I was coming," said Belinda.

"Mr. Riddings is worse," said her mistress. "I think we ought to fetch the doctor. He's got a temperature." She left the kitchen, giving the two men a haughty look.

Belinda was following.

"I've got a temperature," said Bill, slyly, to Belinda.

"Look here—it's four and a blank," said his companion, irritated. "Leave th' women a-be."

"It's her eyes," explained Bill, when Belinda had gone. "I once had a bull pup—"

"Oh, get on wi' thy game," said the other.

When Belinda walked into the hall, she found Mrs. Riddings waiting for her at the foot of the stairs.

"Do you know anything of sick folk, and how to treat them, Higgins?" she inquired.

"I once had a session at the Home Nursing Class," said Belinda, modestly.

"I'd like you to see Mr. Riddings and give an opinion of him," said Mrs. Riddings. It was a surprise. Belinda had been treated as having no opinions. They went upstairs, and on the way could hear Mr. Riddings coughing. When Belinda went into the room, the green-shaded lamp at the head of the bed was lit, and she saw a change in Mr. Riddings. He smiled feebly when he recognized Belinda.

"Going to die after that stuff—like your father did," he said, trying to joke. He was breathing badly. His face was flushed.

"Pneumonia, I think," declared Belinda, after a little investigation.

"Nonsense, Higgins!" said Mrs. Riddings.

"That's what I think," said Belinda. When she brought the doctor back, half an hour later, his opinion coincided with Belinda's. Belinda crept down the stairs after him.

"I say," she said, in a timid voice.

The doctor turned.

"The bailiffs are in," said Belinda. "Can't they be kicked out until Mr. Riddings is better?" She explained the situation in a few minutes. The doctor rubbed his chin, then promised that he would see what he could do. An hour later, the two men removed, by written order, until Mr. Riddings was fit to attend to business or dead.

"Where's Cora?" asked Mrs. Riddings, tearfully.

"I'll go up and see," answered Belinda.

She went upstairs again, calling on her way up to look in at Jerry, who was in bed. He was reading *Huckleberry Finn*, and Belinda had to stay and hear a few paragraphs. Then she tucked him round, blew out the candle, and went along to Cora's room. A bar of light showed under the door. All the rooms had gas but Belinda's—and that had been cut off to stop the servants reading after they had gone to bed.

"Come in," said Cora.

Belinda entered the bedroom.

"You're not going, *now*, are you?" she asked, in surprise.

"Why not?" inquired Cora. She was sitting on the box that was strapped and labelled.

"Your pa's got pneumonia," said Belinda, simply.

Cora looked at Belinda like a wild thing at bay.

"If I stay—they'll talk me round," she said. "Don't you see? I couldn't stand it. When dad gets better—"

"*If* he does," said Belinda.

Cora stared at her and went very pale.

"There's another man, now poor old Denvers is gone, and if I saw dad getting up from a sick bed—to face a Bankruptcy Court—I should surrender, *and sacrifice Tom.* Don't you understand? To sacrifice Tom—to get them out of their difficulties and let them go on the same old careless way. It sounds cruel to you, I know, but I know I'm right." She stared appealingly at Belinda. The church clock outside struck nine.

"What do you think, Belinda?" said Cora.

"I wouldn't have left my dad in pneumonia for the best chap that ever walked shoe-leather," vowed Belinda. "I'd wait till he got better and fight him then. But I wouldn't go away and perhaps come home to find him a corpse."

When Cora had finished crying, she ripped the labels off the box and took off her hat.

"So you're not going," said Belinda, with a sigh of relief.

"I'm not going," said Cora. Outside, the clock struck the quarter.

"Tom will be waiting," said Cora. "Will you run along and tell him, Belinda, that I cannot leave my father?"

Belinda went. When she got clear of the street, she experienced the delicious sense of freedom that always came to her when she had her back to the place. The lamps made the trees cast soft shadows on the walls. She stared up at the night sky, and had the rapture of seeing stars. Then she fell to wondering what Annie was giving her mother for supper, and if the bed was shaken soft enough for the pain-sore limbs. Thinking in this strain, Belinda walked on to the station platform just the clock pointed to five and twenty minutes past nine.

Belinda waited twenty minutes.

"He's fallen soft," was her verdict. "Well, I shouldn't have thought it."

At ten o'clock, however, an overcoated figure, with a porter carrying his box, hove in sight. Tom Baines never forgot the sight of Belinda waiting for him under the big station lamp in her jacket that made her look so squat.

"She isn't coming?" he asked, in amaze. There was heartbreak in his voice, too.

"Her father's got pneumonia."

"Then, she isn't coming?" he repeated. He looked sick with disappointment.

"She couldn't go away and her father on the point o' being a corpse," said Belinda, defensively. "But I can tell you this—she'll stick to you, or my name isn't Higgins."

Tom was satisfied.

Belinda watched him go off the station platform a half-disconsolate, half-bitter droop about his walk.

That night, she sat up with Mr. Riddings, in company with Mrs. Riddings. He coughed horribly and the fever was increasing. What did Mrs. Riddings think of, as she sat in that sick-room, in her pink dressing gown, yawning with fatigue as the night wore on? Belinda could not guess. Once she caught herself nodding, and just saved herself toppling off the chair. The jerk thoroughly awakened her. She started with a "I didn't mean to go to sleep —" and saw Mrs. Riddings, a weary-eyed, worn woman, holding her husband's hand. He was asleep—his face a flame against the white of the pillow.

"There's a bit of human nature left yet," thought Belinda.

Cora took Belinda's place at seven.

Belinda took Mrs. Riddings a cup of tea.

"The bailiffs is gone, that's one good thing, ma'am!" observed Belinda, respectfully.

"How shall we live until Mr. Riddings is better?" said Mrs. Riddings. "Thanks, Belinda." She took the tea and the biscuit with something like gratitude. "*I* don't know," she added, wearily.

"I once pawned my fiddle when dad lost his job," said Belinda. Mrs. Riddings winced at her slavey claiming financial troubles along with her. But a rare gleam of humour trailed across the horizon of her artificial superiority. There was something about Belinda's "cheek" that was irresistible.

"Well, what would *you* do?" asked the mistress.

"I should sell those marble ladies on the drawing-room fire-shelf," said Belinda. "Just to be going on with."

"But the bailiffs—"

"What the eye never sees the heart never grieves," said Belinda, who was as chock full of maxims as her dad.

So it came that Belinda carried off in a black bag the exquisite marble copy of Venus. She proceeded down Jenny Lane, towards a by-way, where was a very old-fashioned curiosity shop. The window was full of books. Belinda lingered over the sight wistfully.

"What have you got there?" inquired the young man over the counter. Belinda was perspiring and panting.

Her hat had toppled awry. The black bag looked mysterious.

"Venus," said Belinda. "An' glad to get rid of her."

"Bring the vixen out," said the young man, smiling. Belinda then saw that an old man with a white beard was sitting at a table on the other side of the counter, examining a piece of glassware by aid of a magnifier.

"Seventeenth century," exclaimed the old man, in jubilation, turning to the young man.

"Jolly good, dad," replied the young man.

He went over to look at the glass through the magnifier.

It was at this moment that the shop door opened, very gently. There came in a man, down at heel, in threadbare garments, a man who carried with him a distinguished air of refinement, an aroma of dreams, an exquisite presence. Belinda looked into the fine face, and felt something stir within her, a new shyness, an awe.

"Are you in a hurry?" asked the young man of the shop, addressing Belinda.

She shook her head, dreading the sound of her own voice. Hence she witnessed the pathetic transaction between a shopkeeper and a poet, who was parting with his book-treasures for bread to keep him alive. The old man and the young man fleeced him. He must sell. Belinda's business eye saw that. But he winced and expostulated gently when they offered him one shilling for a beautifully illustrated copy of Shakespeare. He went out with three shillings and sixpence, and an aching place in his soul.

"I'll take that copy of Shakespeare," said Belinda before she began negotiating the marble Venus.

She managed to get it for three shillings, after much haggling, and was positive that if she had not seen with her own eyes how much they gave the poet for it they would have charged her thrice that.

"The autograph alone will be worth pounds some day," said the old man. "He's a real poet. Some day he will be famous."

Belinda did not tell them that she had bought the book to give back to the poet.

She sold the marble for two pounds fifteen, and left the shop feeling that she had not been "done" very much.

When she entered Browning House, she was surprised to find Mrs. Riddings in the kitchen— cooking.

"The doctor has been. He says Mr. Riddings will pull through, he thinks. You look tired, Higgins. Suppose you lie down until lunch. We shall have to be up all night again."

Belinda looked as though she could have been knocked down with a feather. She planked the money down on the table, telling the whole story.

"Life is very sordid," sighed Mrs. Riddings.

"It's a bit of a fight," agreed Belinda, cheerfully.

Within a week Mr. Riddings was out of danger. Belinda saw that some sort of an understanding had grown up between mother, father, and daughter—a strained sort of understanding, it is true, but, none the less, a better feeling than they had known for some time. One evening, Belinda answered the front door bell and found herself face to face with Tom Baines.

"Oh——!" she gasped.

"You were right, Belinda," he told her, in a whisper. "She's going to stick to me, and—we're going on fine—so far. It's all through you."

Which amazed Belinda.

Amazing things continued to happen in Browning House during the week following the burial of Mr. Denvers. Tom Baines was at first reluctantly accepted as the fiancé of Cora. When he said that he did not wish to marry Cora until he could give her a good home, the air cleared. Perhaps the parents clung to the hope that by that time Cora would be tired of waiting. Nevertheless, Belinda saw thát there was a chance that Mr. Riddings would grow fond of Tom and take his side. These were two of the amazing things. The other was the withdrawal of the claim on the furniture. An unknown friend had paid off fifty pounds. The other amazing thing was Belinda trying to sing the "Marseillaise" in French, and doing it with English pronunciation—or, to be more correct, the English of Syke Gate. Mr. Riddings never looked behind him after that.

But the great thing was when Mr. Denvers' solicitor called on the Riddings to inform them that Cora had inherited all the old man's money.

Mr. Riddings then proposed a smaller house, and, to his surprise, his wife assented.

Belinda made an excuse for leaving their service.

"But what is the real reason?" asked Mrs. Riddings, dryly.

"I want a quieter place," she said. "This has been too mixed. And—I won't wear a cap."

"Well, I think we could improve," said Mrs. Riddings, when Belinda had left the room.

"She's a heart of gold," said Mr. Riddings.

"What good is a heart in a servant?" said the other, but more kindly than usual. "Though, I'll admit she has her good points."

Thus Belinda passed out of the lives of the Riddings. She refused Cora's invitation to keep house for her.

On a rainy evening, Belinda left the house, going to the expense of a shilling cab ride to take her to the car. She got out and left a parcel at the post-office, registering it. It was addressed to Sim O'Keith, Poet, Back Grammar Street, Heathill, and contained a cabbage, his beloved copy of Shakespeare, and—well wrapped up, so as not to taint the cabbage—a tablet of Parma violet soap. She had enclosed a letter:

"Dear Sir,

"Excuse me, I am sure you will, for I have followed poets since I was a little child, and have known quite a lot of them, for there was a society of them in the town where I lived. If ever you are famous I should like your autograph, and enclose my home address. My father could poet about anything, but never got nothing published. I think because it was too good, for he sent it up often. He once poeted about a beetle, it was beautiful, for he took it up the hill of life and brought it down on the other side, an old man. I hope the cabbage will be nice. I pinched it and it felt tender. Those thieves at the book shop fairly did you in, for I had to give three shillings for the book back, but don't worry. It makes me feel rich to give it back to you. We owe so much to poets and I hope you like the scent of the soap. Hoping you will accept it as a humble tribute to genius, for I am sure you are one,

"Your humbly obedient servant,"

Belinda Higgins.

"P.S.—If you will fill the pan half full of water and keep the lid on till the water evaporates, you will get all the juices, and it's good for cancer.

"B. H."

"There!" said Belinda to herself, coming out of the post office. "Won't he be glad to see it back again!" After which she took her box into the luggage office, and went towards the public news-room to look up a fresh place, wondering what kind of folk she would fall amongst this time. She had already posted her month's wages to her mother. Only fifteen shillings now stood between her and destitution, and yet—she felt absurdly rich. She had served a poet—a real one.

CHAPTER VI

Belinda Stays—and Goes

BELINDA found nothing in the advertisements to suit her, so was reluctantly compelled to return to Syke Gate. Her mother was overjoyed to see her; indeed, she might have been away half a lifetime to warrant the look she got as she came through the doorway of the front downstairs room where Mrs. Higgins lay in bed. Belinda saw at once that her mother was thinner. When Annie had gone from the room both women broke down.

"I wonder what we're crying for!" ejaculated Belinda, as she wiped her eyes.

"Eh, Belinda!" murmured her mother. "Eh! Belinda!"

In those two words were chronicled all her loss of Belinda's presence; all her humiliation at being where she was not wanted; all the sad downfall of having no hearthstone of her own.

"How long can you stay, Belinda?" she asked, trying to keep the eagerness from her voice.

"I'm staying three days," announced Belinda. "Will that do for you?"

The prospect of having Belinda near her for three days brightened Mrs. Higgins up wonderfully. She started to take the tablets again, with her an unmistakable sign of new hope.

"Well, tha hasn't reigned long,' said Jonathan, as he came in from work and found his sister at table.

"She could have gone with the family," said Annie.

Belinda nodded assent.

"I think it's a mistake to leave a place just when people are getting used to you," added Annie.

"But I hadn't got used to them," said Belinda, smiling. "I shall look before I leap next time, you bet! I'll go where they pay their way whatever else they do."

With this determination she scanned the papers, sitting in that front room where her mother basked hungrily in the fine and cheerful presence, even beginning to feel that Belinda was lucky to be able to go out on such adventures.

"Terrible lot of strong young women wanted," gibed Belinda, genially. "All duties! Christian character—whatever that may mean—eighteen pounds a year, and good outings. Pork butcher's shop that is. H'm! We'll not go there."

"And tha'rt not strong, after all, Belinda," moaned her mother. "Eh, do take care o' thyself."

Belinda said she would.

Belinda read hundreds of advertisements during the first and second days of her enforced holiday. She dreamed of them at night; they danced on the ceiling when she looked up at it; finally she let her mother decide where she should go. Mrs. Higgins, screwing her eyes tightly so that she could see nothing, jabbed a pin into one of the advertisements. It read as follows: "Reliable young woman wanted temporarily; housework and assist in small country stores; good home; moderate wages; apply personally to Wells, Newburton Stores, Newburton."

Jonathan found Newburton on a local map. It was ten miles away.

"A bonnie village," said Jonathan, who had fished in the reservoir there.

Belinda did not tell him that her mother had acted as blind Destiny in her choice. "Temporarily" rather upset her apple-cart. Why temporarily? she wondered. Perhaps it was a widower wanting help until he remarried; or some old woman whose powers were failing. She experienced the keen curiosity of a child which is promised a lucky-bag and wishes to look inside at once; nevertheless, she did not go until next day.

"She might be going to America!" said Annie to Mrs. Higgins, who wept to see Belinda ready to depart.

"Take care o' thyself, Belinda," said Mrs. Higgins, ignoring her daughter-in-law's comment.

"I will that," responded Belinda. "But, if it doesn't suit me, I shan't take it, and shall be back to-night—sometime."

Annie's look as Belinda said this told plainly enough that, so far as she could see, "beggars could not be choosers." Belinda bent down to kiss her mother. She reached the door, turned back again and said "ta-ta" once more, then, with a firm resolve not to make a fool of herself again, said "Good-morning" to Annie and left the house carrying a change of clothes, Napoleon's *Book of Fate* and Hugo's *First French Course*, and a little copy of *Silas Marner* which she had found wet with rain in the street when she was on an errand for Annie.

Once she had got over the pang of parting from her mother, Belinda looked about her with interest. She had left Syke Gate behind by the time the melancholy, flung over her by her mother's grief at her going, was passed away. She was on the highroad, hard and white with frost. The scarlet of hips in the hedgerows, the litter of yellow leaves in the dykes, the tall grasses all run to seed, tattered, beggarly-looking, made a little picture to Belinda. As the wind swayed the bare trees, those lines of Longfellow, in which he compares the boughs to the keys of a great instrument, came into her mind. Belinda's mind was like that—a room full of corners hung with poetic extracts, quotations, misquotations, and, here and there, an original idea of her own.

It was ten miles to Newburton, ten up-and-down miles, with hill country melting into wood country, and wood country turning into pasture country. She crossed little bridges, rested under many hedges full of the last gold of the year, and greeted many people, asking how far yet to Newburton. One man, a labourer, clothes the colour of earth, said it was "a goodish stretch"; another said it was "a two hours' walk"; and yet another that it was "a fair distance." Belinda trudged on. Sometimes, when the road was quite empty, she sang bits out of old school songs she remembered, though her schooldays had been brief. She saw an old woman peddling, a chocolate-box suspended around her neck—holding her pathetic wares. Who knew? Belinda saw herself in some remote future, when she was too old for service, peddling like this. She gave the old woman sixpence—the sixpence she had kept for refreshments. Supposing she went back to Syke Gate and did not take this place. After all, why not? There were sadder fates. Belinda liked the feel of the road under her feet, of the sky over her head. Newburton burst on her suddenly on the crest of a hill. It was a pretty village. Little streams spread out in all directions from it glinting in the sunlight. Two children in snowy pinafores were trundling hoops along the quiet road just beyond another of the little bridges. There was a stone wall running alongside the road, and near one of the bridges stood a tiny girl with very light hair, an unattractive child with stubborn or stupid look; it was difficult to tell which.

"Which is Newburton Stores?" asked Belinda.

The child pointed out a small shop set in the middle of a row of cottages. Over the door was a sign. This was Wells' shop.

Belinda opened the door and a rusty bell tinkled loudly. A female face stared into Belinda's—a round, fat, curious, country face swathed in a white woollen shawl. Belinda waited. This was a customer being served. She wanted multitudinous things.

"Perhaps I can serve you," said the woman behind the counter, "if you don't want much?"

"Oh, I've plenty of time," said Belinda.

The woman behind the counter was the ugliest woman Belinda had ever seen; her voice had a weary apathy.

At length the curious fat woman went out with her mountainous bag, the rusty bell tinkling again.

"I've called about that there place," said Belinda. "You are Mrs. Wells—"

"Yes, I'm Mrs. Wells."

"Thought you were," said Belinda, and smiled. "Something told me," she added.

"You'd better see Wells," said the woman.

"Oh, he's not henpecked," mused Belinda.

"Jack!" called the ugly woman.

He came, a man of suave, diplomatic manner, a little man whose sandy head came just to his wife's shoulder.

"I've come after that there place," announced Belinda.

"Oh!" said the suave man pleasantly. He was very pleasant, always pleasant; even when he and Belinda struggled about the wages he never lost that pleasantness. Sixteen pounds a year. Belinda made a quick reckoning. Not much to keep her mother on! Then she remembered the "Temporarily" in the advertisement. The ugly woman had retreated into the kitchen in front of the shop.

"Why 'temporarily'?" inquired Belinda.

"She'll never get better," said the suave man in a whisper. "No, she'll never get better, that's why."

"Oh!" said Belinda, pitifully.

"It's a lot of expense," said the man, but still pleasantly. "Otherwise—perhaps I could have afforded more."

Belinda did not believe a word he said on this score.

"I'll take it," she said decisively.

"Go through into there—make yourself at home," said Mr. Wells.

Belinda went into a poky kitchen furnished in country style. Upon the settle the ugly woman had laid herself down. Belinda was not drawn to her either, but she had seen that she had been crying; she saw now, in the brighter light of the two windows of the kitchen, ravages of pain and disease on the woman's face. Belinda sent a wire to her mother to say she had taken the place.

For a week Belinda and Agnes Wells fought shy of each other. Belinda made certain discoveries in the household: under the names of economy and thrift, pinching and scraping went on. The child she had seen against the stone wall, the child of the pale hair and stubborn-stupid look, was not called Wells but Mortimer. Mrs. Wells let it escape that her maiden name had been Mortimer. Lucy Mortimer was a strange child, living as solitarily outdoors as she lived in the house. Sometimes she served resentfully in the little shop. She never played with anyone. Her chief post was against the wall watching the life of the road, the people, even hens that passed, with a dull resentful stare. To try and get inside that child-heart was like getting inside a Chinese puzzle.

Lucy wore little grey drawers stitched with red and a grey straight dress in which she looked like an amateur convict. Belinda could not tell if Mrs. Wells loved the child or not. Lucy always looked at her mother when she asked for more at table, and Mrs. Wells looked at Mr. Wells, who gave the decision.

"Mr. Wells wants to get on," said Mrs. Wells one day.

Belinda said nothing.

"He's always been a tryer," said Mrs. Wells, warming up. "We'd to borrow to take this shop. It's well-stocked now," looking round it proudly.

"Well, you've always plenty to go at when you live in a shop," said Belinda. "Now, have a good cup o' tea, do. Have something in the middle of the morning. Do as the doctor tells you."

"There's some tea left in the pot," began Mrs. Wells.

"Don't stint yourself," advised Belinda. "There's folk got right—even with your complaint. Buck up!"

The ugly woman smiled. Belinda saw the look in her eyes. It passed quickly, but it was a revelation. She did not want to get better. From that moment Belinda and the ugly woman were in one camp and Mr. Wells in the other. As for the little Lucy, that child of restraint was in neither. Belinda tried to win her in a thousand ways. She regarded the advances with fear, like a wild thing. She went to a school three miles away, setting out every morning, carrying her food for the day. She was a dull scholar according to the teacher's report. Belinda began to wonder if "temporarily" lasted long, how she could augment the sixteen pounds a year. She approached Mr. Wells on the subject, and he eagerly consented to her taking in a little washing and earning a little more in that way.

It was on a misty afternoon, as Belinda sat in the little low-ceilinged parlour behind the shop, helping Mrs. Wells mend sheets, that Mrs. Wells said abruptly, "Never leave me, Belinda."

Belinda was staggered. This was the first mark of appreciation she had received from Mrs. Wells.

"I never meant to do," said Belinda.

"They're—poor wages," murmured Mrs. Wells.

She gave a cautious, guilty look through the little window, fearful of Wells hearing.

"They are good wages," said Belinda, meaningly. "I make it—a bit easier for you, don't I?"

Mrs. Wells' eyes filled with tears.

"I don't know how I did before you came," she acknowledged.

Belinda knew this was not a reference to the physical aid. Mrs. Wells was dependent on Belinda now. Sitting in that low-ceilinged room, with the little spotted mirrors and photographs of people mostly dead, Belinda and Mrs. Wells mended the almost defunct bedlinen every Tuesday afternoon when the shop closed. When Mr. Wells went out, which he often did on Tuesday afternoons, they talked. Belinda learned a great deal. Lucy Mortimer was the child of Agnes Wells and her cousin, Gilbert. People had tried to persuade her years ago to father the child on him. She had loved him. It was the one romance, the one foolish, extravagant chapter in a life of monotony and restraint and common sense. She had married Wells after—four years ago. He had said the child would be no encumbrance, indeed, would be a help by-and-by. She gave him her savings—thirty pounds—and they had started this shop. He never showed resentment against little Lucy, he never showed anything but the asset she had chosen him for—common sense. He had only one passion—the passion to "get on." Nothing wounded him but *waste.* He was saving, would some day be a prosperous man. But she wanted to die.

Mr. Wells thought that he got on immensely with the general. He was glad to see that she liked books. Education was never wasted, he said. *Silas Marner* was a gem, he considered. Belinda marvelled. Excellent sentiments, she discovered, did not always mean excellent examples. Here was a man who could appreciate *Silas Marner* and yet think of nothing but getting on. Were we all mixtures—one self contradicting another in us?

Mrs. Wells grew gradually worse. More and more she leaned on Belinda. When little Lucy fell ill, her love revealed itself like a lightning- flash to Belinda.

"Never mind me," she said, "see to Lucy."

Yet Belinda had never seen her kiss the little one.

Belinda looked after Lucy, played with her on the bed when the measles were going back. Belinda scarcely knew when little Lucy began to like her. The first sign of any affection was the sight of Lucy waiting for her one evening at the end of a lane. Belinda had been home, calling at the doctor's for Mrs. Wells' medicine on the way back.

"Waiting for me, Lucy ?" asked Belinda.

Lucy hung her head in assent. Belinda had now been with Mrs. Wells several months. This was the first sign she had got of winning the heart of this child.

After that, when Belinda went on her weekly visit home, she was always at the lane-end waiting, watching. Scents of blossom stole out into the dusk now when Belinda came from Syke Gate into Newburton. Spring was coming. There were baby ducks on the little streams all about Newburton. Belinda took the little Lucy one day into the woods to gather primroses. She got nearer to the child's heart. They came home tired in the evening loaded with primroses. Lucy ran into the kitchen that evening. But she stopped when she saw her step-father.

"Now, then, not too much noise," he said, but not angrily.

"Is the missis worse?" asked Belinda.

"I'm afraid she is," said the rational one. "The doctor says so."

Belinda went up to the lonely room. Mrs. Wells was laid in the dark. The white curtains looked ghostly, waving in the draught from the window. Little Lucy had crept up after Belinda. Belinda lit the lamp.

"I got these for you, mother," Lucy told her mother.

The ugly woman smiled.

"They're bonnie, Lucy," she said.

Belinda got Lucy to bed.

It was on the morrow that the first bit of awkward friction occurred since Belinda's arrival. It happened not between Mr. and Mrs. Wells, but between Belinda and Mr. Wells. Every Monday he went to town to bring back such probable things as would be needed during the week. Mrs. Wells had mentioned in a timid, casual way that she would like a "taste" of halibut, if it was not too much trouble. Mr. Wells returned without it.

"Where's the halibut?" asked Belinda, genially.

"I—clean forgot," said Mr. Wells. He had an excellent memory. Belinda knew it for what it was—a lie.

Belinda opened her mouth and did not pick her words. Mr. Wells quailed. It was so sudden.

"Well—the shops will be shut now—before I could get there," he said. He was quite pale. "Do you never say things you regret?" he asked, in his rational way.

Belinda wanted to spit in his cold, grey eye.

"No," she said, very quietly.

"I should have thought," began Mr. Wells.

"Where are you going, Belinda?" asked Mrs. Wells, in a trembling voice.

"For some halibut," answered Belinda, buttoning her clumsy boots up.

"You can't do it," said Mr. Wells, looking at the shop. "For a whim, too—"

Belinda looked up.

He really thought she was going to come to him with the buttonhook.

Belinda went. How she had done it they never knew, but she brought home the halibut in triumph, fried it, and gave it to Mrs. Wells for supper. Mr. Wells retreated. No, he did not want any. Little Lucy had some, too, taken up to her by stealth by Belinda.

From that moment Belinda assumed in the eyes of the dying woman the aspect of Providence, and when Belinda told her of how the choice of the place had been effected, Mrs. Wells was the more convinced.

For many hours now every day Mrs. Wells lay on that settle enduring great pain with a fortitude that was Belinda's awe and admiration. The sight of his wife's agony wrought some little changes in Mr. Wells. He regarded her with something of awe. She was something more than an ugly convenience whose thirty pounds had given him his start. Mystery had touched her—she was going to die.

But Mrs. Wells was too far gone to care now for these outward tokens of an affection she did not believe in. It was Belinda whom her gaze followed with pathetic hunger. Belinda gave up one out of every two of the visits she usually paid her mother. The hot weather came on; it sapped the remaining strength of Mrs. Wells. She lay on the couch all day now, watching Belinda.

"Belinda," she said, cautiously, one hot afternoon, opening her eyes to see Belinda trying to fix a new head on the dilapidated trunk of Lucy's old familiar.

"He's not near," said Belinda, without looking up from the task.

"Suppose he asks you to marry him," said Mrs. Wells. It was curious to Belinda to recall what things they had said to each other so quietly, in so commonplace a tone.

"He won't," said Belinda.

Her gaze met that of the woman on the couch. Belinda had long since got past the barrier of the utter ugliness of Agnes Wells.

"Want my opinion on such a cat-as-trope?" asked Belinda, giving the doll's head a forceful stab.

There was a short silence.

Belinda's eyes blazed.

"There are some men," said Belinda, meaningly, "whom I should like to shoot."

"Ah!" There was relief in the sigh of the suffering woman.

"Only," said Belinda, with a return to her usual humour, "I couldn't hit a haystack, not if it was set right under my nose. But folk like Mr. Wells explain suffragettes. I used to think they was mad. Men and women always strikes me as human beings—but when you travel you learn— and when I see about a suffragette hitting a bobby in the eye, I shall know she was hitting at Mr. Wells, really. Has he always been like this?"

Mrs. Wells shook her head from side to side.

"That thirty pounds—" she said, "it ruined him."

"Never!" said Belinda.

But Agnes Wells was emphatic.

"He saw the chances," she said, feebly, "and—everything else faded away."

"There are folk can't stand money, like folk can't carry their drink," said Belinda.

That afternoon Belinda was reproached by Mr. Wells. She had let mould gather on the top of a dish of stewed rhubarb.

"Are you mad?" asked Belinda, meaning to ask if Mr. Wells was indignant.

"I never get angry—it's a waste of energy," he said, gently. "I've got past that stage long ago."

Mrs. Wells died that day at tea-time. She died holding Belinda's hand, gazing into Belinda's eyes; and that night, under the bedcloths, little Lucy heard Belinda say, sobbing, "There are some men I would like to shoot!"

Mr. Wells showed a few symptoms of emotion during the next day or two; but, as he said to Belinda, it was a sin to mourn her, for she was now out of her sufferings, and their loss was her gain.

"It is," said Belinda, with vim.

Mr. Wells' gaze slunk away from hers. The dignity of death had wrapped itself about the commonplace woman—she won respect now.

As for little Lucy, the child followed Belinda around like a timid animal. Three days after the funeral, as Belinda was dressing Lucy, the child said, "Perhaps you'll stay and be my mother now." There was a ray of hope in the unchild-like eyes.

"Who said that?" asked Belinda.

"Father said you might," said Lucy.

That afternoon, as it was shop-closing day, Belinda took Lucy out. The lanes were a flush of red and white roses, bees sucked clover and vetch blooming in the short grass by the road. They walked along gathering flowers. Sunshine made the grasses shine like green fire as they sat down by a dyke-side. Belinda broke to Lucy the news that she was going away.

"Take me, too!" begged the child.

Belinda wished, in agony, that she was a bloated millionaire. But she was not.

"You'll soon grow up," said Belinda. "The years'll pass, chuck. So soon as you can work you can go away. And you'll come back to Newburton sometime, when you're a nice young woman in long frock and your hair pinned up, and you'll remember all this time as a bad dream. Nothing more—a bad dream, with little nice bits stuck in, like the ducks on the water and the posies you pick. You'll grow up and you'll be happy."

Lucy stared at her.

"Do you understand, chuck?" asked Belinda.

Lucy nodded her head.

"What's that for?" asked Mr. Wells, that evening, as Belinda trundled her box into the kitchen.

"I'm hopping it," said Belinda, genially.

"No!" protested Mr. Wells.

"But I am," said Belinda, firmly.

"But—"

"I've got another place," Belinda told him.

Mr. Wells walked over to the window.

Then he said, "Perhaps it could be arranged that you could stay. I can't pretend to offer anything romantic—but, I offer you marriage. I am not badly off."

"Don't mention it," said Belinda.

Mr. Wells ought to have understood the challenge in Belinda's eyes; but he did not.

"Lucy is very fond of you, too," added Mr. Wells.

Belinda sprung from the box side. In her hand she still clutched a pair of combinations, darned and patched beyond knowledge.

"So you'd make even the poor kid's liking for me a step to your getting on!" she exclaimed. She brandished the combinations at Mr. Wells.

"You ought to die in a ditch," said Belinda to the man, who had collapsed into a chair, "but you'll not," she added, beginning to pack again. "You'll flourish like a bay-tree, like it says in the Bible. However, no man'll ever have *me* for a convenience. It's the genuine article for me, mister, if I wait till I'm a thousand!"

Belinda left next morning. It was terribly hot. She was overtaken by a brewery cart on the way, and accepted the offer of the young man with it to jump up and put her bag on. She looked back at Newburton. It lay down below her now. The little streams all molton gold spread out on all sides. The hills rose all round. A tiny, childish figure grew into a speck at the lane-end. Belinda watched it fade. Then she burst into tears.

"Leaving home?" queried the young man, sympathetically.

"Lived there nearly a year," snuffled Belinda.

Sixteen pounds a year! For a long time never a day passed but Belinda thought of Mrs. Wells, the little kitchen, the low-ceilinged parlour, and of the little child who had almost made her marry a man she would rather have shot. For a long time Belinda sent letters to little Lucy, and Lucy rushed eagerly to count the number of kisses. Then Lucy sent a letter to say that her father was marrying again—marrying a Mrs. Jones, and Belinda said merely "Nemesis!" for Mrs. Jones had said what she would do if she were Mrs. Wells, and Belinda knew the widow would do it. For once Mr. Wells had made a mistake. Belinda breathed more easily now that she knew Lucy had such a step-mother.

CHAPTER VII

In the House of a Literary Man

BELINDA'S next place was quiet and uneventful, though she got it rather oddly. She had been back with Jonathan and Annie only some days when a letter addressed to "B. Higgins" came to the door. Thinking it was for herself, though the handwriting puzzled her, Belinda opened it. This is what she read:

"No. On no account do that. You have got to kill him.
"*JESSIE.*"

Belinda turned pale. Here, evidently, was a murder plot. She ran to the door. The postman was out of sight. What B. Higgins could this letter be intended for? Belinda made casual inquiries and learned that at a tumble-down farm, two miles from Syke Gate, lived a man of the name of Bartemus Higgins. Sunset found her approaching the farm. It had been newly whitewashed, and under the windows was an unfenced garden in which dark red sweet-williams, purple pansies, white rock-flower, and golden moss blazed in the mellow light. Swallows flew over her head as she knocked at the door. Belinda heard a voice within, reading in a peculiar way. Shivers ran down her back. She had come to confront a potential murderer. When footsteps answered her knocking she wanted to run away, but recalling the eulogium her father's colleagues had heaped upon him, braced herself up for the ordeal.

The door opened.

A middle-aged man looked out at Belinda, Belinda in a white dress fashionable ten years ago, Belinda in dusty boots, her black eyes looking at him as though he were a criminal.

"Is this letter for you?" inquired Belinda.

She held it out.

Bartemus Higgins took it, recognized the handwriting, and smiled.

"Why, yes," he said.

"It came to Syke Gate," Belinda told him.

"And you've come all that way," he said, in surprise. "Come in and have some refreshment."

With the sensations of a gallant fly going into the spider's web, Belinda entered a cosy kitchen and sat down on an old-fashioned settle.

"I—read that letter," she said, suddenly, challengingly. "Who is it you are going to kill?"

Her host looked at her—then burst into a roar of laughter. Her conclusion had never entered his head. Then he explained. He was an author, and "Jessie" was his sweetheart and his critic.

He had written her on the question of killing one of his characters, undecided whether or not to let him die a natural death. Belinda laughed then, and accepted the explanation, when he put into her hands his latest novel, in a bright-coloured jacket. He asked her things about herself, and when he learnt that she was a servant out of place, said it was queer, but he had just lost his housekeeper.

"What's she gone for?" asked honest Belinda.

"Wanted to marry me," said the author.

"Oh!" said Belinda. "Now, that's why I left my last place—*he* wanted to marry me."

"Quite a coincidence," said the author.

Belinda brought her box and her books three days later, also her testimonials, which the author glanced at casually and handed back to her.

Belinda blushed at the compliment.

She set out by feeling herself a very superior person to be living in the house with a real live author. But, as she told her master, it was quite natural, after all, for she had followed the poets ever from being a child, and her father had "poeted" in his lifetime.

It was only a tiny house, two up, two down, a passage, and a little cobbled yard where nasturtia were trailing up the walls. B. Higgins was not exacting. But he let meals spoil, and that irritated Belinda. Many people came to the house, and Belinda had to make a good spread out of a lean purse. She thought him a little mean at first, having the idea that authors rolled in money, until she discovered that in an author's life there are two seasons—the fat season, when royalties come home, and the lean season, when they are some way off. Belinda had come at the lean season. But, as B. Higgins said, plain living and high thinking were very good at times. Belinda read a great deal here. The little sitting-room was full of books. Besides being an author, B. Higgins lectured. His chief subjects were Burns, Blake, and one which he read to Belinda in its entirety. This was entitled "Genius and Poverty." It took Belinda many days to look on him as an ordinary man, after he had read that lecture. She told him she would like him to read her father's "works," but the author was not encouraging. He said he was very busy, which rather surprised Belinda, seeing that he sat hours in the sunshine of the cobbled yard, staring at the green, blowing leaves of the nasturtia. By degrees it was borne in upon her that the author was a very human human being. When she told him that a woman brought up in a factory, used to standing on her feet ten hours a day, would *not* faint at the tension of sitting by a patient so many hours holding that patient's hand, he was annoyed. So Belinda began to keep her judgments to herself.

Perhaps it was living in the atmosphere of books and the influence of people who wrote (there were great gatherings almost every Sunday), but Belinda herself was guilty of trying to write in the secrecy of her bedroom. The only thing she produced was "sweat."

Twice a week she walked over to see her mother.

Mrs. Higgins was taking the tablets regularly and benefiting so much that she could sit up several hours a day. She even began to darn stockings.

Belinda hit on a novel plan by which the treatment could be continued at less cost. The firm who supplied the tablets to drive uric acid out of the blood gave samples to people who applied, paying one penny postage. B. Higgins sent up for a sample, likewise many of his friends, also Jonathan and his friends, and then Bill Greenwood, acting under orders from Belinda, sent up for some for his mother.

A month later, when another friend of Belinda's wrote up for a free sample, she received this letter:

"Dear Madam,

"There has been such a run on our free samples in your district that we are out of them just at present. But we send you a full-size bottle, free of cost, hoping that if you receive benefit you will tell people of it.—We are, dear Madam, etc."

Belinda laughed until she cried when she saw the letter.

"Must think Syke Gate an awful place for rheumatism!" she said.

She liked Jessie Smith, the sweetheart of the fourth-rate author. Jessie was middle-aged, too. The couple had courted twenty years. Belinda said that would be too long for her. Jessie had a mother. Thereupon was the drama. Jessie, knowing the idiosyncrasies of the author, likewise the idiosyncrasies of her mother, preferred the idylls of courtship to the reality of marriage. But Belinda could not see it, she said. There were people with whom Belinda got friendly, people living in the scattered farms who asked Belinda if she thought the author would ever marry Jessie. Belinda knew nothing—nothing at all, she said. Loyal Belinda! She went to see Jessie in her own setting, and was further impressed by her. After seeing her mother, Belinda realized some of the wisdom of Jessie. Mrs. Smith was very fat, very pessimistic, and unable to do anything but crochet and read. Belinda realized why Jessie looked so worn. After teaching all day in the school she did all the housework.

"Strikes me, she'll wear you out," said candid Belinda, whereupon Jessie was indignant, and Belinda liked her for it.

Belinda was living in clover and knew it, knew that at some time, near or distant, she should look back on this happy oasis as she liked to look back at the sunset sky or a nice scene. She dipped into Plato's *Republic*, wept over *Les Miserables*—which she said she would not have missed coming across, no, not for worlds! Fantine, poor unfortunate, was the cause of Belinda's giving away a skirt she really wanted. A woman in Syke Gate had asked Belinda's mother, when visiting her, if Belinda had any clothes she did not want. Belinda's mother said she did not think so, but would ask. Belinda, with seven shillings a week as wages, out of which she sent her mother six-and-sixpence, had certainly not much hope of renewing her wardrobe, and, when her mother asked her, said she would be having to go about in her birthday suit in a bit.

"Well, 'Linda, tha knows best," said Mrs. Higgins. "But Sarah said this woman she wanted them for had hardly a rag to her back and *such* a lot o' childer."

Belinda walked back, and that evening read about Fantine, the candle flickering on the rush-bottomed chair by her bedside. It was odd. As she read of Fantine, as the warm tears gushed right from the warm heart upon the badly-printed page, Belinda thought of having refused the skirt she wanted to the woman with the lot of children. She took it at week-end. She had now no Sunday dress save the old-fashioned white one, but, to Belinda, it was the inevitable. Could one weep over the miseries of Fantine, that child of the people, and wear, without guilt, a skirt that another child of the people badly needed? Belinda's sincerity was immaculate. Perhaps that was why she walked through the world with so fresh and beaming a look. Ever afterwards Fantine and her own reluctance to part with a good skirt, when she did not know where the next was to come from, were associated in Belinda's mind.

There were lovely walks in the neighbourhood. Sometimes the author, Belinda, and Jessie went into the woods, lighting a fire and taking sandwiches.

"I think tha'rt settled yonder for life, Belinda," said Mrs. Higgins, on one of her daughter's visits.

"I think I am," said Belinda.

"A rolling stone gathers no moss," said Annie, sententiously.

"No, no dust, neither," retorted Belinda. "And it gets the corners knocked off."

Annie's behaviour towards Jonathan's mother was improving. Belinda did not know how to account for this, and had not the opportunity of finding out. It was sufficient for her to feel that her mother was not quite in the way, and either because her health was mending, or as a reflection of Annie's changed demeanour, Mrs. Higgins wrote very cheerfully to her daughter. This made a great psychological difference in Belinda. When she left Syke Gate now she did not feel that she was leaving behind her a broken-hearted woman.

It was not long after Mrs. Higgins had told Belinda that she was going to stay in the place she had, when Belinda began to realize that she might not be there very long after all. Mrs. Smith was very ill, really ill, having got severe bronchitis worse than ever she had it. Belinda trotted to and fro from the white-washed farm to the house of Jessie and her mother, bringing back bulletins to the author.

"Don't you feel fluttery like at the prospect of marrying her, after all these years?" asked Belinda.

B. Higgins paced several times across the room, before answering.

"Do you think you should ask such a question, Belinda?" he said, in turn.

"You do look nice in that velvet jacket," said Belinda, in her motherly way. "But it sort o' fulls a bit under the arm." There was a short silence. "But don't you feel fluttery?" she asked.

"It's been a dream so long," said the author, evasively.

"Now, what's that you say about putting folk on the psychological dissecting table?" began Belinda.

The author wheeled round.

"I have not been able to pay you much money, Belinda," he said, proudly, "but from an educational standpoint you have certainly profited."

"I have that," said Belinda, warmly; "but come on—place yourself on this psychological dissecting table."

She waved her hand as though there was really an operating table in the room.

"Well?" queried the author.

"Are you afraid of marriage?" asked Belinda.

"H'm!" said the one being dissected.

"But are you?"

"Somewhat," admitted the author.

"Reason ?" asked Belinda.

"—— has taught me that there are so many illusions." began the author.

"But, the real reason?" asked Belinda.

"It sounds so beastly commonplace," confessed the artist. "Think of the myriads who have said 'Will you marry me?' And—I'd like it to be unique—original—artistic." He caught the glance of Belinda's eye. "Can you understand that?" he asked, pathetically. Belinda shook her head.

He grew warm on the subject.

"But can't you think out a unique proposal of marriage," asked Belinda. Then she added, "Why ask her at all? You've asked her once?"

The artist scratched his head.

"It's so long since we mentioned it," he said. "It's grown into a quiet friendship, so I've got to ask again. Besides, I want a similar scene for my next novel."

Belinda glowed.

"But I can't think of anything unique—for Jessie," he said.

"That proves it's the real thing," she said, delightedly.

"Oh—it's real enough," grumbled Mr. Higgins. "But it's got to be artistic. I have made so many people propose marriage, in railway carriages, on board wrecks, on the sea-shore, at garden-parties, but I'm blowed if I can think of anything unique for Jessie. I should like to think of something absolutely and entirely original. Now, will you try and think of something?"

Belinda racked her brains vainly during the next few days. Meanwhile, Mrs. Smith grew worse. Mr. Higgins went to see her, in duty bound, and found all the windows open. The unfortunate woman was really ill now, fighting for breath. Jessie, filial, warm-hearted, was enduring agony with her mother.

"Go away," she said, "you'll only make her worse!"

The author told Belinda that this was distinctly original, as he should not, under any circumstances, have dreamed Jessie would say that.

"The coal-hole," said Belinda, hugely pleased with herself, next morning.

"What about it?"

The author was sleepy and had just got up.

"Propose marriage there," suggested Belinda, beaming.

The author glowed.

"Belinda!"

His tone was grateful.

"You really are brilliant, sometimes," he admitted. "But—how am I going to get her into the coal-hole?"

"Send her for some coals," advised Belinda.

"I hope it's never been done before," said he, several times.

The doctor went to the Smiths' three times next day. Mrs. Smith died at midnight, and Jessie, who came down next day to ask her fiancé if he could spare Belinda for a day or two—Jessie, red-eyed, weary, a forlorn and pathetic figure, had little to say. But Belinda could see that whilst the author was undoubtedly sympathetic, he enjoyed the sensation of trying to understand what Jessie was feeling.

It was quite possible, mused Belinda, that the people who made other people weep on their printed pages achieved their success, not from greater feeling, but a shade less feeling, which allowed them to stage-manage their effects. When the author came home one evening, badly knocked about by running his bicycle into a motor-car, and confessed that his first conscious thoughts were what a realistic scene he now had for his fifth chapter, Belinda was further staggered.

Jessie, meanwhile, lived on in the little house, and went out teaching in the daytime. Belinda believed that not even Jessie was sure of the author.

But a fortnight later, when Jessie came to tea on Sunday, the author had gone to lie down. Belinda went up, knocked respectfully on the little door, and said, "Excuse me, sir, but Miss Smith has come to tea."

"What is she doing—now?" was the unexpected answer.

"Gathering the nasturtia seeds ready to put in vinegar," Belinda told him.

"Good," said the author. "Wait a moment, Belinda."

Belinda waited. A slip of paper appeared under the door.

"Don't read it, Belinda," said the author.

"No," said Belinda.

Neither did she, though the paper almost burnt her fingers.

Jessie Smith was pulling off the hard, green knobs of the nasturtia—and dropping them, with an abstracted air, into a china pot on the little strip of grass under the wall. Belinda silently held out the note. A quick light of expectation illumined Jessie's face. Belinda was suddenly aware of tragedies going on under quite commonplace exteriors. The grey hair blew softly about the gentle face, and the autumn sunlight turned it into a silky halo.

"Tell Mr. Higgins, Belinda, 'Yes,'" said Jessie.

"You mean—?"

Belinda's warm and eager tone of wishing to share in the joy, made Jessie look at her rather oddly.

"Mr. Higgins and I are going to be very happy," said Jessie, gently.

"I shouldn't like to risk it myself," said Belinda.

Jessie laughed.

"He has a fancy," said Belinda, "to stitch his own buttons on. He says they never come off."

Belinda winked at Jessie.

Jessie understood the depth of Belinda. Belinda stitched the buttons on after him, and never said a word.

"You're rather a wonderful person," said Jessie. She took Belinda's arm. They entered the kitchen that way.

"Belinda!" called Mr. Higgins.

Belinda went upstairs.

"What does she say?" asked the author.

Belinda set her mouth to the keyhole.

"Yes," she said.

"Nothing more?" queried the author.

"Nothing more," said Belinda.

"Good," said Mr. Higgins. Then, as Belinda was moving away, he said in a low voice, "I don't think, Belinda, it's ever been done quite like this."

Belinda gave him up.

"And—I say—Belinda—" came the voice.

"Yes, sir," said Belinda.

"Did she look glad?"

Belinda was silent a moment.

Then she said, "Oh! Sir!"

"I'm coming down," said the author.

Belinda was always puzzled, when she thought of it afterwards, whether it was the artist or the man who had asked if Jessie Smith looked glad on knowing the temperamental one was going to marry her, Belinda had her doubts about B. Higgins being an artist at all. She heard him called a journalist.

As royalties fell due a week later, Mr. Higgins decided to marry at once, by special licence. They went down to a lonely fishing village on the East Coast, Mr. Higgins finding out that it had not been written up. Jessie was radiant.

"I'll have the house as clean as a pin for you to come back to," said Belinda.

The die was cast. Belinda knew that they could not afford to keep her. Jessie was taking her place, adding to the duties of housekeeper those of wife, and Belinda was glad that she did not stand in her shoes.

She received a postcard, with the picture of a string of fish on one side and a message on the other from the bride. Belinda kept that card for years. The card merely said they were having enjoyable weather, and that Mr. Higgins was working on his book. It took Belinda's breath—working on his book—on his honeymoon!

"Oh, Belinda!" exclaimed Jessie, when they stood within the little kitchen. Everything varnishable had been varnished. Belinda had re-papered and whitewashed, as the whitewash yet clinging to her eyelashes testified.

The bridegroom looked a happy man, despite all his fear of disillusions.

"And now, I'm leaving you," Belinda told them, at the jolly supper table that evening.

They looked reproach.

"You can't afford to keep me," said Belinda, bluntly; "so—if I wanted to stay—what odds?"

"If there's anything in this house you'd like to take," said the author, "you're welcome to it, Belinda."

"There's one thing—" said Belinda.

Jessie and Bartemus wondered. There were many things in the house.

"That picture—in my bedroom," said Belinda. "The 'Fighting Temeraire,' it's called. I've read about it, in Ruskin—or somewhere. It's being dragged away, that old battleship, to be broken up for lumber. I—like that best in all the-house. I think—I'll be like that old ship some day. But —it's grand—it's a grand picture."

She looked apologetically at the pair across the table.

Jessie Smith felt a lump rising in her throat.

Then Belinda made her want to laugh, by saying, "You can keep the frame. I can't cart the frame round the world with me."

On a Monday morning, when Syke Gate was hanging its clothes out, Belinda departed from the house of literature, with a vague presentiment, destined to be true, that never again, in the whole of her domestic service, would she have so easy a time. She had been treated as a human being, nay, as a friend. She stopped to look back at the house, and the white patch amidst the green, swam through her tears.

"I get too darned fond of folk," ruminated Belinda, wiping her eyes on her sleeve. She went on, and never looked back again, the picture of the 'Fighting Temeraire' banging against her legs at every step, the little bundle of clothes, Hugo's *First French Course*, and *Silas Marner* travelling along with her, on the other side. She allowed herself a penny bun and a bottle of ginger ale at a little shop on the way home. When she undid her parcel, at Annie's, something tumbled out. It was a copy of Plato's *Republic.*

"Well, if ever!" said Belinda, "Now fancy him thinking o' that. He was just a bit short o' greatness, somehow." She was thinking of Charles Lamb and Victor Hugo, their lives indissolubly one with their writings, not a contradiction, and, had she only known it, she had discovered a rare truth. There can be mediocrity with sincerity. But there can be no greatness without it is deep and intense.

CHAPTER VIII

Belinda Protects Her Character

BELINDA decided to go a little further afield, and her next place was thirty miles away from Syke Gate. She sent her luggage on in advance, Jonathan suggesting this. He said it was idiotic to go about burdened like a donkey.

She arrived on a foggy day when the town streets were thick with mud. A long and wearisome car ride brought her to what Belinda called "the garden city." The house was called "Cedar Lodge," and the great fact that hit Belinda in the eye as she stood on the curved path, was the number of small windows there would be to clean. She learned later that this house was built in the old English style.

As Belinda stood waiting after having rung the bell three times, she heard voices raised in altercation.

"All that glitters is not gold," mused Belinda.

She pulled at the bell again. Surely they would hear that.

"Well?"

It was another maid who opened the door. But for her cap, Belinda might have been mistaken in taking her for the lady of the house.

"I'm come after the situation," announced Belinda.

Mr. Higgins had told her that this sounded better than her former way of announcing herself.

"Come in," said the maid.

Belinda followed her into a beautiful room and sat down. A few minutes later Mrs. Mayton came in. She was exquisitely dressed and evidently knew her business, for with a few adroit questions, she soon had Belinda weighed up. She scarcely thought Belinda would be able to fill the place—but after staring through the window some moments, said she would take her a month on trial. Belinda later learned from the maid who had let her in that she was to take her place. She likewise learned that she had come to a household where things were, domestically speaking, at sixes and sevens. But she did not believe what Flossie said of the master and mistress, for she saw that the girl was spiteful. Flossie was to stay on and show her her duties, which she did conscientiously enough.

Belinda served at table, in regular high style, that evening. It was surprising how the black dress and white apron suited Belinda. She scarcely knew herself as she passed the mirrors, and the place was full of mirrors—mirrors and aspidistras. There were no books. That gave Belinda a pang. Sporting papers, fashion journals and the weekly papers were the household literature.

Mr. Mayton was a successful business man, a self-made man, Belinda learnt from a charwoman who came in to help on Fridays. He had worked in a hat factory in his youth and was still under forty, but now the boss of that hat factory.

"We all have our gifts," said Belinda. "My father had a sister with second sight. She's dead."

"She's a . . ." The charwoman winked, referring to the mistress.

But Belinda had no taste for scandal, and said she liked to speak of folk as she found them.

Flossie went at the end of the fortnight.

Mrs. Mayton thought at the end of that time that Belinda might do, and offered her the fashion journals as a token of thought, but Belinda only got time to read them in bed which she did, her chief sensation being one of wonder that people could for shame spend so much on robes and furs when so many poor creatures were up and down the world half naked.

Belinda appreciated the fact that she was not stinted of tea and had a decent room to sleep in—also the electric light. The family cat had kittens, and Belinda was allowed to have one of the kittens, which became her pet.

Besides Mr. and Mrs. Mayton there was a son of eighteen, a weedy-looking lad for whom Belinda volunteered to make rice pudding every day, vowing that would fatten him up. He had a latchkey and used to let himself in, sometimes tumbling amongst things, as Belinda, in her little room, could hear. She told him once that if she were him, she would sign the pledge, which amused him and his mother, though Mr. Mayton said gruffly that he might do worse. It shocked Belinda to see whisky and wine so much in evidence in the house—but with the benign tolerance which was part of her composition, she told herself that it took all sorts to make up a world.

There was an old gentleman, a constant visitor to the house, particularly when Mr. Mayton was away, and Belinda thought him very nice. He dressed like a regular dandy though he was seventy and he and Mrs. Mayton were very good friends. It was not until Mr. Mayton, finding her alone in the morning room, asked her, with a peculiar glance, if Mr. Ingleton had been again yesterday and if he had stayed to supper, that Belinda suspected anything wrong. She coloured up, recalling little incidents that had not struck her at the time.

"Watch," said Mr. Mayton.

Belinda was too concerned to be able to get a word out, and just then Mrs. Mayton came. But on the first opportunity—it was in the hall, as she took her master's hat to hand up—Belinda showed Mr. Mayton the fibre of her mind.

"I came here as a servant. I'm not a spy," said Belinda in a low voice.

"Oh, very well!" said Mr. Mayton, indifferently.

Belinda, in bed that night, thought grievously of what her mother would think did she know she was in such a household. Domestic servants were expected to bear immaculate characters, but their superiors gave no guarantee of any kind, and might for anything anyone knew, be the most immoral rogues under the sun. It was odd to read *Silas Marner* here, in an atmosphere charged with modernity and suspicion, and not know what a day might bring forth. It got on Belinda's nerves. People affected her very much. She began to knit her mother a pair of undervests, doing three rows every day after meals, and any time she could snatch. She had read somewhere that knitting was soothing to the nerves.

One day there came to the house a man very plainly dressed. Belinda had to take him a glass of wine. As she entered she heard these words: "So far, Mrs. Mayton, we have discovered nothing."

In one of those flashes that sometimes came to her, Belinda realized, to her horror, that Mrs. Mayton was having Mr. Mayton *watched.*

Watched! And they lived in the same house, ate at the same table, slept in the same—no, Belinda pulled herself up. They did not. But she had thought it a sign of the higher hygiene of the upper orders. To say that she was horrified at this double discovery, is to put the thing mildly. A pity that was near to contempt was in her mind for all these poor people. An old man, a friend, a close friend of the family for years—venerable of aspect—a man who had not much longer to live! Belinda, without passing a ban on such people as a class, could not help but recall things she had seen in various newspapers, or the morals of her class. Yet here, in an atmosphere of good manners, were educated people, living a lie, and spying on each other. She thought of her father and mother—illiterate, simple, and they became ennobled by contrast.

At the end of the month Belinda gave her notice.

"Very well," said Mrs. Mayton.

It was that evening, when Mr. Mayton had gone to the city, that old Mr. Ingleton called. Belinda showed him into the drawing-room, and went back into the little kitchen, with its blue-and-white checked curtains. She had to pass the drawing room door, to make supper in the sitting room, later on. She heard a sound and looked in—and stopped. Mrs. Mayton must have heard something. She looked out. Belinda stood on the mat, tray in hand, looking at them—at Mrs. Mayton's arms around the old fool—horrified, speechless, her horror a sufficient condemnation.

"Well?"

It was the old man who spoke, looking at Belinda.

"I think," said Belinda, "you're an old fool!"

She passed on into the kitchen. Mrs. Mayton came in a little later. She was absolutely indifferent to Belinda's opinion—Belinda saw that.

"And you're another," said Belinda. "I'll speak my mind, if it costs me my wages."

"We can't go on like this any longer," said Mrs. Mayton. "We want you to be a witness, Higgins."

"Against you?" ejaculated Higgins.

"Against us," said Mrs. Mayton.

"And—your Eddie?" queried Belinda. Her eyes filled with tears. After all, one can't make rice puddings every day to try and fatten a poor boy up, without getting some affection, even for boys who carry latch-keys and tumble against the furniture.-

"Oh—he'll be provided for," said Mrs. Mayton.

Belinda gained a new conception of life.

"But—you can't tear him in two, and take half a-piece," she said, "if you can provide for him."

"Oh, he'll marry sooner or later; sooner, I should think," said Eddie's mother.

"God help her!" said Belinda, devoutly.

"What are you doing, Higgins?" asked Mrs. Mayton.

"I'm going," said Belinda, folding her apron over the back of a chair.

"Going!"

It was Mrs. Mayton's turn to be surprised.

"But a railway strike is on. There are no trains running," she said, a little testily.

"I'll walk," said Belinda.

"But—see, I'll give you twenty pounds to give evidence against us. You will be subpoenaed. I wish you to say—"

"Not for a thousand!" said Belinda.

"But—it's thirty miles, didn't you say, from your home?" she asked. "You'd have very little to say. Just that you saw us kissing—" Her voice faltered. Perhaps Belinda's eyes worried her.

"I know," said Higgins. "I've seen such-like. 'What the servant saw through the keyhole'—I *know*. But I'm not being mixed up in it. I've come from a decent home."

"Very well!" said Mrs. Mayton.

She gave Belinda her wages, and Belinda, half an hour later, set out, lugging her baggage, the "Fighting Temeraire" bumping against her legs.

It was raining. The cars were ten minutes' walk away. They were crowded. People were hanging on to the straps. The ticket man could not get round with the tickets. Everything was jumbled, like Belinda's mind. She went to the station in a forlorn hope that there might be a train. All in vain. But on her return she heard that there was a waggonette going to Long

Moreton, then on to Blackpool. Long Moreton was seven miles from Syke Gate.

Belinda got a seat in the waggonette. It had other passengers, several of whom had mouth organs, and concertinas. They played tunes Belinda loved. Belinda felt that once again she was amongst her own people. But she eyed askance the youth who had his arm round a girl's waist, until she found out it was his girl.

"It was time I came away," mused Belinda. "I'd get suspicious, else."

What a night of adventure it seemed to Belinda. They set off, after the driver had got the waggonette full, and the driver promised not to get even a pint. The roads were a miracle of vehicles, vehicles of all kinds, from motors to donkey-cars, and when the lights of a passing car lit up the otherwise dark roads, it made Belinda tremble. Dark trees, the sky—a shade less dark—dark walls, and a vision of two men once, drinking from a barrel that had been got from an overturned brewery-cart. People laughed and tumbled, and sang, and the concertinas played "Home, Sweet Home" and made Belinda, in her corner, where she guarded the "Fighting Temeraire," wish she was home. They appeared to crawl. But as the driver said, he dared not go any faster; once, they pulled up only just in time. Near the Yew Tree a trap had been overturned. A motor-car went by on the other side with ridiculous speed, and lit up for a second the road, the overturned trap, and a figure stretched out on the grass.

"Dead!" said someone compassionately.

There were people in attendance—a policeman. Belinda's waggonette crawled past.

But the worst was when she had to get out at Long Moreton. It was still raining. Other people were walking, people coming home from their holidays, courters carrying luggage between them and trying not to fall out, married people carrying luggage, and not trying not to fall out. Belinda carried a baby for a mile, for one couple, and then left them to their fates, hearing the baby cry, in imagination, for a long time. She passed through P—, a barracks town, and was terrified of the soldiers. But nothing happened.

Half-fainting she reached Syke Gate. She wept with joy as she saw it stretched out in the darkness before her eyes.

She had to knock them up. Jonathan shot up the window.

"Who's there?" he asked.

"Only me," said Belinda.

Jonathan struck a match and looked at his watch.

"At half-past four—" he said.

Belinda sat on the doorstep.

"Eh!—our Belinda!" came a voice. Mrs. Higgins had awakened, and heard.

Love and comfort flowed out on that sound and wafted her round.

"Wet to the skin," said Belinda cheerfully, as she staggered in. "Well, it can't go below the skin, anyhow—."

CHAPTER IX

In Search of an Antidote

BELINDA set herself to find another place. Within two weeks she had tramped seventy miles. Either she did not suit the advertiser or the place was already filled. Belinda blamed having walked under a ladder when going for the milk.

She went one afternoon to see Bill Greenwood's mother.

"Why won't you have our Bill?" asked Mrs. Greenwood, during tea.

"He can't afford to keep a wife."

"But that isn't the reason, is it now?" said Mrs. Greenwood, coaxingly.

"No," said Belinda, lingering on the word. "But I am married—or as good as married," she added. Which made Mrs. Greenwood almost drop her cup.

"Married!"

Belinda nodded.

"I shall never leave my mother," said Belinda. "I've taken my father's place. She leans on me."

"But—couldn't she live—"

"No, she couldn't. As long as she lives, I'm hers—all hers. Catch me deserting a sinking ship!"

Belinda helped herself to the nicest cake she could find on the plate.

Belinda did not get a place for five weeks. Jonathan paid for her boots soling, taking care not to let his wife know. It was plain from Annie's demeanour that she thought it was too much of a thing, two of them dumped on her, but there had been no quarrelling.

Even Mrs. Higgins, sorry though she was to have Belinda leave her, was glad for Jonathan's sake that Belinda at last received a letter, saying the writer thought she would suit them very well.

"I'll be only six miles away, mother," said Belinda. "I'll try to come once a week. Five shillings isn't much," she added, "but crumbs is better than no bread. How will you do about the tablets?"

Mrs. Higgins had finished the free samples sent for by half Syke Gate. The rheumatism was certainly allayed.

"You must have some more, mother," advised Belinda. "A pennyworth of ease—"

Belinda said "Good-bye" to her mother, hurrying away as she always did. She had been in service now a year and a half. The shadowy hope that something would turn up before long to do away with the necessity of leaving her mother was fainter now. Again she was faring forth, again she had had to say "Good-bye," again her mother was weeping the slow tears of age at being left. It would be always like this, thought Belinda—comings and goings, the comings tinged with regret because they had to sponge on Jonathan, the goings saddened by the recollection of her mother's clinging gaze, which worried even whilst it touched Belinda, touched her more than anything in the world touched her, and her heart was yet as susceptible in its sympathies as a young girl's.

"Well—it ought to be a good place. I've got it on my birthday," mused Belinda, tramping the highway from Syke Gate.

Her destination was Beldon, a small industrial town with thirteen thousand of a population. It was typical November weather. The dark trees on each side of the road were strung with raindrops.

They looked like garlands of tears hung on black bayonets. Belinda did not often get downhearted. This being out of work so long had got her down. But by the time she had done three miles, she had left her dark mood behind.

A man on a cart gave her a two-mile ride and refused the threepenny-piece she offered.

"Nay, nay, I can give a lift without being paid for it," he mumbled.

Belinda's face lit up—her heart, too. She did the rest of the journey humming.

It was five o'clock when she reached Beldon, and she found she had got to the wrong end. The house was yet a mile and a half distant. The village road wriggled along like a watery worm, in the slimy darkness of the November fog. Belinda found there would be a car, later, and decided to wait for it—a workmen's car. Belinda lingered about, looking in at shop-windows, until she reached one that held her as a lamp holds a moth. The window, a very blaze of light and beauty, flashed on the greyness around. There was a man with his nose almost pressed against the pane. Belinda stood for several minutes, the outside world forgotten. Gardens blossomed in that window. There were quaint uphill cobbled streets, with skies showing at the narrow openings, such skies as are only near the sea. There were camel-riders in a cloud of fine desert sand. Belinda, when a tiny girl, used to tell her father she would paint pictures, and had crayoned blue seas with red ships on them.

"That's a bonnie un," said the little man to Belinda.

Belinda noticed two things about him. He limped slightly and his moustache was something between lavender and pink. Had he been trying to dye it and made a mistake?

"Ten guineas." Belinda whistled, peering at the price of the picture.

"I should want a house o' goods for that," said the little man.

"Me, too," said Belinda. "Funny how if you like a thing it's always a big price."

"This your car coming?" asked the little man.

Belinda looked reluctantly away. Two lights were swimming towards her through the mist.

"Grandon Road," she said.

"This is it, then," said the little man. "It's mine, too."

They got in and sat side by side. The little man bought a ticket for Belinda.

"No, no," objected Belinda, holding out twopence, "I always buys my own cherries."

He had to take the money.

When they got out, it did not seem strange to them that they should walk along together. Somehow—how, Belinda never knew—they got to talking about poetry.

"I've followed the poets all my life," confessed the little man.

"So've I," said Belinda. "My father, he could poet about anything."

"I'd like to have met him," said the other, warmly. Belinda's heart grew warmer towards him.

He was in lodgings, he told her, and worked at a dye-works. So that was the cause of the pink moustache!

"Are you on a visit?" he asked her.

"Going into service," said Belinda.

"I'll happen bang into you on the street," said the little man, wistfully. Belinda was something of a find. She followed the poets.

"Call and see me sometime," invited Belinda, warmly.

He wrote down her address, with a stumpy pencil, in a notebook of his own manufacture, a notebook containing ideas for epic poems and dramas, which never got written.

"I shall come," he said, threateningly.

"I shouldn't have asked you if I didn't want you to come," said simple Belinda.

"I shall come!" he reiterated. "It's like an oasis," then, waving the notebook, he vanished into the mist.

Belinda found No. 176 with some difficulty. The street was one of those best described as being inhabited by people who regard themselves as the better-end of the working class. Belinda called them "washed workers."

Belinda knocked at the door, with a thrill of wonder, hope, and curiosity. An inner door opened, letting a flood of light through the passage, and Belinda saw, through the blue and red glass of the vestibule door, an umbrella-stand with a swan painted on it, and a young woman in a white blouse.

"Are you—Miss Higgins?" said the young woman, when she opened the door.

"I am."

"Come in."

Belinda was shown into a bright, neat kitchen furnished with modern working-class taste, chiefly an imitation of things seen in pictures of better houses. There were reproductions of well-known gallery pictures on the walls, engravings in good frames.

At the table, a sandy-haired man was eating ham and pickles, and reading a daily paper.

"Joe—" said Mrs. Pickett, looking at him.

"Oh, settle it between yourselves," said Mr. Pickett. He went soon afterwards into the scullery, and washed himself. He went upstairs and came down in his week-end clothes. When he was going out, Mrs. Pickett followed him down the passage. "You won't be long, Joe," Belinda heard her say.

In a moment she was back with Belinda.

"They are not high wages, but all I can afford. You won't be overworked. You see, I dressmake, but since the baby came—"

"Baby!"

There was pleasure in Belinda's voice. She looked around for the baby.

"In bed," explained Mrs. Pickett. "Yes, it's been such a toss—oh, he always goes to bed at half-past five yet—I've really thought I should have to give it up. But that would be a pity, too, because, you see, I have to help my parents a little —so I thought I'd see if I could get help, and not give up my business."

Belinda saw that the young woman was very thin. But for that, and that she looked so timid, she would have been good-looking. She dressed well, explaining to Belinda that she must do credit to her trade. She promised to show Belinda how to cut out patterns, then she could make her own clothes.

"Now, that'll be a godsend," said Belinda, "for I've been thinking I'll soon be going about like a Fiji Islander."

Belinda wrote a card to her mother and had to run to catch the post. She wrote:

"I've got that job. Think I shall like. Send clothes by carrier. Home first half-day off. B."

Mrs. Pickett was fitting people on in her front room, the "fitting-room," until nine o'clock.

Belinda had supper ready, home-made chips, and fish in batter. Her mistress stared at the quantity.

"You're like two laths nailed together. You want to eat plenty," Belinda advised her.

Mrs. Pickett admitted that it did feel nice to have it made for one. She cast several anxious glances at the clock, during supper, thinking Belinda did not notice. Belinda washed up, got in coals ready for the morning, and sat on the sofa looking at music copies. Mrs. Pickett asked her, if she would like to go to bed. But Belinda knew that Mrs. Pickett did not want her to go to bed, that Mrs. Pickett was frightened of something. So she said she was not tired.

"Gets drunk, does he?" asked Belinda, putting down *When the Swallows Homeward Fly.*

Mrs. Pickett coloured.

The same pride that made her dress well, made her strive to conceal even her terror and her anxiety.

"Sometimes," she said, rather weakly.

Her smile was weak, too.

"But—what are you scared on?" asked Belinda.

"I—well, Joe has been in India," said Mrs. Pickett, "and it goes to his head. He's like one —"

"Possessed," prompted Belinda, as she paused.

"Possessed," agreed Mrs. Pickett.

They heard footsteps, something stumbling. Mrs. Pickett whitened.

"We're two to one and can lick any man," said Belinda. "You're not much, but you can count me one and a half."

"Don't—don't go up to bed until I do," pleaded Mrs. Pickett, her terror stronger than her pride.

"Will a pig fly?" said Belinda, and there was time to say no more. The front door banged open and Mr. Pickett came in. Belinda poured his tea. He looked at her in a puzzled way, then at his wife—all in a gloom, as Belinda styled it. He started quarrelling on the least pretext. Mrs. Pickett's share was silence and panic.

"Sit you down and shut up," said Belinda. "Don't you know it's Gunpowder Plot? You'd have looked better having a bonfire round the back and letting off flip-flaps, than being where you have been."

"Ee ay—it's the Fifth—Gunpowder Plot," he muttered, inanely. For three solid hours Belinda manipulated his plastic mind until he was worn out and fell asleep.

"Upstairs with you!" said Belinda to his wife.

"But I can't go and leave him here," she whined.

Belinda marshalled her upstairs, but she would go into Belinda's room. It was midnight by then. They talked until three o'clock. Then they heard Joe stumbling aloft. Mrs. Pickett dodged into her own room. He was almost sober now. She appeared fast asleep when he entered.

Next day, when Joe had gone to his work, Belinda set off on a mission of light. Belinda had persuaded Mrs. Pickett to try to cure her husband of drunkenness—"unbeknowns to him." Belinda had great faith in the printed word. She believed all quack advertisements. It was her belief that had she known of a certain quack remedy now on the market, her father would not have died when he did.

She fared three miles, until she came to a town where the newspaper had said she could get the cure for drunkenness.

"Hersfield," was the name. "Hersfield, Lingwood."

This was Lingwood. Belinda wandered up and down inquiring for the shop kept by Hersfield. She asked two people who said they were sorry, but they were strangers.

"Hersfield," said a young man, out with his sweetheart. "Oh, let me see." He looked into the blue eyes of the girl as though he might find the directions there.

"Isn't it the herbalist's?" said the girl.

"It will be," said Belinda. The advertisement had said that the magical cure was a herbal remedy.

"Right away up that hill, past the workhouse," the young man directed her. "Yes, Hersfield, Herbalist. I've seen it—it's up there."

Belinda toiled past the workhouse, and found at last a shop. She opened the door, and walked in. There was no bell on the door. She knocked on the counter with her umbrella, but it might have been a dead-house. Herbs, loose and in boxes, scented the air. Everything seemed dry, dusty, aromatic. Belinda thought she would like to keep a shop like that, scented with dry herbs. There was a weight on the counter. She thumped with that. Nobody came. Just as she was about to go out, she heard feeble steps descending wooden stairs, somewhere behind the shop. A pair of dark curtains parted, and a picturesque figure came through. Belinda stared at the patriarchal old man. The herbalist wore a velvet jacket which reminded her of Mr. Higgins. A long white beard flowed to his waist. He wore a velvet cap with a dangling bob, and his face was crossed and crinkled. He walked with a stick, tap-tap, looking at Belinda in a far-away manner.

"What can I do for you?" he asked in a courtly way.

"Oh, it's not for me," said Belinda. She raised her voice. He was old, and probably deaf. But no, he seemed to understand.

"I know. I know," he said, shaking his head. Belinda was puzzled. Then light broke on her. Perhaps he was a wizard. Belinda believed some people were so much wiser than others that wizards were possible.

"It's for a friend of mine—her husband drinks — we've seen it in the paper—four shillings a bottle. Cure for Drunkenness," said Belinda, beaming. She spoke at the top of her voice.

The old man came towards her.

"Yes, your eyes are yellow," he said, in a firm voice. "Yellow—and your tongue is coated of morning."

"No," thundered Belinda, shaking her head." It's not for me."

"Let me see—how old are you?" asked the professor. Belinda eyed him with anxiety, then burst into a peal of laughter.

"You should not laugh. This could be serious," said the old man. "Now—if you will follow my instructions—"

Belinda shook her head.

"What!" said he, indignant.

"It's not for me," yelled Belinda.

Apparently he heard nothing. She heard him say something about obstinate cases yielding to proper treatment. Just then she saw an ear-trumpet on the counter. She held it out to the old man. He put it to his ear.

"Cure for Drunkenness," shouted Belinda down the trumpet.

"Yes, yes, it's what I said," said the stubborn man. "Can't deceive me. Now, if you'll follow my treatment—"

Then, to Belinda's great relief, she heard someone enter. A woman of about seventy.

"Ey, you'd never make him hear," said the old woman.

"Are you his daughter?" asked Belinda.

"His wife," said the woman. Tell me what you want."

Belinda explained. The old woman shook her head.

"It's Hersfield, the chemist, right past the workhouse, back at Lingwood, you want," she said. "So you're going to try the cure. I've a son drinks. If he was at home, I'd try it on him, but I daren't ask his wife. She might tell, and he'd never forgive me. But—if he'd been at home, I'd try."

The old man looked impatient.

"It's all right, Josiah," she called down the trumpet. "It's Cure for Drunkenness. No. It's not for her."

The old woman was firm, but the patriarch's look, as Belinda went out, conveyed that he was not sure that Belinda did not need something for herself. Belinda, a blister on her heel as big as a pigeon egg, hobbled back to Lingwood. She was cross, but the recollection of the old herbalist made her smile, and caused several people to turn round to look after her, wonderingly. Near the workhouse gate, Belinda saw two of the inmates. Her eyes filled with tears. The Bastille! She prayed that she might never have to go there, and trudged on to the chemist's.

"Have you got a cure for drunkenness?" she inquired, adding quickly, "not for me." She did not want that nice young man to think she had need of it.

He had.

"Is it dead certain?" she asked.

"It's a good thing," said the young man. "It allays the craving. Be careful how you administer it —"

"It isn't poison?" asked Belinda, scared.

"I mean—it's best in water. It tints tea, they tell me. But, of course, that does not matter if it's for someone taking it of his own accord."

Belinda shook her head. She knew well enough that Joe was not in that category.

Belinda landed the bottle safely at Grandon Road.

"Have you got it?" asked Mrs. Pickett, looking scared to death and motioning Belinda towards the kitchen. Joe was home for dinner.

Belinda said something about gripe water and the baby, as she went in. "And how's your head this morning?" she asked Joe, smiling in a challenging way.

Joe looked pathetic. He was wishing he could give up the "racket." But somehow—well, he had tried. But it always ended in the same way. He could do with a drink, he said—water. Belinda brought him a glass, into which she poured a trial dose. Mrs. Pickett turned tail, and fled into the fitting-room. Belinda watched Joe drink that water. He may have fancied it tasted queer. He left half of it, but said nothing.

"Next time I'll put less water in," Belinda told Mrs. Pickett when he had gone back to work.

"If he finds out he'll kill me," said the other, trembling.

"But he isn't to find out."

"I wish I was like you."

"And I wish I could make clothes like you. We have our own gifts, haven't we?"

They sat down and had cups of tea, Belinda telling her adventures. Mrs. Pickett laughed until tears stood in her eyes.

"That's the first good laugh I've had for a long time," she said.

"I'm glad I'm good for something," said Belinda.

CHAPTER X

The Muses Call to Belinda

DURING the week, Mr. Pickett complained that Beldon water was tasting of fish, whereupon Belinda dilated on the vagaries of the imagination, and how, in a house where she once lived, she could always smell coffin-wood when she went into the parlour. She told Mr. Pickett that, judging from the shape of his nose, he had the gift of imagination highly developed.

Mrs. Pickett lived in fear that Joe would discover the trick, but Belinda always had a pot of water ready doped, waiting to be taken from the cupboard, though she let the tap run to deceive him. A day before the stuff was finished, Belinda was to procure a further supply. But Joe, his repentance having run out, or because he had missed two doses, broke down utterly.

Mrs. Pickett wept.

"Well—we've tried," commiserated Belinda, and suggested that they send for leaflets on hypnotism, and cure Joe by suggestion. Mrs. Pickett whimpered that she would not "t-t-try a-any m-more," now that Joe had broken down after all she had "g-gone" through that week.

"Very well, then," said Belinda, impatiently. "Don't cross him when he's in liquor. Laugh with him. Get him singing. Don't cross him."

Mrs. Pickett took the advice with commendable results.

Belinda had fine times with the baby. She took him with her once to Syke Gate. Her mother said, "Ey, Belinda, tha does look nice wi' a baby," and Belinda blushed and admitted that she had often wished little Frankie was her own. He was a laughing baby, with ginger hair, and big blue eyes.

Belinda perceived that her mother wished to tell her something, but could not get started, so she said, "What's bothering you, mother?" Perhaps the tablets had run out. Belinda had sold a plait made from her hair-combings to get her mother the last bottle of tablets. She would have sold her head, if necessary. Her mother was now able to walk about. She had mended astonishingly. But neither she nor Belinda suspected how much will-effort had contributed. The woman, sheltered by Sam Higgins, slaved for by Belinda, had been aroused by the late upheaval, by the heartburning desire to be as little dependent as possible on her daughter-in-law.

"What is it bothers you, mother?" asked Belinda.

"There's somebody wants to wed me," said Mrs. Higgins, flushing.

"Never!" said Belinda, astounded.

"There is," avowed Mrs. Higgins, tartly. "I don't see—" She stopped, looking at Belinda, who was dandling Frankie.

"But who?" asked Belinda.

She could not have dreamed that her mother would be so pleased to have an offer of marriage.

"Oh, a man up this street," said Mrs. Higgins. "He came to get Jonathan to sign some papers for him, about his pension money —"

"Pension money?"

"Old Age," explained Mrs. Higgins.

"Oh!"

"He kept coming after that, just to pass a half-hour, and one day he throws the key of his house in my lap and says, 'Pick it up or leave it.'"

"Well?"

"What could I do?" said the old woman, plaintively.

"You picked it up?"—chokily.

"I picked it up," said Mrs. Higgins. "So— you'll have somewhere to come, like coming home again, when you have a day off, Belinda."

"Mother!" cried Belinda. "Did you do it only for that?"

"No, no. I like him."

There was a long silence.

"Linda!"

"There is no man fit to follow my father," said Belinda. That was the only reproach she made. Mrs. Higgins wept. Belinda thought this winter-marriage was utterly mad. She felt that it was treason to her father's dust. But she comforted her mother.

"He has some wed childer," said Mrs. Higgins. "Six of 'em. They give him two shillings a-piece, so with his pension, we'll be able to manage. The house belongs to his son. But he pays no rent."

All the flush of happiness had died out of her face. She had expected Belinda would be delighted. Belinda saw this, and strove to eradicate the pain she had given. Her own heart was very disturbed. She saw things as they would be—her mother hobbling about on a stick, doing the housework with pain and weariness, the old man in the corner, the six children perhaps grudging the meagre allowance now that a strange old woman was sharing. On the other hand, she saw no hope of being able to make a home for her mother again. Mrs. Higgins was between the devil and the sea.

"There, mother. It just took me by surprise, that's all," said Belinda. She strove to enter into her mother's dream, and, by-and-by, managed to think it might not be so bad after all. Her mother would not, at least, be lonely.

"And I'll send you my wages, just the same," said Belinda.

"Nay," said Mrs. Higgins, with streaming eyes. "That wouldn't be right, Belinda. What will you do when you're old?"

"Somehow," said Belinda.

"Well, there was never a better lass," said Mrs. Higgins, wiping her eyes.

Belinda went back to Beldon, wheeling little Frankie. She was all "fluttery." She strove to analyse her emotions fearlessly. Was she against this match because it cut across old memories? Belinda never saw her mother without being conscious of the presence of her father. Her mother often used Sam Higgins' very words. She swore by his opinions. His influence, the influence of long years, had left its indelible mark.

"You look worried," said Mrs. Pickett, two days later.

Belinda told her all about the coming marriage.

"I'll tell you what we'll do," said Mrs. Pickett. "We'll go and see a spiritualist."

Belinda was excited. She wore, at Mrs. Pickett's request, an old brooch that her father had given her when she was a girl, though she could not see what spirits had to do with that.

"How much will it be?" asked Belinda, a little anxiously. She wanted to look into the future for once in her life, but having stripped herself of all save half-a-crown, must know the cost beforehand of this glimpse into the abyss of futurity.

"Oh—about—but you give anything," said Mrs. Pickett.

"What's usual?"

"Oh, a shilling." Belinda breathed again.

They set out. It entailed a car-ride which further depleted Belinda's resources. They entered a grey, working-class district, where slip-shod women, bleak of eye, sat nursing pallid infants in doorways.

"Poor things!" said Belinda, pityingly, forgetful of her own lack of gear. "It makes me mad," she told Mrs. Pickett.

"You should think about yourself," said Mrs. Pickett. Belinda dropped a threepenny piece into the tin cup held by a blind woman sitting in a doorway.

"I do think about myself," said Belinda. 'I think I do—when I think of them."

"There, you nearly went under that car!" cried Mrs. Pickett, aghast. "Didn't you hear it?"

"I was thinking," said Belinda.

"You should notice things more. It would go against you in service, not noticing things—if ever you left me."

"Oh, I shall never leave you," said Belinda warmly.

Mrs. Pickett said nothing, which might have struck Belinda as queer if they had not just then been crossing the street. Mrs. Pickett had been very anxious that Belinda consult this spiritualist. There was something she herself badly wanted to know and on it would depend Belinda's staying or going.

"Now, I did not think anybody in touch with the spirits would live in a place like this," declared Belinda. "You'd think the spirits would have more sense than come back to a hole like this. But perhaps they are pitiful spirits."

They dived down a narrow street, past a marine store, then Mrs. Pickett said, with relief, "Thank goodness, it's here!"

Belinda fluttered. She was where spirits communicated with mortals.

"Have you been before?" she asked Mrs. Pickett, suddenly.

"Once. Before Frankie was born. I wanted to know if I'd get through."

"And she told you correct," said Belinda, breathlessly.

"To the letter."

"Well, we all have our gifts."

"You knock," said Mrs. Pickett. But before Belinda could do so, the other said, "No, don't knock. Walk in. They might be watching the house."

"Watching the house?"

"Don't talk so loud," Mrs. Pickett advised.

"Go in. It's a shop. Go in as if you want something."

The place was half-dark, red merino curtains being hung across the windows. A few toffee-bottles, a pair of scales, some weights, and a half-empty box of chocolates, stood on a table, against which leaned a small boy watching his sweets being weighed by an old woman, somewhat untidily dressed, an old woman who might have sat for the figure of Penury. She eyed Belinda suspiciously. The boy went out.

"What do you want?" asked the old woman.

"We want you to tell us something," said Belinda.

"Have you been before?"

"No. But my friend has—she's outside."

"Oh!"

The old medium's face cleared. It was hard to turn half-a-crown away. Had the police nothing better to do than watch the house of a struggling old woman, dying of gall stones and bronchitis? They said "it" was unlawful, a trespass against the public intelligence, whilst a whole world of big fraud went on, under big names, in big places.

"Did anybody see you come in?" she asked, when Mrs. Pickett and Belinda were seated.

"No. Nobody saw us come in," Belinda assured her. "Only a woman two doors away."

"And she's no friend," said the old medium.

She drew a pack of cards from under a newspaper spread on a round table.

"Shuffle them," she said, and sat back coughing.

Belinda's keen insight enabled her to feel deeply this tragi-comedy. Here was a poor old creature, telling others' fortunes, and in sore plight herself, trembling lest anyone should come and catch her earning an honest shilling.

The medium addressed herself to Belinda.

"You've a good look with you, young woman," she said. "You carry a fine light round your head. Do you know?"

Belinda did not.

"I've seen a light like that round only one head before," said the old woman. "He sat where you sit now. He was an author."

"My father was a bit o' one," said Belinda. But Mrs. Pickett gave her a look which said, "Don't tell her anything. Let her tell you."

"Shall I go out?" asked Belinda, delicately.

"Well, perhaps you'd better. Sometimes it disturbs the conditions," she was told. Mrs. Pickett looked relieved. Belinda went through a curtained doorway, into a back kitchen, where were many cobwebs, a wringing machine, a tub of dirty wet clothes, and a lot of unwashed pots on a rickety table.

"Poor thing!" mused Belinda, sitting on a little stool. "I wish I lived nearer, I'd come in and do a bit for her, now and then."

If Belinda had not a light round her head really, it was not her fault.

She sat for what seemed an age, the utter silence from the other room being broken only by such phrases as "Cut 'em again," or, "You've cut the same again," or, "I see it for you, on a roadway, quite plain." At last Mrs. Pickett came through the curtained doorway. To Belinda's surprise, she looked pale and downcast.

"Go on. She's waiting," said Mrs. Pickett, and sat down on the stool Belinda had vacated, the figure of despair.

"Shuffle 'em well, or you'll cut her cards," said the old spiritualist, wheezily.

"You've got bronchitis," said Belinda, sympathetically.

"Ay. But I shan't have it long."

"Ey, don't give up," said Belinda, cheerfully.

The old woman sighed.

"I think you've never handled a pack before, have you?" she said.

"No."

"Cut 'em," she was told, but had to be shown how.

"Do you know anything about a man, between-colours?" asked the old woman. "He stands up to you with a wedding ring, and good hearts, but there's a coffin between—"

Belinda felt creepy. Bill Greenwood sprang into mind. A coffin between! Was his mother going to die?

"There's a death," said the old woman, matter-of-fact. "Look!" She held up the ace of spades. "Looks like the death of a woman. You're here. Spades, I call you. You've black eyes, haven't you? There's tears for you. You swim in 'em, fair swim in 'em—they're all round you, like the sea. I'm sorry to have to tell you this, but I reads 'em as I find 'em—not like some, telling all sorts o' stuff. Then you go on a roadway. You go living by water—it might be the sea—"

"Or the canal," suggested Belinda.

"No, when we see the water-card it means the sea, generally. The ring comes up to you, with good hearts, but you turn your back on it. Do you know aught about that?"

"There's a man wants me to wed him," said Belinda, simply. "But he's a mother and I've one."

"This coffin is for a light woman," said the old medium.

Belinda's heart lost its terror, though she felt sorry. "His mother is light," she said, cheerfully. "It'll be for her."

"You seem to go wandering up and down," said the old woman. "You seem like you can't rest. You're here again with your back to that ring. He's here again with it. And there's a dark woman here—with a dark man—

relatives, they look— who are they? Have you a brother your colour?" asked the old woman.

Belinda nodded. It took her breath away.

"Well, they both are here, with good hearts to you. They'd do anything for you, but you've your back to them, too, though you don't turn it on a child. Have they a lad?"

Belinda leaned back in her chair. Here was an old woman, clad in the rags of poverty, an old woman, not over clean, ill, struggling to pay her rent, and dealing, with absolute confidence, in destiny!

"How do you do it?"

"It's a gift," said the old woman, smiling. "And but for that I'd have starved. But I'll have to give it up. They watch me so. It makes me I can't sleep."

"The spirits watch you?" asked Belinda in horror.

"No—the police."

"But what harm do you do?" asked Belinda, tenderly, her hand reaching towards that of the medium. The old eyes filled with tears. Many came grabbing at good fortune, but none before had pitied her sad one.

"I wish there'd been better luck to tell you," said the medium, sorrowfully.

"Well—you have told it as it is," said Belinda.

"This child clings to you, too," said the old woman in a musing way. "You seem to have words with the dark man and woman, and the child comes to make peace. But you turn your back."

"I think," said Belinda, gently, "that must be wrong. I'll never drop our Jonathan."

There was silence.

Belinda blushed as she asked the momentous question.

"Shall I get married—ever?"

"It doesn't show," said the old woman. "But cut again. And pitch thirteen cards, throw 'em out without counting—and—wish."

Belinda thought of money, having only one and threepence left in the world. No. She set that aside. She wished, intensely, holily, almost mystically, for her mother's happiness with the old man taking her father's place, stepping into a post which for thirty-five years Higgins had held worthily, unselfishly.

How anxiously Belinda watched those cards spread out!

"You get your wish," said the old woman. "But not just as you think it. There's some black cards goes with it, but they are up against you." Belinda beamed. She could stand black cards against herself.

"Are you satisfied?" asked the old woman.

Belinda nodded.

"You don't write poetry yourself?" asked the old woman.

Belinda shook her head.

"Nay—there's a poetess lives at Beldon. They put some of her things in the paper, and I thought—"

"No, I've not met her," said Belinda. "I have tried to write—"

She was getting out her purse.

"No. Don't pay me. Not that way, anyhow," said the old woman. "I want you to do something for me. If you can put lines together put some together for me. I've children, and they never send me a penny piece. They don't like me telling fortunes, either. Couldn't you put something together about a poor old woman?—just to touch 'em, and make 'em see they are doing a wrong in never coming to see me."

"If only my father had been here!" said Belinda. "I'm not a poet. But he *could* poet."

"Try," begged the old woman, earnestly. "Think! It might mean ten shillings a week to me, and the comfort of seeing 'em as well. I shan't be here long. I've gall stones and bronchitis."

"I'll try, then," said Belinda, pushing a shilling under the newspaper.

The old woman gave her the addresses. Belinda was to send the lines to each of the five children, posting them from Beldon. She was to ascend Parnassus not to sing songs sacred to Poesy but to touch the hard hearts and close pockets of undutiful offspring. It had at least a useful purpose. It was fitting that Belinda, ascending Parnassus, should carry a household lamp, burning humble paraffin, to return, not with immortal flowers, but bread and butter—and not for herself.

Mrs. Pickett and Belinda had too much to think of on the home journey, to say much to each other.

That evening, the man with the pink moustache paid his third visit within a fortnight. Belinda had grown rather fond of him. He asked her if she would mind going with him to the pictures. Belinda did not mind.

"You aren't struck with ready words to-night," said Belinda, when they came out.

"I've been thinking, Belinda. I'm not doing right by you."

Belinda stared at him.

"I've been thinking," he said, sadly, "that I ought to have told you I've a wife. She ran off with a bobby, twenty years ago. That was when I took to poetry. I'd got to tell you to-night."

"Good lord!" laughed Belinda. "Was you thinking of committing bigamy with me?"

The little man looked pathetic.

"Me going through all that to tell you, and you taking it as a joke!"

"Come and have some chips," chaffed Belinda. "I can understand your wife running away with a bobby if you looked like that often. Don't worry. These Platonic affairs is quite correct, though there's a terrible lot lands in the Divorce Court. But you're safe with me."

Belinda beamed at him, benignly.

"Oh, I never thought nothing wrong," said the little man.

Returned, Belinda flopped into a chair, giddily. She was franker with Mrs. Pickett.

"Glory, he's married!" she almost shrieked.

"Who? Mr. —"

"Pink-Tache!"

"You weren't —" began Mrs. Pickett.

"Not me," denied Belinda.

But she had blushed—to the roots of her hair.

CHAPTER XI

A Wedding—Conflicting Auras—and Tragedy

SEVERAL times during the next week Belinda caught Mrs. Pickett crying, and finally learned the cause.

"But it's only natural," Belinda assured her. "And they always say there should be two to fight, and another to separate them."

Mrs. Pickett shook her head sadly.

"And you'll have me to help you," said Belinda.

Mrs. Pickett broke down at that.

"But Belinda, Joe says I haven't to sew any more, with two children. So I'll have to give you up. You might as well look out and get as good a place as you can."

It was a sore blow. Just when her tent was pitched she must move again.

"Shall I go now?" asked Belinda. But Mrs. Pickett had work in to finish. After September, she was not sewing any more, so Belinda promised to stay till then.

Belinda was busy, too. Ascending the slopes of Parnassus to sing a song that should bring bread and butter to an old woman, and, javelin-like, strike stony hearts, is a big order, in spare time. Belinda burned many candles, being by nature a slow mover, like her father. In two weeks she brought this down from Parnassus:

Think of your mother dear before she goes away
She is your mother who has brought you up
Who raised you gently when you tumbled down
Think of her ere she pushes daisies up.
She has not long to stay, be kind and good
You know not who writes this but I wish you would
Lift up her latch and smile on her once more
Before she saileth to the golden shore.

Mrs. Pickett was amazed.

"Belinda!" she gasped.

"Do you like it?" asked Belinda, blushing.

"It's beautiful," said Mrs. Pickett. "Of course, I don't know much about poetry, excepting bits I read in the school-books. But *I* couldn't do it."

Belinda went off and posted five copies of her first "poem". She surveyed the streets through new eyes, as she went to the pillar-box. She had the fire of poetry in her, if only she could get it out. Her shoes certainly were as down at heel as ever poet's were, and of all those who have sung in the choir invisible, none had a warmer heart.

But her great anxiety was, what effect would her "poeting" have on the offspring of the old medium? After a week she received a card. The old woman's message was brief. It merely said, "It has worked," as if Belinda's song was a new purgative. Belinda danced round the room when she had taken in its meaning.

"I reckon that's pretty good—for a first," she told Mrs. Pickett.

"Who knows, Belinda, perhaps you may someday make money with it," said Mrs. Pickett, businesslike.

"My father's some lovely things—mine's not a patch on 'em, and nobody would even print his," said Belinda. "No, I'll be satisfied if I can just do a good turn now and then, like this."

A month later, Mrs. Higgins married. Syke Gate *Herald* called it a romance. Belinda swallowed hard, and bought twelve yards of narrow width stuff, had a wedding frock made, and went to the wedding. Despite her fears, the old man's children were glad to see him take a wife. He was a nice old man. They married quietly, and asked Belinda to stay with them for the week-end, which she gladly did, flinging the halo of her own cheerfulness over the three-roomed house. She left them a pound, her past month's wages, and a stamped addressed envelope.

At the tram terminus, she saw Bill Greenwood. But he was not alone. He had a woman with him.

"Hello, Bill," said Belinda.

He stared at her, then reddened.

"An old friend o' mine, Miss Higgins, Dorothy," said Bill, turning to his companion. "You'll be surprised, Belinda, to hear I'm going to be married."

It was decidedly a tremendous blow. But Belinda said she was surprised at nothing, and wished them much happiness.

"Have you heard my mother's married again?" she asked.

Bill was staggered.

Only the conclusion that Mrs. Higgins would live twenty years had made him waver, and whilst he had wavered Dorothy had pounced.

"Why, it was in the *Herald*—Old Age Pensioner's Romance,'" said Belinda.

"Last week's paper got ripped up before I saw it," said Bill, ruefully.

"*Our* car," said Dorothy. She had her fears.

"Oh, ay," said Bill. He went a few steps with Dorothy, then ran back to Belinda, Dorothy watching, cattishly.

"I shall rue it all my life," Bill muttered. "Belinda—can't I —"

"No," said Belinda. "You can't. But I'll tell you this, Bill—I'll like to think you said that— *'all my life.'* " She smiled in a bashful sort of a way, and then ran off to the car, which had started.

"Nothing in spirits," she declared when she reached the Pickett kitchen.

"Been on rum?" asked Joe.

"Nothing o' that sort," said Belinda. She told Mrs. Pickett that the medium with her tale of a man offering a ring was wrong. He was marrying somebody else.

She left the Picketts at the fall of the leaf. Mrs. Pickett had a friend, near Manchester, who wanted a domestic. Belinda had been recommended. After visiting her mother, finding her fairly comfortable, and able to knock about the little house, Belinda set her face from Syke Gate. Instructions there were from both sides, Belinda telling her mother to be careful, her mother telling Belinda to be careful, too, and keep her shoes mended, not to strip herself of every penny on their account. During which, Belinda's stepfather sat smiling in his corner.

"Take care of her," Belinda asked him.

He liked his stepdaughter.

"I will that," he said.

Belinda kissed her mother.

"It hasn't made a bit o' difference 'tween thee and me, has it, now?" asked Mrs. James (now), referring to her remarriage.

"Not a bit," said Belinda, bravely.

She took her mother in her arms and hugged her.

"And isn't the matting nice?" asked the old woman, proudly. And so the shadow passed away.

"I'm happier, thinking you are," said Belinda.

But she did not go to see her father's grave this time, though she was going further away than ever before.

Belinda arrived at Home Lodge on the edge of dark. Her new mistress met her in the last lane. Belinda was reciting from *Bliss Carmen*, like a pagan devotee, as she came along, carrying the "Fighting Temeraire."

Mrs. Bairns made Belinda feel hushed and nice, the feeling she got when there was snow on the ground. Though there was something a little cold about Mrs. Bairns, she asked Belinda if she had had any difficulty in finding her way and was, in other ways, considerate. Forty years of age, she had white hair, and wore a little straw hat, rather old-fashioned.

The house was a dream of beauty, and a model of simplicity. The floors were inlaid, polished wood. No gorgeous furniture, but simple chairs and tables, and a beautiful grand piano. One vase in art ware, filled with fresh flowers of foliage, adorned each room. There were roses in Belinda's room, an exquisite little room—Belinda had never slept in the like. Over her bed was an oval picture of a woman in trailing draperies, gathering shells on a dim shore, her head against a sky of melted pearl, her bare feet on dim, shimmering sands, lapped by a sea of blue moonbeamy lustre. Belinda knelt on the bed to read the tide. "The Sea hath its Pearls," she read.

It was all like a dream. Something in her uncurled and peeped out, tremblingly. She had always had an almost uncanny longing for culture.

Mrs. Bairns was surprised at the taste Belinda showed for music. When Edgar, the hope of this intellectual household, was playing Beethoven, Belinda would steal to the door to listen, and though unimpressed by Chopin, she discovered a strange love of Russian music—the Slav sadness, its barbaric gaiety (when it *was* gay).

Mrs. Bairns was a psychologist and regarded Belinda in the light of a study, hence that remoteness, that coldness, likened by Belinda to a field of snow. She claimed to have reached beyond passion of any sort. Belinda was also told that, undoubtedly, her delight in music, her uncommon taste for the best, had been carried over from some other life. Belinda was openly staggered at the preposterousness of returning to the same old place, time after time.

"How if the shell of the earth cracked?" Belinda wanted to know, for she had read of the possibility of the earth going "bust."

"Matter is indestructible," said Mrs. Bairns, gravely.

She lent Belinda books about auras, astral bodies, and passion-quelling, which Belinda read with an open mind. Belinda would have liked to have, a thousand lives.

"I suppose, if you were sure of coming again," said Mr. Bairns, one evening, "you would not want to do menial work."

Belinda pondered.

"I'd like to be in service again," she said, thoughtfully, "that is, if I could be treated as a human being."

"I hope you think we treat you as a human being."

"I eat by myself," said Belinda, slowly.

"Most servants do."

Belinda smiled.

"Do friends eat in a place by themselves, when they come?" she asked, removing his tray.

"You are impractical."

"No. I'd like to be able to practise what I preach."

Mr. Bairns laughed, and retired behind his paper, intent on markets. He was on change.

Belinda had been at Home Lodge seven weeks, when the big blow fell. It fell on her birthday. The family had had a big bonfire, and let off ten shillings' worth of fireworks for Edgar. Belinda was washing up in the kitchen after supper. As she wiped the cups she was staring out at the Great Bear, which Mr. Bairns had shown her how to find only that evening. She was grateful to these people grateful with her mind rather than with her heart. Yet, despite their consideration, she could not get as fond of them as she had of the Picketts, though Joe did drink, and Mrs. Pickett babyish, and little Frankie such a howler—when he did cry.

Mrs. Bairns came into the kitchen. Belinda smiled though she was very tired.

"I'm afraid I'm going to upset you," said Mrs Bairns, gently.

"Upset me?"

"Do you think you could get a new place within a month?" asked Mrs. Bairns. She looked as near ordinary common feeling as ever Belinda had seen her.

"What have I done?"

Belinda looked like a thrashed child.

"I'm sorry. You do not meet our requirements."

"I should like to know where I've missed it."

Then Mrs. Bairns told her. Belinda had set the tea-things wrongly. Instead of setting the cups in a row, she would persist in setting them in a triangle. It irritated Mrs. Bairns.

"And you are not very observant," continued Mrs. Bairns. "Visitors have to knock a long time before you hear. It is the same in other things. I am not blaming you. The qualities we have not got, we shall have to cultivate, in other lives—"

Belinda was crying. There was something so clean-cut in this demonstration of her deficiencies. It was like the last straw, after her mother's marriage, and Bill's mistake.

"Personally, I like you very much," said Mrs. Bairns, unemotionally. "But we have to learn our lessons. We have to cultivate qualities we have not got—"

"I'm a bit dreamy," said Belinda. "But I hope to take more notice—with trying."

Her eyes were dry again now. A sense of shame wrapped her round, a nasty sense of inferiority, for which she felt there was no justification. The cat she had fondled opened its eyes and blinked at her. She heard Edgar run his fingers over the piano keys, in the room she had polished only that morning on hands and knees. There were things she loved here.

"Yes, I had noticed you are a little dreamy," said Mrs. Bairns. "But, as I was saying, we are born with certain tendencies we have developed in our last lives. In this house we need someone with acute observation. I do not care to tell people time and time again—"

Belinda could not resist a shot.

"Maybe you'll have to cultivate that, next time up," she said.

Mrs. Bairns flushed.

Belinda had not believed that possible.

"You understand. I am not angry with you. You don't just meet our needs," said Mrs. Bairns.

"Am I short in any other direction?" asked Belinda, curtly.

"You put too much energy into things, and it takes too long."

When she had gone, Belinda sat and stared the window with its pretty muslin curtains, and the starry sky showing through. Her tent was to move again. According to Mrs. Bairns, eternity was full of moving tents, every life a tent, every life a new "place." Belinda was tired to-night, tired, and sad, crushed, daunted. "I hope it's a long sleep," she mused. Then she wept, ashamed of such a thought. But as she lay her head on her pillow, she was sure of one thing—she could not serve a notice with the Bairns. She must go at once. It was odd. They were much nicer people than the Wells, the Picketts, but nowhere else had she felt so written over with demerit.

She left two days later, not refusing the book on Theosophy that Mrs. Bairns offered as a parting gift. On the spring cart that took her to the station was a huge bunch of Michaelmas daisies, a parcel of vegetarian sandwiches, and "The Fighting Temeraire."

Her mother stared on opening the door and seeing Belinda there, rain dripping from her hat brim. When she had heard the story she said. "Well, you'll happen soon get another place."

"Why doesn't she stop with us, and go out days?" asked the old man in the corner.

Belinda's eyes shone. "Do you mean that? she asked.

"Never meant aught more in my life," he said, pulling at his pipe.

"Well, then, happen I will," said Belinda. She went next day to town to see if she could get a place as day-woman. One had been advertised for, but was filled. Belinda walked back in the rain. It was like seeing a door half-open, then close with a bang.

"Belinda," said Annie, bursting in on the trio, as they sat at dinner. "They want a servant at Barnfield Police Station."

"Police Station!" Whenever Belinda saw anyone being "took up," her sympathies were with the one being taken.

"You'd have a good chance. The inspector knows Jonathan," said Annie.

Belinda did not like going to a police station. It was like going back on Jean Val Jean. She had wept over his life in the hulks. He would not like to know that she had gone as servant at a police station.

But it was forced medicine. She had only two shillings left, and could not live on the old folk! She left "The Fighting Temeraire" hanging in the spare room they called hers. She would not take her "altar-picture" into a police station. She got there at three, in a sun-shine shower.

"Come in," called Inspector Moreton.

Belinda went in.

"I'm after that there place," announced Belinda.

"Jenny," he called out.

His wife came, a stout, jolly person, with ginger hair and the map of Ireland in her face.—

"She's after that there place," said the inspector. Belinda laughed, for he had said it just as she had, and he had put his finger across his mouth to show how simple and unsophisticated he was.

"Oh, not as green as cabbage-looking," Belinda reminded them, pulling out her testimonials. They were excellent ones with respect to her honesty, though vague otherwise.

Belinda got the place and soon became one of the family. There were three girls, whose fair hair she plaited every night, whom she got ready for school every morning. There was also P.C. Kerton, twenty-seven, who came to dinner every Sunday, and to him Belinda lent the dog-eared copy of *Les Miserables*.

"That's my Bible," Belinda told him.

It never failed to upset Belinda when anyone was "took," and brought to the cells. P.C. Kerton said she would get used to it. But she hoped she never would.

Early one morning when Belinda was making herself a pot of tea, she heard a tremendous thumping, in a cell into which, the night before, a woman had been put for being drunk and disorderly. Belinda knew her history, or rather, the history of her misdemeanours. She was of the same class as Fantine.

Belinda lifted the peep-hole door and looked into the cell. The woman, thinking a constable would look in, had stripped herself naked and stood there challenging and shameless. Belinda cringed. What had been done to the woman to bring, her to such a pass? Then she recalled Fantine spitting at the mayor.

Belinda acquainted Inspector Moreton. He had a pot of tea by him and took it to the miserable wretch whom Belinda had persuaded to dress.

It was a revelation to Belinda, but she knew that Inspector Moreton was one in ten thousand, and would get no medals for that.

Ever after, Maria Pilkington would submit to none but Inspector Moreton. They got him up at all hours. "There's your friend kicking up a row, it'll take ten if you don't go," he would be told, and then he would bring her in, arm in arm, like bride and groom to the altar, Maria cursing the constables behind.

Little boys with faces like cherubim came for various offences. P.C. Kerton told Belinda she did not know human nature. He talked about the criminal instinct. Belinda could not agree.

"After all," she said, "it's all a toss-up which comes to be which. A thief to catch a thief—one's as deep as the other or he wouldn't know how his brain had worked."

Said Mrs. Moreton, one day, "Do you know P.C. Kerton is a bit sweet on you, Belinda?"

"He needn't be," sharply.

"Why?" in surprise.

"I'd never marry a bobby," said Belinda, with finality.

"It's only prejudice," said Jenny. "They're human under their clothes."

"They daren't be human in those clothes," averred Belinda, in spite of the pot of tea incident. "You give him a hint, if he's that way. It's no good letting him make a fool of himself."

Belinda sent her mother nine shillings a week, every week for six months. She went "home" once a fortnight, relieved to find the old couple always comfortable.

One April evening, as Belinda sat in the kitchen, mending brown stockings for the three girls, and incidentally watching a boiling pan of apricots, she heard P.C. Kerton on the telephone. Inspector Moreton was out, his wife was shopping.

"Where's the inspector?" asked Kerton, looking into the kitchen at Belinda, placidly seeking holes in the long stockings.

Belinda told him.

"Anything particular?" she asked. The man who had seen a lot of the tragic side turned coward suddenly. He mumbled something and went away.

Belinda fell asleep in the chair after taking off the jam. When she awoke she heard voices in the room next the kitchen.

"No. I haven't told her," Kerton was saying.

"You darned idiot," said the inspector. "She'll have to be told —"

"I know."

"Then, I'll have to tell her."

"It's three hours since," said Kerton.

"What's up?" burst in Belinda.

"Some awful news on the 'phone," said the inspector. He was pale himself. Belinda's laugh had endeared her to them all.

"Go on —" said Belinda.

She stood, a brown stocking on her arm, staring at him.

"They've sent word that two old folk in Syke Gate are burned to death.

Belinda tried to get the stocking off her arm. She stared at the inspector as though she was in a nightmare. She tugged at the stocking, then toppled heavily forwards. When Mrs. Moreton came in, ten minutes later, she found Kerton and the inspector giving Belinda brandy.

"Burnt to death—burnt to death," she was muttering. It was all she had said, since recovering consciousness. They took her in a car to Syke Gate. Annie and Jonathan were expecting her. Jonathan was all broken up. Reggie cried to see his aunt's discomposure, for she was associated in his mind with all that was valiant.

"Don't look at her, Belinda!" begged Annie.

"How did it happen?" asked Belinda, almost inaudibly.

"Nobody knows. The police think the lamp toppled off the washhand-stand, not being set on properly, and mother must have tried to carry the lamp out, got on fire, and he's tried to put her out, and they've both gone."

Jonathan was as pale as Belinda, as he spoke. It was he who had encouraged his mother to re-marry—for Annie's comfort. All his days this would haunt him.

The inquest took place. It broke Belinda's heart over again to hear Mrs. Lee, a neighbour, say that she heard the old woman call, " 'Linda, 'Linda!" just as though Belinda could have heard her.

Belinda had no faith in telepathy after that.

The coroner said it was a thousand pities that old people like them had not someone to look after them.

At Jonathan's, Belinda sat for an hour without moving. Reggie came to her. Suddenly she roused herself.

"Burnt!" she cried. "There is no God— there is no God. Burnt!"

Belinda said a bitter thing to Annie, when leaving Syke Gate—at the very point of departure, her coat on, ready to go:

"If you hadn't made her feel in the way, if you hadn't shown you were fain to be shut on her when the old man threw the key in her lap, she'd never have gone—she'd never have been burnt to death. I never want to see you or our Jonathan again. She'd been alive this minute but for you."

Reggie ran after her, trying to make peace. Belinda kissed him.

"I'm not mad at thee," she told the lad. "No. Never forget, Reggie—there's nobody in the world I like as much as thee, now."

It was as though the injustice she did her brother and sister-in-law were made up to the boy. She could see her mother in him, and her father, too, as he stood and pleaded.

"Always write to me, Reggie," said Aunt Belinda.

Reggie promised. "But where are you going—now?"

"I don't know."

She walked quickly away, did not once look back. Reggie stood, tears in his eyes, watching.

CHAPTER XII

Belinda Strikes a Smashing Blow Against Pan and Pot Worship

IT could not be said of Belinda that at any time of her life was she utterly miserable or without hope. But the nature of her mother's death was a cruel shock. Most people change by slow degrees, mentally as well as bodily, thoughts and beliefs falling away like dead skin. Belinda's faith had been ripped away from her in one moment. Belinda's God had been a God who decently marked the fall of a sparrow. He had let her mother burn. So it was, when Belinda walked out of Syke Gate, that she walked out of it naked and bleeding of soul. She was not harder—that would have been self-torture. It was that between her and all the things she had loved, the sky, the dear friendly trees, the songs of birds, was the charred body of a woman.

During the following year, she lived on farms, in restaurants, in private houses, once in a doctor's house, rarely staying more than a few weeks anywhere. Where they did not "sack" her, she "sacked" herself. Luckily, she was always able to get work quickly, or she would have been destitute. She gave to the blind, the lame, and, the other maids said, to the lazy. Nevertheless, she saved a few shillings weekly towards the grand objective of her life. She meant to have published, the works of Samuel Higgins—published, not in paper covers but in cloth and gilt. It was the imprudent maid, Sally, who, in the kitchen basement where they sat snatching a meal before the rush of tea-people came to the café upstairs, gave Belinda the idea of going to London.

About this time, too, she frequented the Sunday evening services of the Spiritualists, burningly eager for a message from her mother. Time after time she went, only to come empty away.

"I see beside you the form of an old lady—"

How Belinda's heart would start—like something coming alive again!

"No, not beside you—she comes to the gentleman behind."

At last Belinda saw the advertisement she wanted, and was invited up to London.

She left the café, left Sally and the others and their giggling with commercials, left the shrivelled narcissi in the glasses, the pots with "Blue Rose Café" on the sides, the greasy mirror with letters advertising Beef Tea, left the big windows fronting the public lavatories, left everything but the vision of her mother as she had seen her in that upper room.

"If you want to know the way, ask a policeman," sang Sally.

"Think the white slave traffic wants her?" Polly had said, in jest.

"Oh, she isn't bad looking—well, she hasn't been," Sally had replied.

Belinda had given her a brooch for a mascot.

"I wish I'd never put the idea into her head," uneasily.

"Oh, come on—there's sixteen beds to make, and a chap to topple out o' one"—and giggling and screaming, they had scampered up the dark staircase.

Belinda reached London in the dark, and, bewildered and frightened, stood wondering whom she ought to ask. But everybody seemed to be busy.

The dimness, the lights, the vastness—she never forgot that first glimpse of London as she rode towards the place where she was to be "General." She felt perfectly sure the vehicle would go "smash" when shadowy buildings loomed up as if out of nothing.

When she reached her "place", someone came up from the basement.

"You Miss Higgins?" came a voice like a man's—though a servant girl's.

"Come down here, then. Oh, the boss'll fetch the things in. Drop 'em at the door. Supper's ready."

Belinda entered a basement kitchen. At the table sat a coarse-looking man in middle life, and a thin, worried-looking woman, over kippers and porter.

"I said it was her, Bessie," said the man. "Got her traps in?"

"You can fetch 'em in," snapped Bessie.

"Oh, all right—all right. Don't get nasty," said the little Cockney.

"Sit down," said the thin woman. "I forgot your name. Had a pleasant journey?" Belinda nodded.

"Take your things off," said Mrs. Freebootle. "Beer or porter?"

"Tea, if you don't mind." But the fire was out. "Water will do, then."

Belinda went to her room, ninety steps high, with Bessie, a fresh-complexioned auburn-haired beauty, spoiled by that rough jarring voice.

"Nice little room, ain't it?" Bessie giggled, in the English of "Shikespeare spoke nysal."

"I've had one before—nearly as bad," said Belinda, sitting on a bed with a hideous counterpane.

"Do you sleep near here?" asked Belinda.

"There," said Bessie, thumping the pillow.

"Oh!"

There would be little reading in bed, then!

But Belinda had not been in this house long before she found that she had only strength to crawl up those ninety steps, at the close of the day's work; and often, as she sank on the bed, wondered if death came with such weary satisfaction.

She had one Sunday evening to herself a month, and every other Saturday afternoon. But she had been in London a month before she went any further than the shops round the corner. People smiled to see her run when crossing even a quiet road.

In the best room lived a very well-preserved old lady, eighty, if a minute, but looking not more than sixty. It was Belinda's duty to carry in her meals, and the table was what Belinda called a "tableau," so finely was it set out. There, the old lady dined in solitary splendour. She had her own china, her own pictures and plate, and a small but splendid library. Belinda felt very nervous when waiting upon her, but the old lady liked Belinda, despite her clumsiness, and asked that only she attend her.

Up at seven, to bed at twelve!

"I'm three months behind with my sleep," said Belinda, one morning. Spring was passing into summer. London, the city of enchantment, was all about her, yet she had seen nothing of it but the Tower, and that had merely depressed her.

Utterly body-weary, Belinda arose one morning in that hideous room.

"We must rise and shine, I suppose," she yawned to Bessie.

It was a day of misfortune. When she was slicing bread into—"fly-wings," she called them—the knife slipped.

"Oh, Higgins!" cried poor Mrs. Freebootle, and turned faint.

Blood was streaming from Belinda's hand.

Mr. Freebootle, cleaning boots at the time, had been in the army and was, therefore, dependable. Belinda's finger-end was hanging off, so he stuck it on.

"Shall I have to report?" asked Belinda.

"Oh, I don't think so," said the boss, knowing that if she did report she would be expected to stop work. So Belinda developed her crooked finger!

Then she smashed one of the old lady's soup dishes whilst washing up. It was an heirloom. Mrs. Freebootle turned pale.

"I'll buy another," said Belinda, valiantly.

"You can't. And I daren't tell her."

Belinda faced the old lady and there was a short passage at arms.

"I wouldn't care if you were sorry," said the old lady.

"People shouldn't worship pots and pans, it's heathenish," said Belinda.

The old lady blushed. Belinda got her notice, but threatened to leave without if she did not get a day off. She spent that day on London's bridges, watching the people, hearing the murmur of feet, engrossed. She watched the lights shine on the water—then walked slowly back.

She got into bed, and, lighting her inch of candle, began to read Maeterlinck's wonderful description in *Pelleas and Melisande*, of the sheep passing on their way to slaughter.

"I must have eaten quite a lot of sheep," thought Belinda, touched. Maeterlinck had made them seem like humans going to destruction.

Next day at lunch, Mrs. Freebootle asked. "How much?"

"No meat for me," said Belinda, cheerfully.

Mrs. Freebootle was horrified. It was no use telling her of Maeterlinck and sheep, so Belinda said nothing, and chose cheese, and half-starved during the next fortnight, until the stairs seemed unreal under her feet.

"I want Higgins to bring in my food again," demanded the old lady, at last. She could not bear Bessie. So Belinda carried in the meals once more.

"You don't look well, Higgins," observed the old lady.

"I'm all right," smiled Belinda.

The old lady looked at her curiously. "Perhaps you were right," she said, as Belinda set the supper tray on the table. Belinda did not understand. "Perhaps it *is* heathenish to worship pots and pans," smiled the old lady. "But that soup dish had been in my family so long, and there were so many associations—but there, we'll say no more about it. Do you mind carrying my candle up, Higgins?"

Belinda carried up candle and tray to the magnificent bedroom with its toilet table laden with perfumes, creams, and silver-backed brushes. The old lady followed, very stateful and graceful, and more nimble than Belinda. Belinda's notice to quit was rescinded. She felt nothing beyond a relief that, for the time being, she could settle.

Two nights afterwards, Belinda awoke Bessie. "Something's burning," she said, sitting up.

Bessie had heard Belinda talk in her sleep about burning, and believed Belinda was a bit crazy.

"But there is," said Belinda. She ran out, in her coarse night-dress, sniffing—and then thought she must have been mistaken. But as she descended the second flight of stairs to the landing on which opened Madam's room, she saw smoke issuing. She burst open the old lady's door—the room was full of fire and smoke—snatched her out of bed and on to the landing, raising the house with cries.

The old lady lay in bed all next day, suffering mainly from shock. Belinda, with one hand bandaged, took up chocolate. Madam was effusive and grateful.

"Oh, call it quits for the soup dish," said Belinda.

"I shall remember you, Higgins," said the old lady. "Yes. Be quite sure I shall remember you."

Mrs. Freebootle, who was passing, asked Belinda what had been said.

"That she'd remember me," smiled Belinda.

There were two letters from Syke Gate, one from Jonathan, saying that he thought it too hard that she did not write to them. He had only one sister, he said. He also said that if she were in need, she knew how gladly they would do anything for her. The other from Reggie, confiding his first love affair. He had sent her a photograph of himself, which Belinda nailed on the wall. Reggie was the only being she loved. She found it impossible to forgive Jonathan and Annie.

Belinda, rigidly a vegetarian, stayed with the Freebootles a year, then Reggie sent a letter that made her leave London. His father was ill, he wrote, would Aunt Belinda not come home?

Belinda went.

She arrived early one autumn morning. Syke Gate looked strange and small to her. She looked anxiously towards the windows when Jonathan's came in view. No. The blinds were not down.

She passed the house where her mother had been burned to death. It looked different. Others saw an ordinary house. Belinda fought hard with herself. But the memory of the burning! She shuddered, and passed on.

Annie opened the door. She was glad to see Belinda, and began to cry.

"Is he ill?" asked Belinda.

She followed Annie upstairs.

"'Linda!"

Jonathan sat up in bed.

"Our Jonathan!"

Belinda ran to him and the tears she could not shed before, rushed out now, freshening her heart. But they frightened Jonathan.

"But what I can't understand is—God. What was He doing?" complained Belinda.

"There's a lot we can't understand, 'Linda," said Jonathan.

Belinda stayed two months, helping Annie in the house. She was more like the old Belinda, though with fewer dreams. Bill Greenwood had married. The man with the pink moustache *was* married. Her mother, dead. It did not bother her now to think that, to the end of her life, she would live in other people's houses. But a sad, autumnal film of unfulfilment pervaded her heart.

All her hopes and dreams centred in Reggie. Some day he would cut a figure in the world. Reggie's future and the publishing of her father's works—these filled her life. She thought of them, dreamed of them, when scrubbing passages, steps, scullery floors, polishing door-knockers—"muggin' around" as she called it. Her father's book would cost twenty-five pounds for five hundred copies, the printer had said. Belinda had saved ten.

"Wanted," read Belinda, aloud, one night, as they all sat for the usual chat after supper. "It's by the sea-side, too."

"Oh, are you moving again?" asked Reggie, anxiously.

Belinda began to sing about the moving tent.

"I feel I could do with a breath of the sea," she said.

So she got to Long Marsh, near Seadale, as domestic in a boarding-house—the usual sort, inside and out. The mistress was a tired, cross-looking woman, living, apparently, in the kitchen.

"Isn't the sea lovely?" said Belinda.

"It is—if we ever got to see it, I suppose," said the woman wearily.

Later they began to turn out the fifteen rooms, ready for the holiday rush.

"We must make things as nice as we can for 'em," said Belinda, "for they have to work hard all the year."

"You haven't been in service long, I think," said the mistress.

Belinda told her just how long.

"I can stand working for them as works," said Belinda, "but, my hat! —when you're working for them as never works and they're so exactsome, it gives you the hump."

Belinda learned the full meaning of slavery in the following months. It was a radiant summer. The first rush came with Gadby Wakes. Folk tumbled in, like waves. There was one roomful of girls, cotton weavers from Gadby, in whom Belinda took a special interest, her father having worked there. Two of the girls were sisters and very pretty. One was on the lively side. The other was quiet, with big grey eyes and clear, pallid complexion of one who worked in a cloud of steam.

"Full moon and a low tide, Annie," said the lively girl to the quiet one, one evening. Then to Belinda, "Does it matter if we're a bit late tonight?"

"The missus likes 'em all in at eleven," said Belinda. "But you must feel like letting steam off once in a while. I'll ask her."

The missis said they must be in by half-past eleven. What a time it took them to get ready! Jenny had pinned an immense blue bow on the front of her blouse, and Annie, the quiet one, had a pink bow.

"Now, be careful and mind the trams," said Belinda, tenderly, as they were going out. Jenny laughed, and Annie gave Belinda a serious look out of her grey eyes.

The thought of the two girls troubled Belinda all evening. It was their first time away from home without their friends. Jenny was only seventeen, and Annie a year younger. They had put their hair up, to go out.

"Could you spare me a run out on the front for half an hour?" asked Belinda. Permission was given with bad grace. Belinda put on a wrap and went out, almost racing up the street. A high old wind was blowing. There were people on the front. The strains of a band came to her, just the high notes, like little staccato cries. She heard the sea—boom—boom.

"Going for a walk, dear?"

It was a man's voice.

Belinda looked to see whom he was addressing, and discovered with disgust and amazement that it was herself.

"Go home, and die," said Belinda, cheerfully.

He turned away, chagrined.

"Those girls!" moaned Belinda.

She could see it all—the low tide, the moon, the escape from dull lives, mechanical toil. She recalled her own youth, the stirrings she had smothered because her mother had rheumatism.

The sea was like a great pulse, beating near, or something restless for the unattainable. Belinda went on the pier. There were many lovers about, some dancing. She went then along the promenade, the lovers' walk, where were many figures in dark recesses.

"Those girls!" thought Belinda, grievously.

As she was walking back, thinking it had been a wild goose chase, she saw two girls passing an arc-lamp. Surely that was—but people looked so much alike in this bewildering light and shadow. Belinda raced on. Two youths were following the girls. As she got nearer, she heard Jenny's laugh, and followed with palpitating heart. She saw the boys join the girls, she saw the girls, strange to Seadale, being led into the quiet part of the town. Belinda hastened her steps. The quartette were so intent on their own business they did not hear.

Belinda followed them a mile.

One of the boys had his arm round Jenny's waist. Annie walked a little apart, apparently distrustful.

Belinda, breathless, came up nearer when on the outskirts of the town, where lamps ended and darkness began.

"We're not going any further," said Annie, clearly.

Belinda heard it.

The boy held Jenny by the waist and she screamed.

"Here, you come out o' that," cried Belinda, her white wrap appearing, sudden and ghostlike. "You let those girls go."

Annie, in great relief, ran to her.

"What have they been saying to you?" asked Belinda.

"Nothing—much," said Jenny, sulkily.

The boys disappeared. Belinda saw that Jenny's face was pale, despite the stiff upper lip she kept.

"I expect you'll tell 'em at the house," said Jenny. "Grasshopping us like that! We can take care of ourselves. We've not been brought up in cotton wool."

Belinda gazed at her with admiration. *There* spoke another Belinda Higgins!

"I shall do nowt o' th' sort," said Belinda. "But let your first scare be your last."

"We weren't scared," lied Jenny, but her voice wobbled.

"I couldn't rest," said Belinda. "Had to be. Told you their fathers were rich, didn't they? "

Jenny was amazed.

"Most likely sells oysters and chips," gibed Belinda. "Throwing yourselves away like that—nice lasses like you, too!"

"Oh—shut up!" said Jenny.

Annie said nothing.

That night a piercing cry of "Mother!" rang out twice. It came from the room of the two girls. And how they teased the sixteen-year-old Annie next morning!

"Might shout for somebody worse," said Belinda, who had understood.

But how full the house was!

"I'm sure you're tired, Belinda," said the worn mistress, one day. "You're thinner."

"I'll be nothing but a grease spot in a bit," said Belinda. "But, I've enjoyed it."

"Enjoyed it!"

Mrs. Willoughby gasped.

"I like to see folk enjoy themselves, when they've had to work," said Belinda.

They poured out, those trippers. They poured in, almost before the beds could be changed. They came from all over, rushing in with joyous expectation, going away with cheerful resignation to another year of toil. One party, from near Syke Gate, took Belinda out with them on a motor drive. She was the life of the party, singing, reciting, yarning, feasting her eyes all the while on the sea and country. She went to the Aquarium with one group, and, as she stood with a ginger-haired, jolly little man, wondering at the strange fish, he said, "Let's see, didn't you say you'd been in service in Beldon?"

Belinda told him where, and with whom.

"Mrs. Pickett died—confinement," he told her.

"And—Joe?" asked Belinda, with a tear in her eye.

"Went the way of all flesh," said the man.

"Died?"

"Died, be hanged! Married! If ever Joe dies, it'll be through beer. Wed a woman who'd make three o' the other, and fairly bosses him, I believe."

"Boy or girl?" asked Belinda.

"Girl," said the man. "A dumpling."

Belinda hesitated, then she inquired if he knew the man of the pink moustache.

"Wife run off with a bobby? Works at Beldon Dye Works? Ay. Queer old stick! Always looks like he doesn't know where he's going. Green, he's called. Saw him, not long since, in black. Ay. A proper comic-cuts, he is. Do you know him?"

"A bit," said Belinda, casually, and they walked further up to look at a mud-cat.

She could not help thinking of the man with the pink moustache during the weeks that followed. But why did he not write? Then she put him out of her thoughts, as she had put the old lady's saying: "I will remember you." All her life she had been building on dreams. None had come true.

When the season was over, all the house was to clean, which took weeks. Rain set in. Belinda got out more now. She liked to walk by the sea-wall, quite close, so that she could hear the sea, boom—boom, in thunder and song. She loved the spray, to rush through showers of it, to smell the salt. If she could have analysed her own feelings, she would have realized that the sea, its ceaseless, endless warfare with the shore, was symbolic of the freedom she hungered for. She used to talk to herself at such times, and people would stare on seeing her in a cloud of flying spray, lips moving, hands on her hat, fighting her lonely way on. She got to love the sea. When it was calm, she took Eric, Mrs. Willoughby's imbecile boy, down to the shore. He laughed at the sea in his foolish way, and Belinda gathered shells for him, and pebbles, which he put into his pockets, laughing quietly. She knew that his mother was saving up for him, fearful that he might be left alone; so when the tea was like dishwater, Belinda did not mind too much.

When October was at its close, Mrs. Willoughby said she did not need Belinda any more, but, if she liked, she could come next year for the season. She insisted on giving Belinda five shillings for a present, and Belinda put it into Eric's savings-box—all but a shilling, which she spent on a trumpet for him.

"Good-bye, Belinda," said Mrs. Willoughby, on the station platform.

"Good-bye and keep your heart up," said Belinda.

Eric blew a blast on the feeble, gay trumpet— took it out of his mouth, smiled foolishly, the train screamed, and Belinda's tent was moving again.

"Where next?" wondered Belinda.

"What did you say?" inquired a man on the seat opposite.

"Only talking to myself," said Belinda, smiling.

"Queer fish," thought the commercial. He looked at Belinda again. But she was staring out at the window, waiting for the moment when the yellow sand-dunes, the curve of dark hollow sea, would show up.

“I’d love to live at the top of a cliff, in a castle, where I could hear the sea,” mused Belinda. “But I’d want folk in it.”

With the romance of the poets, and all loyalty, she went from pillar to post. People looked at her hands, judging her from them. But it would have taken more than a camera to reveal Belinda!

CHAPTER XIII

Belinda Refuses to be a Burnt Offering on the Shrine of Mammon

BELINDA heard that old Sam Wiggles wanted a housekeeper. She applied at once, knocking on the back-door (there was no front one) of No. 12, Grammond's Yard at a quarter to seven on a wet evening.

The door was opened by Sam himself—a soiled-looking man in his shirt sleeves, which were frayed round the wrists. "Twenty years ago I used your soap," thought Belinda. Aloud, she uttered a benevolent, "Good evening."

"Good afternoon," said Sam, whereupon Belinda knew that he had not had his tea yet. She told him she had come after the vacant post.

"Come in," said Sam, slamming the door on a few inquisitive gossips. He inquired into Belinda's experience. Belinda was summing up the position as it affected her. He was a man with rows and rows of house property, shares in factories, and—too mean almost to live. They haggled ten minutes over an extra two pounds a year.

"I believe in economy," said Sam.

Belinda did, too, but not in the way Sam meant.

She got the job, and when two women saw her buy a whole eighteen-pennyworth of meat at the butcher's cart, they began to look for her rapid exit. There was certainly a long and close argument that day at dinner, and old Sam said "they couldn't go on at that rate," and Belinda said, "if she didn't eat, she couldn't work," at which Sam stopped. He was staring at a letter which Belinda had reared against the tea-caddy on the table. He snatched it, saying, "When did this come?"

"This morning."

"God! She's gone!" said Sam, staring at the letter. The letter was shaking.

"Steady up!" said Belinda. "Who's gone?"

"My—wife," he said. "She's been in the asylum fifteen years. She's gone—went last night."

"Poor thing!" said Belinda, compassionately.

Sam shook his head.

"She were a good un," he said, "a rare good un. So thin she peeled the pertaters. We scraped and pinched, an' we allus meant to have a good time, an' then she went 'queer'."

He became aware at this point that he was taking Belinda into his confidence. It surprised him.

"If you've bacon an' eggs for breakfast, and only spring onions for dinner, it's safest to eat the good stuff first. Then you're sure of it, an' anyhow, you can allus think of it," said Belinda.

"Now, if I'd been Mrs. Wiggles, you wouldn't have catched me wasting my time on seeing how close I could get round a potato-eye. Don't you think you made a mistake, mister? Your wife's gotten neither the ha'penny nor the cake!"

Sam Wiggles stared at her dazedly.

"What'll I ha' to do first?" he asked, still staring.

"You'll have to bury her," said Belinda.

She crossed over to the window and pulled down a ragged blind. The gloom seemed to worry old Sam.

"Ay, she's goan!" he muttered several times, and did not even notice Belinda throwing more coals on the fire.

She persuaded him that he would have to wear black, and wondered what he would look like in a new suit. Three days later, when he returned from the funeral, Belinda hardly knew him.

"Why, you don't look a day over forty-seven," she said, childlike.

"That's just my age."

He stared down at a rug, nearly new, laid across the hearth. "Where's that come from?" he asked. Belinda explained that Mrs. O'Hanna had sold it to her for seven shillings, and it had cost a pound only a few weeks before.

"But—" began Wiggles.

"I saved you that seven shillings," said Belinda. "Look there!" Wiggles looked and saw an apparently brand new kettle on the hob.

"Old Mother Clarke threw that amongst the ashes," said Belinda. "I soldered the spout on, bought a four-penny lid, and it's as good as what you'd get in a shop at eight bob. So I thought you wouldn't mind the rug. The kettle's paid for that."

Wiggles was staggered. This was a new sort of economy. His was one of going without—Belinda's apparently was one of getting.

All he said was, "H-m."

During the week that followed, Wiggles did a lot of thinking. Something had slightly changed his ideas of life since he saw his wife framed by that coffin which he had ordered should be of the best oak, with silver ornaments. Belinda's words had rung in his ears. Suppose Alice *had* been different? Death loomed up a very real thing. Wiggles began counting off the probable number of years he would live. Alice had always given in to his idea of saving and scraping. He almost wished now that she had not done so.

A gipsy woman came offering lace curtains to sell, one sunny afternoon.

"No, no, we don't want any," said Belinda.

But the gipsy stuck her foot in the doorway.

"Cross my hand with a bit of silver and I'll tell you your fortune, my dear," she said.

"Not on your sweet life," said Belinda, smiling. The gipsy peeped further in, and saw Sam. She had also noticed Belinda's hand.

"A bit of lace—real hand-made—"

Belinda smiled at the "hand-made" lace at five pence a yard.

"Here, come in!" said Sam. "Tell her her fortune. Here's sixpence," tossing a coin on the table.

A knowing look came into the gipsy's eye. She understood Sam.—

"You are not married," said the gipsy, taking Belinda's hand. "But you soon will be."

Belinda looked startled. Then she laughed "Not on your sweet life," she said. "But what is he like?"

"A man slightly older than yourself," said the gipsy.

Belinda was staring down at the hand whereon her destiny was written.

"H-m," she muttered, "and how shall we get on?—"

The gipsy went on to paint a glowing picture. Old Wiggles surprised Belinda by buying two pairs of curtains. The gipsy then departed, looking picturesque and many-coloured as she crossed the grey yard, where children as dirty as her own but not as brown, shouted and gambolled.

Belinda put the curtains up that night. She pulled them into place as pleased as a child. The hovel she had come into was changing.

"H-m," said the women of the yard, knowingly. "She's goin' to twist him round her finger."

Their eyes followed Belinda respectfully whenever she went to the ashbin.

"Nice pattern, them is," observed Mrs. O'Hanna, referring to the curtains.

"Don't you feel better when you let yourself be comfortable?" Belinda asked Wiggles as they sat at the table over Yorkshire duck.

"There's summat in it," he allowed, "so long as it doesn't go too far."

Belinda was dreaming of effecting a transformation upstairs soon, and got Wiggles to let her have the gas-boiler down from above, for he had taken it away so that the last woman could not use it. She tackled Wiggles about oilcloth, on the theory that it was best done whilst his heart was warm. He demurred a little, but after seeing Belinda banter down the oilcloth vendor to half price, he gave way.

"They allus put a lot on, expecting to be knocked down," said Belinda. "Ey, this is a right clean-looking bonnie little pattern."

She told Wiggles that she was going to the pictures that night.

"I've half a mind to go myself," he said.

"Ay, do," said Belinda, warmly. "It'll take trouble away."

"Well, I'm blessed!" said Mrs. O'Hanna, as they crossed the yard.

"Come on wi' us to the pictures," shouted Belinda. "It's Mary Pickford."

"But I'm not dressed," said Mrs. O'Hanna.'

"Go on. It'll not take you long to jump in your clothes," said Belinda. So she and Wiggles waited whilst the poverty-stricken Irishwoman with the two fatherless angel-faced demons of children, "jumped" into her clothes.

They all came home with chips and fish wrapped in paper, and a sense of great deeds seen.

Pictures and chips became the order of the evening once a week, for Belinda, Mrs. O'Hanna and Wiggles. Wiggles believed that Belinda would marry him. So did Mrs. O'Hanna, and told him so.

"An' he's the fine man, Mr. Wiggles is," Mrs. O'Hanna would say to Belinda.

Belinda agreed, for Mrs. O'Hanna was having the time of her life.

It was after their return from seeing "Tess of the D'Urbervilles" (Belinda had wept and been unashamed to weep, and Mrs. O'Hanna had been Irish and indignant!) that the interesting moment came. Belinda was serving out the tripe for supper.

"Belinda," said Wiggles, "I have an offer to make."

"Ay," said Belinda, slashing the tripe across into equal portions.

"Of course, I'm seventeen years older than thee," said Wiggles, stumbling.

"A bit o' fat?" queried Belinda.

"Ay, ay. As I said, I'll marry thee, Belinda."

Belinda stared at him and dropped the knife. "Me!"

Wiggles was startled.

"Why, who else?" he asked.

"I thought it was Mrs. O'Hanna," said Belinda.

"Mrs. O'Hanna!" gasped Wiggles. "But Belinda—"

"Not *me*," said Belinda, dredging salt and sprinkling vinegar on her tripe. "I couldn't throw my youth and beauty away like that."

"Come, come," said Wiggles. "You're none so good-looking, Belinda—"

"I look well in my clothes, when I'm dressed up—though that isn't oft, and I couldn't think o' throwing myself away like that. Anyhow, I'll be off to-morrow to a fresh place. The curtains an' oilcloth won't be wasted. They'll suit Mrs. O'Hanna down to the ground. She said she liked both the patterns."

Belinda gave no intimation that she had been working dodges for Mrs. O'Hanna.

CHAPTER XIV

A Doll's House

BELINDA stood outside the door of a tiny villa, with its "rustic" bench under the window, and its basket of geraniums swinging just overhead. Alongside the gravel path, white pansies fluttered gently, as if discussing the dilapidated state of Belinda's shoes.

Everything was very still.

"Bills, bills, I'm sick to death of bills!" came a man's voice, between anger and despair. "Anyhow, if any more come, I shall refuse to pay them. It's preposterous. I might be made of money."

"Oh, Tony," answered the sweetest voice Belinda had ever heard, "if only you were! Tony, don't be angry, don't Tony! It was that cloak. I simply couldn't resist it. And you know, Tony, I gave up quite a lot to come to you —"

There was a muttered exclamation, which Belinda did not catch. Then she saw the curtains at one of the windows sway.

"They are kissing," thought Belinda. "She's young, and silly, and selfish. I don't suppose I'll stay long."

She gave the doorbell a furious ring.

"Oh, come in!" said the same pretty voice.

Belinda stared into a face perfectly angelic, but was not deceived. Belinda had ideas on women who ran their husbands into debt. She was of that type that would stump up its last farthing to discharge a debt despite where the next meal was to come from.

"May I see your last testimonial," inquired the girl-woman, her yellow hair framing her face like ripe corn. "I don't like taking anyone without testimonial, you know."

Belinda stared at the Doll, as she mentally termed her.

"I haven't asked *you* for one, have I?" she asked calmly. "For all I know I could lose my character here. But I'm quite prepared to take you on trust."

Doll Burnham gasped, crumpled up, and engaged Belinda.

Two days proved to Mrs. Burnham that Belinda was not an efficient servant. She could not understand why furniture should be "muffled up" before sweeping began. She could not cut bread thin enough for afternoon tea, and she was too intimate. But she said one thing to Doll that touched the heart. Said she, one afternoon, "If you'll not be hard on me, I will not be hard on you. Seeing as you're none too flush, I'll reduce two pounds from my year's wages, on conditions I go to the picters once a week."

"You are under some misapprehension," said Doll, laughing. "We've plenty of money." But she had blushed.

Belinda went to the pictures.

"Have you any religion, Belinda?" queried Tony, one evening, as she brought in supper.

"Not that I knows of," answered Belinda, seriously. "Except I tries to do by others what I'd be done by, and my father always said, ''Linda, always tell the truth, pay thy way, an' trust to the Lord.'"

Tony laid down a book.

"There's a book here," he said, tapping it, "says we live over and over again, and that you might have been a princess in your last life, Belinda. Supposing you could choose your next life, what would you be?"

Doll looked up with sudden interest.

"Myself," said Belinda, with dignity. "Myself, treated as a human being, an' not sittin' gettin' my meals like

I was nothing. Myself, given a free hand to do my own work, an' my opinions asked on things—and—I'd like to be a sort of servant an' mother an' all that sort, you know, rolled in one. I want to be no princess!"

"Oh, well," said Tony, "I suppose it's a sign of the times!"

Next day at breakfast table, Doll and Tony had a violent quarrel—indeed, the first since Belinda had entered their house. It was the old trouble—bills.

"Don't mind me," said Belinda, calmly, steering her way through the doorway with the tray. "I've heard it in better families than this."

"Don't be impertinent," said Doll.

"Am I?" asked Belinda, in child-like surprise. "I only wanted to make you feel easy."

Tony burst out laughing.

"All the same," he said, kissing Doll behind the door, "I sha'n't pay those bills. Fact is, seraph, I can't!"

He had said that before, and if his tone was bitter, Doll had often coaxed him out of what appeared a worse humour. She went to a concert that evening with the sister of the young man Belinda did not like.

Belinda took Tony's lonely supper in. She was about to go, but he stayed her.

"Can you keep a secret?" he asked.

Belinda looked at him.

He had ceased to be her "master." He was just another human being. She nodded. Her mouth had tightened to show it could shut itself.

"I'm broke," said Tony. "Bankrupt!"

"You mean 'busted'." Her eyes had filled with tears, though she had nothing in the world but that tin box of old-fashioned clothes.

Tony nodded.

"What will Doll do?" said the young man. "I think you can read character, Belinda."

"She'll have to do her own work till you pull yourself round."

Tony shook his head.

"Ey, never say die!" said Belinda. "I'd an uncle went bust three times an' got up every time —a tailor he was—an' ten childer. You've no childer."

Tony looked a little embarrassed.

"May be, Belinda," he said, "that's what makes it so hard. And—I shall have to go abroad—there are no other openings here. I shall never have courage to tell Doll." He groaned.

"I'll tell her," suggested Belinda.

She did so, next morning, when she took up a cup of tea.

"Your husband has bust, ma'am," she said, handing the cup. Doll was used to Belinda's bow-legged remarks—but this one needed explaining. When she understood, she began to go into hysterics.

"Stop that!" said Belinda, sternly. "I expect there's a woman somewhere under the doll in you. What's the good of it?"

"Oh, what shall we do? What shall we do?" lamented Doll.

Tony was coming up the steps.

Belinda opened the door.

"Go back," she told him, eyeing the smelling-salts he carried with scorn. Tony went.

An hour later Doll came downstairs, her eyes very red, her face very white. She looked at Tony with a twisted sort of smile. Then she said, "Oh, Tony, I've been a little beast. But—why did you let Belinda tell me? Couldn't you have told me? You—you thought her more of a woman than me."

"I have a great respect for Belinda. What did she say to you—to make you change so?"

Doll laughed tremulously.

"She—she said if I'd teach her how to be a better servant, she would teach me how to be a woman—which she guessed I'd never been called on to be in my life before."

"And to me, she said she hoped when I came back I'd be a man fit for you."

"The impertinence —" gasped Doll.

"She has a rude way of telling the rude truth," said Tony, chastened. "If she hadn't been a domestic, I think she'd have been a reformer. But in this case—she has been both."

Doll and Belinda watched Tony set sail from Liverpool. Doll did not cry.

"Good-bye, old sport!" yelled Belinda. "Keep thy pecker up."

It was the courage of a nature that had got up after many hard knocks—since cradlehood.

CHAPTER XV

Poets—Burglars—and Belinda

BELINDA got work with a childless couple at Bransworth, within ten days of leaving Seadale. The place was really what it was advertised as—a nice, good home for a willing worker. The "light duties" did not include shovelling a ton of coal into a cellar in pouring rain. Her master would not have the mess and slop of washing in the house, so the washing went to the laundry. The couple had a small but sufficient income and were very kind to Belinda, but it was a kindness that stooped to her. What opinions they had were few—and not their own. Mr. Hingborough's interest was bowls. Belinda told him the story of Drake and the great sea captains. He was delighted.

Belinda found life deadly dull there, after the first restfulness had worn off. "Wouldn't I make things hum," she said to herself, "if I'd their money!"

She bought a game—"Snakes and Ladders," and played left hand against right, of an evening. Mrs. Hingborough only smiled at Belinda's invitation to try her luck.

Her master was fond of walking, but the mistress could not bear it—on account of her legs. Belinda would have stuck it without legs—it was nice, she thought, to see married people go out together.

They had a white Pomeranian dog with big dark eyes that stuck out a bit. Every Friday, Belinda bathed

Tim, who barked aggressively at her all the time. He had seen her on a ladder and had not liked it. But he *could* be affectionate. He had his meals on his own little saucer, set on a red-and-white kerchief spread across the corner of the carpet, and, every evening, Belinda took him for a little run round the streets and back again—Tim tugging at the leash, barking and trying to get away. Belinda liked dogs—but rough dogs, working dogs. Irish terriers and Airedales were her fancy. Her dad once kept such a dog.

Belinda had been "off" one evening and returned to find that Mrs. Hingborough had been crying.

"What's up?" she asked.

"Tim's lost." And Mrs. Hingborough burst out anew.

"When did he get out?" asked Belinda.

"Just after you went."

"I shut the door. Happen he's only gone courtin'."

The clock stood at a quarter-to-ten.

"Where's Mr. Hingborough?" asked Belinda.

"Lo-o-king for Tim."

Belinda went looking for Tim, too.

Mr. Hingborough, wet through and very worried, came back just before Belinda did.

"Tim got in?" he asked.

Mrs. Hingborough shook her head.

They all sat up till midnight, waiting for the dog. Long after she had retired, Belinda thought she heard Tim barking, but no white dog was to be seen.

Mrs. Hingborough was low-spirited all the next day.

"But if he'd been run over, we'd hear," said Belinda. She was not sure, but wanted to comfort Mrs. Hingborough.

"No one knows what Tim is to me!" said her mistress. "When I've been troubled, he knew immediately. He would come and jump on my knee."

"Why don't you adopt a child?" asked Belinda, bluntly. "Dogs is all right, but you never heard of one turning out to be the Lord Mayor o' London—like Dick Whittington."

She stopped. The mask had fallen from her mistress's quivering face.

"I should have loved to adopt a child," she said, "but—he won't hear of it—never would hear of it. At first *I* didn't want to. There's something rises up in you against it. You think you might have one of your own—yet."

"Well, you'd have two then —"

"And then, it couldn't be quite the same, could it?"

"It could be nearly the same," said Belinda, "It could to me, anyhow. Why, see what I think o' yon Reggie! After all, there's a terrible lot o' childer without mothers, and a terrible lot o' mothers without childer—why shouldn't they comfort one another? They put lambs to sheep that's lost theirs. They kick a bit at first—and soon they can't tell the difference. Whenever I see an old woman singing in the streets, wi' her shoe-heels down, I feel like she's my mother—a bit—"

Her voice shook a little.

"How long has your mother been dead?" asked Mrs. Hingborough.

Belinda told her.

"You would miss her."

"Miss her!"

Belinda's face twisted as she tried to smile.

"What was the matter with her?"

"Burnt to death," said Belinda, her voice changing, a note of infinite agony.

"Belinda!"

Mrs. Hingborough got up and walked towards her domestic. Their hands met.

"You poor Belinda! You poor Belinda! My only sister—she—was burned to death."

"We have to try an' get over such things," said Belinda.

Tim did not turn up.

Belinda went everywhere seeking the little white dog.

"Somebody must have pinched him," Belinda concluded. "But if they cared enough to do that, they'll care enough to look after him." It was all the consolation she could give.

Weeks afterwards, Belinda went, at Mrs. Hingborough's request, to a neighbouring town, to get some bulbs for the back-garden. She went into the market house, and was looking at the bulb and seed display when she heard a furious barking.

Belinda looked round.

"Where did you get that dog?" she asked of a young man.

"That's my dog," he said.

Tim barked furiously.

"That dog belongs to my mistress, and I'm taking him," said Belinda. "Listen! You can tell he knows me."

The young man grinned.

"Barks at everybody like that. That's my dog." He began to tell her its pedigree. "Will it follow you?"

Belinda faltered, recalling how Tim had dragged at the leash on his evening runs.

"Ay," she said, with a certainty she was not feeling. "Come on, Tim!"

The dog looked uncertain—hesitated—then followed Belinda.

"Here, come back," cried the young man. "It will follow anybody. It followed me. But I've got to know it goes to its owner." He looked crestfallen. Evidently he had grown very fond of the dog.

"Haven't you seen the reward offered?" asked Belinda. That brought him to. He set out with Belinda and Tim, when Belinda had got the bulbs.

Mrs. Hingborough heard Tim's barking. She had been laid down with a headache, but she laughed, though tears were on her lashes, to see Tim again. He pulled at her skirts. She kissed and hugged him, and wept over him. The young man got the reward, and Tim had so many dishes set round him that he hardly knew which to attack first. Belinda was almost as glad as Mrs. Hingborough. She understood now why some people cared so much for dogs and cats, even parrots.

Mr. Hingborough whistled more cheerfully, now Tim was home. Belinda liked them better for liking Tim so much.

One wet February evening, Belinda made her way towards the room in which were held the monthly meetings of the Bransworth Poets' Society. She enjoyed the rainy streets, the yellow lights, the shininess of umbrellas that bobbed near her. She asked a policeman where the poets met —but he only grinned and said he did not know. She asked several people, none of whom knew, but, recalling at last the name of the confectioner over whose shop the meetings were held, Belinda found the place.

She walked into the brightly-lighted shop. The sudden glare made her blink.

"Does the poets meet here?" she asked.

A man was seated at a little table, eating a pork pie.

"Yes. They do meet here. Go up those stairs," said the white-aproned little confectioner.

Belinda passed through a curtained doorway.

"Another one hit with the barm-stick," said the man of the pork pie. "Let's see. Poets is all poor and lives in garrets, don't they?"

"These are all very respectable people," said the little confectioner, bristling.

"Oh, well, they change like other folk, I suppose," said the man, waggishly.

Belinda went up two short flights of stairs, heard someone reciting, and stopped outside a door until the end, heralded by the clapping of sixty pairs of hands. Someone opened the door gently for her, and she passed in, very humbly, with her tin box hidden under her cloak, and the wet umbrella in her hand.

"Are you a poet?" asked a little fat man who sat at a small table.

Belinda hesitated.

Then she beamed, rubbing a raindrop from her nose.

"No, I'm a sympathiser," she said, in the same low tone in which the fat man had spoken. "I've paid my subscription," she added.

"Oh, then you are one of the society," he said.

Belinda felt suddenly glorified. A shilling a year allowed her not only to come to the meetings, but gave her a chance to blossom into a poet herself.

She found her way to a seat, quite bewildered to see so many poets. They were all dressed quite decently, too—not one, so far as she could see, looked down at heel.

"You are a new member?" asked the young man near whom Belinda had seated herself.

She nodded.

The chairman was waiting for silence. He was very grave and very grey. Beside him sat a little bald-headed, cherry-cheeked man, who looked more like a monk than a poet.

"I will call on Mr. Willoughby to give us an original poem, entitled 'Julie,' " said the grave, grey man, with dignity.

To Belinda's surprise, the young man next to her got on his feet, and, after clearing his throat once or twice, recited, very ably, the verses to "Julie," and sat down blushing at the applause.

"I say, that was very nice," said Belinda beaming.

"Do you think so?" he asked, gratefully. "To be quite candid, I don't think I am one." But he spoke so low that Belinda could not tell what he said, could only see that he was pleased.

"Fancy all that talent in Bransworth!" ejaculated Belinda.

"Do you do much?" asked Mr. Willoughby.

He repeated the question in her ear.

"Only once," she said, naively. She was thinking of the lines she wrote for the impoverished old medium.

"And did it—" began Mr. Willoughby.

"Oh, it worked," said Belinda.

"Sh-sh!" said somebody, gently, behind.

A young woman with a wild glow of eagerness to be heard, was visibly asking the chairman to call on her. He whispered to the red-cheeked man on his right, and after he had drunk a little water from the glass at his elbow, the red-cheeked man evidently decided that he could stand the shock. Miss Anita Blytheman, posing herself like a very Siddons, rose, in answer to the nod of the red-cheeked man. Miss Blytheman's poem was exotic and patriotic, and she flung out her hand, almost hitting the man next to her, so that he had to readjust his glasses. She cast a wild glance around as she gave forth her last line, and sat down, drinking in every little hand-clap. Belinda felt sorry for her.

Willoughby shook his head at Belinda, mildly.

Belinda saw the chairman looking at her. It put her into a sweat. Did they expect her to recite something of her own? She had told the secretary, in her letter, that she was only a great admirer of poets and poetry.

"We have a new member, I believe," said the grave, grey man, when the little sigh, following the exertions of Miss Blytheman, had died away. He looked at Belinda.

"Who proposes Miss—?"

"Higgins," said Belinda.

"I do," said Mr. Willoughby. Belinda breathed more easily.

After a chorus of seconders, the motion was carried unanimously.

"Have you—do you happen to have brought anything with you, Miss Higgins?"

Willoughby nudged Belinda to stand up.

She managed to get to her feet. Her legs shook under her. But the chance was too good to be missed. Now or never was the opportunity of introducing to the world the merit of the unpublished works of Samuel Higgins—those unhappy verses written on ledger-paper, which had in his lifetime always come home, like Bo-Peep's sheep. Belinda screwed up her courage. The first word she uttered seemed to fly back at her from the other end of the room. The platform swam, the lights, the red-cheeked man; not for a thousand pounds would Belinda have got up for a lesser purpose than this—her father's glory, not her own.

"I don't do much," said Belinda. "But I've brought some poems of my father's."

"Perhaps you'd like to come on the platform," said the chairman.

"Nay, I'll do here," said Belinda.

She was calmer now, and opened the sacred little box, grabbing the poem nearest the top. The rustle of the paper was like thunder in her ears. Her heart beat like a hammer at the jumble of faces. Somebody coughed. Belinda dropped one of the big sheets. Willoughby caught it and handed it back, touching her elbow as he did so— quite accidentally. But Belinda thought it was to encourage her. It had that effect.

"It's called *'I'm At Whoam,'*" announced Belinda.

Then she began, and as she read, she was back in the little kitchen, where Samuel Higgins sat back in his chair, smoking his clay pipe, at peace with the world, smiling on her and her mother, the fire-shadows playing about him.

Aw'm at whoam.
Theer's a breet roasy fire,
An' dark shadows are plottin' i' th' nooks.
Aw'm at whoam, aw con weer mi owd togs,
An' aw neednа act lies wi' mi looks.
For it's reight if aw want to be gay,
An' it's reight if aw like to sit glum,
An' it's reight if aw linger hawf-way—
Aw'm i' th' best spot i' th' world—
Aw'm at whoam.

There's folk in a hurry to roam,
They goa treaunchin' north, south, east an' west,
An' they see wondrous seets—so aw'm towd,
But this hearth-stoan, just here, suits me best.
There's heavens o' a' maks' so they say—
Some like tossin' an' troublin' on th' wave,
Some like trampin' their shoe-soils away,
Niver restin' till landed i' th' grave—
An' at whoam.

But for me—aw'm a quate little chap,
An' mi heaven's sittin' coasy at neet,
Wi' a child nestlin' under mi coit,
An' th' fireleet a' roasy an' breet.
When aw scammer them stairs made o' gowd,
A breet angel to oppen me th' door,
As aw come in fro' th* valley so cowd,
Aw'll look out for some fire-leet—noa moor!
For mi cheer, an' mi pipe, an' owd Joan,
An' aw'll say, "Well, thank God, aw'm at whoam."

Belinda had not read loudly. If anything, her voice had been pitched too low. But she had read with the rare art of one whose feelings are fine, though simple. A hush followed. Then the applause burst out, hearty, impulsive. It had not been nightingale music, that of Samuel Higgins. His last rhyme had been faulty. But it had the warmth, sincerity, and the true poetic spark.

"Why did you not bring Mr. Higgins with you?" asked the grave grey man, as Belinda sat down. "I'm sure we should have been honoured to have him amongst us." A murmur of assent ran through the room.

"He's dead," said Belinda.

"Genius," said Willoughby, in her ear. "There was genius in that."

It was Belinda's great moment. She put the script into the box with trembling hands, hands shaking with the joy of her heart. She knew now that some day her father's verses would be known beyond Bransworth. She went out into the rainy streets, back to her place, treading on glory. The very street lamps shone more brightly. She heard again the thunderous clapping of those hands, honouring the thoughts of a humble man who had died as quietly as he had lived. Tears ran down her cheeks, tears of joy, to think she was his daughter, to think that some day his sterling worth would be appreciated. For Belinda knew that Samuel Higgins, the man, and Samuel Higgins, the poet, were one and the same person, not one mocking the other. The beauty in the homely lines was the beauty of a homely life. There was not a word that was insincere in the little tin box of manuscripts.

Some weeks after, Mr. Hingborough was called away on business. There was in the house a lot of money, which Belinda had drawn at the bank for Mrs. Hingborough. Belinda was very careless about money. She had counted it in the doorway of the bank lest the clerk should think she suspected his honour.

A young man had followed her home.

"Belinda!" called Mrs. Hingborough, at three next morning.

Belinda thought she was ill, and ran into her room.

"There's someone trying to get in," moaned Mrs. Hingborough. "Oh—if only Tom was here!"

"Get away!" derided Belinda.

"Oh, can't you hear?"

"Where?"

"He's tried the back door—twice now," moaned the frightened woman.

Belinda threw up the window.

"Oh—don't—"

"What do you want?" Belinda shouted.

She was frightened, too.

She thought she saw a man bob down behind the backyard gate. Then she saw someone, plainly enough, get up, and try the door again. Belinda kept watch whilst her mistress slept.

The woman across the way had heard the dog barking and had seen a man go away.

"Well, he wasn't on a visit. He was a burglar," Belinda told her. "But if he comes again, he'll get a warm reception." To quiet Mrs. Hingborough, she reported the case that afternoon to the police, who chaffed her, but said they would see the place was "walked round" a bit.

When Belinda was leaving the police station, someone banged into her.

"Belinda!" exclaimed Inspector Moreton.

"Ey—bless your heart! What are *you* doing here?" she asked, amazed. Then her face saddened, recalling the old tragedy.

"Got shifted here," said the inspector.

Belinda asked after the little girls.

"Little girls!"

The inspector grinned.

"They don' think they're little girls now," he said.

"And P.C. Kerton?" inquired Belinda.

"Not married yet," said the inspector, twinkling. "Shall I tell him—?"

"Nothing of the kind," said Belinda, blushing. "Think I'd wed a bit of a nipper—even if he wasn't a bobby."

"Still prejudiced, Belinda," grinned the inspector.

"It'll take three or four to arrest Maria, now you've left," she laughed.

"Maria will never be arrested again."

"Has she reformed?" asked Belinda.

"Gone to the last cell of all. Pneumonia."

Belinda ceased laughing.

"And that kid she used to hold upside down when she was drunk—what was his name?"

"Joseph Leo—"

"Oh, I remember after the Saint and the Pope," said Belinda. "What's happened to Joseph Leo?"

"Orphanage."

That night, Belinda did her best to persuade Mrs. Hingborough to adopt Joseph Leo—the child of the drunken woman of the streets.

Her mistress was horrified.

"Gems roll in ditches and can be cleaned up again," said Belinda. "He'll be only—about seven or eight now. It was a bonnie kid—little kinks o' gold all over his head, and eyes as blue as beads."

But it was no use.

That night, Belinda made an effigy of old clothes, stuffed inside a pillowcase, with bits of black cloth for eyes, nose, and mouth. She stood it by the window that would not fasten, and reared tin trays against the others, and asked the woman across to send her son to the rescue if an alarm was sounded on the tin trays during the night.

It was a fine moonlit night. Mrs. Hingborough almost screamed when she saw the "ghost" at the window.

"And if he touches the other windows—cuts out any panes—the tin trays'll fall," said Belinda, beaming.

They put a box behind the bedroom door, and hid the money under the mattress.

But nothing happened.

Before morning came, the two women slept.

"Belinda" called Mrs. Hingborough, jumping up.

They had overslept.

"Yes," said Belinda, sleepily.

"I believe that's the window cleaner," she cried. "He'll fall and break his neck, if he sees the ghost."

Belinda saved him in the nick of time.

CHAPTER XVI

The Great War Shadows Belinda

BELINDA stayed six months longer with the Hingboroughs. Then she got restless. There was not enough for two women to do in that house, she said.

It was whilst she was serving her notice that the Great War broke out. Belinda could not believe that it would really begin—until she saw it in the papers.

"My hat!" said Belinda. "Will they want my Reggie?"

"How old is he?" asked Mrs. Hingborough.

"Seventeen," said Belinda, white as a sheet.

Mr. Hingborough laughed.

"It will be over—in a few weeks," he said. "We'll have them beaten in a few weeks—anyhow, they won't take children yet."

Belinda went to see Jonathan and the others. The lad, Reggie, was fired about the war. He had been taking his chest measurement.

"Reggie," said Belinda, fearfully. "Promise me you'll never be a soldier."

"But we can't let them come here," protested Reggie.

"No—," said Belinda. "And they're all somebody's lads—them an' all, aren't they?"

Mrs. Hingborough was so afraid that Mr. Hingborough might have to go, she begged Belinda to stay on, which Belinda did.

She stayed until early spring, by which time Mrs. Hingborough's fears about Mr. Hingborough were lulled to rest. Mr. Hingborough was pigeon-chested. Oh, how Belinda wished Reggie was pigeon-chested! It was unpatriotic, but human. Belinda felt that she could not live if Reggie went to the War and got killed. He was now eighteen, a handsome boy, with the true Higgins eyes, and that bit of snobbishness, which had been his in embryo, clean worn away. He went to gymnasiums. Whenever Belinda looked at him, she saw Youth, incarnate youth, bubbling over with hope, dreams—Youth with its love of adventure. This spirit of adventure frightened Belinda. Yet, as she read the papers she so implicitly believed, there were moments when her own soul stirred, when she wished she had been born a man to go out into those devastated regions to add her might to that of her outnumbered countrymen. But every day and every night her intense prayer was that it would soon be over. When she read about mere children fighting in the German ranks her heart recoiled. She looked at Reggie. Reggie was only a child. There could not be *that* difference! But when she read of atrocities her blood boiled. She saw the recruiting. Sometimes she went to Bransworth Station and watched men go for training. She saw rather a horrible sight, one Saturday morning. A little man had enlisted, and was going away. His wife, a plain-looking woman, twice his size, tried to keep him by main force. She was crying and fighting at the same time. The man was swearing and trying to get from her. He succeeded at last.

"Oh, my God!" cried the woman.

Spent, she leaned against the doorway of the little station, and wept bitterly. Belinda went home feeling sick.

"Somebody'll be hurt, if this war lasts long," said Reggie, when next they met. Belinda's eyes looked sadly and reproachfully at him.

"Don't joke about it," she said. "We just don't realize it here. It must be like living in a slaughterhouse, with hell-fire raging all round."

"Get out!" said Reggie, a little startled. But Reggie thought often of his aunt's words after.

"How do you like your new place?" asked Annie.

"I don't bother about trifles now," said Belinda, sighing. "I can only think of those poor lads."

"I'd leave off reading the papers," said Jonathan.

"Why don't you do something—knit for the soldiers?" suggested Annie.

Belinda started her knitting career a week later. She did not join a knitting party. She knitted in her very spare spare-time.

Belinda saw the civilian population drifting into khaki. Conscription came, and she realized that, if it was not over soon, Reggie would have to go to the War. Her pigeon-chested master had already gone.

Bombs were dropping on London. An aeroplane was heard over Bransworth in the dead of one night, and had passed on to wreck a town miles away.

Once, Belinda was buying potatoes at a little greengrocer's cart and a woman grumbled at the high prices.

A cold rage shook Belinda.

"Oh, shut up, with your whining!" she said. "Call yourself a patriot? An' grumble at potatoes going up a farthing a pound! If I thought I'd bring the War to an end a day sooner, I'd eat grass for a year."

"That's the stuff to give 'em!" said the greengrocer. But Belinda had marched off, leaving a few potatoes rolling behind her.

She sank into a chair on reaching the kitchen.

Mrs. Mellings came in and found her sitting there, half-an-hour later.

"I can't think," began Belinda, that in all this country, and those other countries, there not folk with brains enough to settle this, without; all this butchery. Johnnie Parks has gone, up this street—him that can't see, hardly, with his 'specks and his soft look. Why, he turned sick when his wife got him to drown kittens. And they've sent him out killing folk."

"Belinda!"

Belinda laughed. She felt like it.

"Well, happen killing isn't murder," she said. "And—the other side is sending folk to kill Johnnie Parks. Why don't they send us? I'd go, if they'd send us."

"But we're women—" gasped Mrs. Mellings.

"If the women of all countries followed the men and took the kids with 'em, they'd soon dish wars," she said. "Let 'em see us with our lovelocks flowin' an' our lips tastin' o' gunpowder—an' yellin' like hanky-panky savages—and—there'd be no more wars."

Jonathan told her afterwards that it was an "impracticable proposition."

Belinda stopped reading the papers. She stood in queues, waiting for bacon and "Maggie Ann," all without a grumble. It made her want to vomit to hear anyone grumble at such small things, when a little bit further on the earth stank with dead men, and the sky was black with gun smoke.

"Where's Reggie?" asked Belinda, entering Jonathan's kitchen, soon after her wrath at the greengrocer's cart.

"Gone!" said Jonathan. He looked ill.

"Something to bring 'em up for," Annie said, bitterly.

Belinda flopped upon the sofa. Her nightmare of the night before had come true.

"Gone!"

"Jonathan will have to have help, now," said Annie. Of course, it will be over before Reggie is trained. They're taking longer, now. And they *do* get leave."

It had taken the wind out of Belinda's sails. She trailed back to her place.

“He’ll be killed,” she kept muttering. “He’ll he killed on April 2nd, just as he was in that dream.”

But she said nothing to Annie and Jonathan about that.

Reggie wrote her an apologetic letter.

One bit of it stuck out in Belinda’s mind.

“I’d just got to go, Aunt Belinda. There was much odds against our chaps. And—anyhow, it will be over, possibly, before they need me. But if it isn’t—well, I shall go, and I shall see things.”

Belinda left Bransworth a month later.

She answered an advertisement for a strong woman, needed in a seaside boarding-house—at Scarborough, thronged with Lancashire battalions. Reggie was training there.

She would be nearer him, she might see him sometimes. Perhaps she could see that he got some decent food; perhaps, joy of joys!—he could come to her place and have dinner with her occasionally.

When Belinda reached Scarborough, a lot of people were waiting to see—

“Is it an accident?” asked Belinda.

For a moment, she had forgotten the War—her luggage had gone astray.

“It’s a draft going out,” said someone.

“Poor things!” said Belinda.

“They’re as lively as can be,” said a man.

“Half of ’em’s drunk,” said another.

A band was heard and there was a rush.

Belinda waited. She saw it all—heard the band blaring away, saw the men come up, some looking pale in the late afternoon light. Belinda crying—crying openly and unashamed for burning pity’s sake and rage—a cry against something or somebody deep from her heart. The men, to her, looked like a lot of corpses, stamping their feet. The station lights swam through

Belinda's tears. She heard people laughing. A little man dancing with a comrade. Both were intoxicated.

"They don't care!" said a man, too old to go himself.

Belinda was amazed at his callousness.

The band blared again, then died down.

The train whistled.

A woman ran, sobbing—clinging to a khaki-clad figure—and Belinda caught just a glimpse of the man's face, as he looked into the woman's.

"Keep your heart up, Bess. I'll be back—sure," he was saying. He stood close to Belinda.

He tore himself away.

The train moved out to the strains of "Auld Lang Syne."

"An' it's going right to there?" asked Belinda, bewildered.

"Oh, they'll take a boat at Folkestone," one explained.

"Well, if that's a draft going out, may I never see another!" said Belinda. "What did the damned band play so loud for?"

"Just to cheer 'em up," she was told.

Belinda moved away, wondering.

She saw several laddish figures, khaki-clad, on her way, and looked out for Reggie.

The horror of her dream gripped her more tightly.

"If anything should happen to Reggie—"

Her brain reeled.

She passed a book-shop on her way to the "place." She saw a book, *The Red Horizon.* She had read a review of it. It was about the war.

"It's rather terrible," said the bookseller. "There's one here, I think —"

"Is it a true book?" asked Belinda.

"Oh, yes, it's written by a man who has been there."

"I'll have it," said Belinda.

She wanted to know where Reggie was going. If it was not too terrible for a kid like him to go to, it was not too terrible for her to read about. Muddle-headed, Belinda had yet the saving grace of courage. She had meant it when she had said she would eat grass if it would help to end the war. She had cut down her usual bread ration, in the hope of winning it. She had lost a stone in weight, ungrudgingly, on that account.

Belinda read the book all night. Dawn was filling her room as she turned to sleep. She went to the table the next morning a changed Belinda. *That* was where Reggie was going. Reggie, scarcely out of his napkins!

Her bread ration went down to nil, that breakfast-time.

Belinda had got food for thought.

CHAPTER XVII

A Draft Goes Out

BELINDA grew to love Scarborough. How much that love was due to Reggie's being there, she would learn later.

To Reggie, Belinda meant Home, now. He was having a rough time of it. With his big pal, Rupert, however, he could joke about it. But it was a shock when he found he was lousy. Aunt Belinda washed his and his pal's clothes, saying, grimly, that *that* sort of war wouldn't last long.

When Reggie was on "harbour-guard," Belinda would take him something to eat during the cold hours when the sea sounded in the darkness like a ravening beast.

Some soldiers' wives were staying with Mrs. Coops, Belinda's mistress. One, Mrs. Pratt, had been a pit-brow lass.

"Where are you going, to-night?" Belinda would say.

"Oh, I'm taking him out—to the theatre."

Pratt was a little man. He came to Sunday tea once, and when his wife had slipped out of the room for her coat, after he and Belinda had been joking together, he said, "My wife seems pally with you. For God's sake get her to go home before we're drafted out. She'll play hell on the platform."

Belinda said she would do her best.

Mrs. Woods, another of them, kept the place in an uproar of merriment. Every day at twelve, she took Bert some little buns.

He's your *kid* as *well*, isn't he?" Belinda twitted her. Mrs. Woods smiled.

"He'll miss his little buns out yonder," said Belinda. "I wish it were all over and they were all back."

"Happen it will be over before they've to go," said Mrs. Woods, going out with the little buns.

Despite all Belinda had said about never again watching a draft go out, Reggie persuaded her to go with him one evening.

This draft was sober. The band played gaily.

"Good-by-ee," a girl shouted.

"Good-by-ee," was the answering chorus.

"My hat!"

Reggie stared at his aunt.

"Pink-tache," was all the explanation he got. To his utter astonishment, he saw his aunt grab a little man in khaki hurrying along at the tail-end of the draft.

"Well, I never thought they'd get thee," said Belinda to James Green.

"My wife's dead, now. I should have written—but I didn't like—after having deceived thee so," said he. "Then I heard thy mother had gone, and I wanted to write, but didn't know where to. But if I come back, Belinda—"

"I'll not promise," she said.

"Belinda!"

"No, I'll not promise. Wait till you've seen them French girls—

Pink-tache smiled at the possibility of falling in love with anyone but Belinda.

"I think we should get 'incompatchibility.' How did the dye come out?"

Belinda had to satisfy her curiosity.

"Washed out when I left the dye-works. I'll have to go, now. Good thing I don't leave anybody worrying about me."

That touched Belinda.

"Only me," she said.

"Thanks," said the little man. "Not got a photo of yourself, Belinda?" he asked, wistfully.

"Only one left—of when I was six months old," she said. "But I'll happen get one took, a new one for Reggie."

The whistle blew.

"I'll send parcels —"

Belinda stepped back.

"I'll write—got your address—when I land," said James.

He held out his hand. Belinda came near and took it.

"Belinda—if I come back—"

The tragedy of the man who had lived in lodgings ever since his wife ran away with a policeman, made Belinda compromise. He had been so unlucky all his life. He was almost sure to be killed. He never had any luck:

"We'll see," said Belinda.

All through the summer and half-way into autumn, Belinda toiled here, spending the best part of her wages on the two lads. She was doing her bit, she thought.

Mrs. Pratt's little man went out before Reggie. Mrs. Pratt vowed she would see him off or die in the attempt. Pratt was in panic. He knew what her seeing him off would mean. Some women had fainted on the platform. His wife was capable of jumping on the train, and threatening to go with them. She had worked on a pit-top, and her attitude towards life was therefore pugnacious. Belinda talked to her half one night, without making any impression. Two nights after, Belinda saw Mary Pratt begin to pack up.

"He's persuaded me to go home," she told Belinda, and Belinda wondered what miracle of speech the little man had used.

Pink-tache wrote regularly to Belinda. His letters did not tell much. She sent him letters and parcels.

They were the only ones "Groggy," as they called him, received.

Then came Reggie's turn.

"We're going, Aunt Belinda," he announced, one day.

"No!" protested Belinda, growing pale.

Reggie went home on draft leave, and Annie wrote asking Belinda to see him off—for them. She had no wish to make it harder for him, she wrote. But Belinda knew that she herself could not watch Reggie off without breaking down. She asked Reggie if it would be any easier for him should she see him off.

"If you won't cry," he said.

"I'll come then."

Reggie got a sleeping-out pass and stayed at Belinda's place the last night in Scarborough.

Belinda could not sleep. All night the wind cried round the house.

Suppose Reggie should never come back!

Belinda wilted at the thought.

Suppose Reggie never came back—nor Pink-tache.

She had never really had time for anything warmer than family affection, and Reggie was Belinda's hero. He resembled her more than he did his own mother. She told herself that Reggie must come back, and hid her head, ostrich-like—for the first time of her life.

The hour of Reggie's departure came.

Belinda had made herself eat, so that she would be better able to keep her face straight. Putting on a new hat, in Reggie's honour, she went to face the great ordeal—to watch, without the solace of one tear, the boy of her heart go to meet the terrors of hell.

Even the streets looked strange. Every stone bore, it seemed, dark writings of human pain. Windows looked mysterious. The houses appeared to stand aloof, hugging their thoughts, knowing only their own anguish.

Children laughed in the street. Reggie was once as small as they, and not so long ago.

A flock of sheep went by, a dog yelping at their heels—a heaving mass, afraid, foolish, huddling together, bleating.

"What's the difference between them and us, only we don't bleat?" mused Belinda.

She passed a church where, only a week ago, a sermon had been preached glorifying war. Belinda's soul grew heavy with a great weariness. Pain-born thoughts—echoes of what she had read—the Kaiser's mailed fist, his ambition to ruin England, collided in her mind, and muddled her.

How odd it was that they could not catch the Kaiser!

There!

A band had struck up.

In front of Belinda tripped a flapper, in black velvet tam-o'-shanter.

The band stirred something in Belinda—Adventure, but it died down when she saw the long dreary station wall. She stopped and watched Reggie pass. There was something thrilling in the way they all kept step, marching along, a harmony of action, whatever inward chaos there might be, and that isolation of thought shutting them off from each other.

Reggie had not looked her way.

Belinda boldly took a ticket for the next station and waited. The men came in through the gate, stamped into line, answered the roll.

Reggie was glad to see his aunt. They walked about the platform a while, up and down, down and up, and Belinda warned him against bad women, and drink, and Reggie promised not to forget.

That was Reggie's chance.

"You see that little girl, Aunt," he said, nervously, jerking his head towards the railings, where stood the flapper in the black velvet tam. "That's my girl."

Belinda felt a jealous pang. Reggie was all the world to her—whereas—

"Well, what's she doing out there?" asked Belinda.

She told the girl to get a ticket, and walked about on the platform between them. NO! They repulsed the idea that they wanted to be alone. Belinda must stay with them. Which was in itself balm to Belinda's heart. It meant, too, that Reggie was really serious.

The troop train was filling—it was a signal of farewell.

A middle-aged woman, well-dressed, was led away, tottering.

"Them sort shouldn't come," said Belinda.

"No," agreed Reggie's girl, shakily.

"Sort of sets other folk off," said Belinda, giving her a warning look.

"I'll get in, I think," said Reggie.

The carriage was dark, being yet unlit. The two women stood close by. Reggie looked out of the window. The shadows made his young face look older, longer, gave it a look of her father's face, as she had seen it framed by his coffin.

The whistle sounded.

Reggie came impulsively to the window, reckless of what his mates thought of him.

"Good-bye, Aunt Belinda," he said, with restraint.

Belinda quivered as the young warm mouth touched hers. She saw him glance at his sweetheart, shyly, innocently.

"Go on!" said Belinda, pushing the girl forwards. "Give him one!"

The lovers kissed. Both flashed a grateful look on Belinda. They had kissed under the brooding shadow of the wings of war. The little love story, starting with lemonade and ice-cream, a light word or two, light laughter, was ennobled into something deeper and stronger.

"Good-bye, Lucy," called the lad.

"Good-bye."

Lucy ran away, suddenly, with a cry.

Aunt Belinda struggled against tears—to keep her promise to Reggie. But they burned her heart.

The train moved, then stopped. Aunt Belinda followed it up.

"Good luck, lads! Keep your hearts up, whatever else you do," she called.

The train was moving again. She took out her handkerchief and waved it. The train moved faster. Reggie watched her grow smaller and smaller. She stood a little stiffly, but the handkerchief waved gaily.

"Regular old sport, she is," said one of the lads.

The train took the curve.

Belinda stared after it for half a minute. The whistle, as the train gathered speed, came to her ears like a scream of agony. Tears rushed up to her eyes like a hot geyser.

The girl in the black tammy was waiting for her.

"I couldn't help it," she said, smiling, alluding to her flight.

"Where are you going now?" asked Belinda.

Scarborough had turned into a desert, all at once.

"I'm going home—back to Sparsell," said the pretty girl.

"Come on, we'll have a cup of tea, somewhere," said Belinda. "I'll pay for it," she added, quickly, seeing the girl's change of countenance. The lass was true blue. She had gone "broke" to see Reggie off, and had only her ticket back.

The two sat half an hour in the tea room, talking. Belinda got to know all she wanted to know. The girl was an orphan, in service. She was seventeen, though she looked younger.

"Do you think Reggie's parents will like him —going— with me?" asked Lucy, timidly.

"They'll have a blue-pink canary fit (both of 'em)," she was told, and her eyes filled with tears.

"But before this job is done they may be glad to have him back if he wed Owd Nick," said Belinda. "I'll work the oracle. You'll see how you and Reggie go on—"

"Reggie said he would write and tell his parents," said Lucy. Her hand shook so that she spilled some tea in her saucer.

"Oh, I admire his pluck, then," said Belinda, smiling. "He evidently means business. Well let me know when he has written them, and we'll pay them a visit."

The girl brightened.

"If I can get off—" she added.

Belinda had fallen in love with Reggie's choice.

Lucy Gardener was as fresh and as innocent as a daisy. Her eyes looked like wide-open daisies. But a little hard note crept into her pretty voice as she spoke of "places" she had had. She told Belinda of a terrible experience when she answered an advertisement and arrived only to find the mistress away. She had not liked the look of the husband, and had taken the precaution of barricading herself in, on retiring. The brute-husband had threatened to burst in the door if she did not open it.

"Got out o' the window, I'll bet," guessed Belinda.

"No—he went away at last," smiled Lucy. "I served his breakfast next morning. He said nothing, and I didn't, but I went out and never went back."

"He wanted shooting, he did," was Belinda's remark.

"It was like coming into harbour, when I met Reggie," confessed Lucy, a tear shining on her lashes.

"I'll bet," said Belinda.

She made up her mind that it would not be her fault if Lucy Gardener did not come into Harbour. But she knew it would be another fight with Annie and Jonathan. They hoped big things from Reggie, and he had fallen in love with a "skivvy."

It was amusing to Belinda, but at the moment she did not like the idea of being up against her brother. Perhaps Reggie would forget this little girl.

Belinda said a characteristic thing as she saw Lucy to the station.

"Well, it's all to try for," she said. "And I'm tired of Scarborough, so don't be surprised if you see me—your way."

"Oh!"

The face, shadowed by the tammy, lighted up.

CHAPTER XVIII

The House of Shirts

BELINDA carried out her intention of going to Sparsell. Lucy Gardener had sent her word that a woman, washing shirts for soldiers, needed help. Belinda applied, and received an answer that might have been written with the kitchen poker.

"Plese kum at wonc," it said.

Belinda went. Lucy was at the station to meet her.

"Heard from our Reggie, lately?"

"To-day," said Lucy, with joy.

"How many is that this week?"

"Oh, once besides—and a little note."

Lucy blushed.

It was now Friday. Belinda had been uncertain about coming to Sparsell on a Friday, recalling the old adage that "A Friday flitting is a short sitting."

"I shall have to go back at once," said Lucy. "Mrs. Jones said I must not be more than an hour."

She left Belinda at a farm-gate, half off its hinges.

Belinda's mind was full of pictures of the sea as she had seen it, passing Robin Hood Bay. She thought with joy of the walks she would have along those heights that overhung the sea.

The house she wanted was in darkness. It was like a bad omen. Belinda knocked on the door until her knuckles were sore. Then she heard someone hammering at the back of the house.

"Hello!" she called.

The hammering went on.

Belinda went round, and saw an old man by a rain tub.

"Here, come and hold this," he said, with relief.

"This" was a loose hoop of the rain tub. Belinda held it.

"Are you Mr. Peters?" she asked.

"I'm old Peters. Hold that tight."

He spoke with the quiet patience of one who had been trying to tighten loose things all his life, with small success. Belinda did her best. He went on hammering. In about ten minutes, he said, "Go on. It'll do." Belinda took the hammer and finished it off.

"I'm the skivvy," she announced.

"She wants *skivvy*!" said the old man, patiently. "She's out, trying to get some sugar without coupon."

Belinda stood, wondering what to do. The road outside the gate was now but a glimmer in the darkness.

Old Peters took stock of her.

"You couldn't lend us a bob till she comes back?"

Belinda was taken aback. But she lent him the money.

He set off as though he had been "resurrected," shouting, "Go on in, she'll not be long."

Belinda opened a sort of wicket gate, set inside the front door, and entered the House of Shirts.

Never in her life had she stuck her head inside such a show. She tried to find a chair, but all had bundles on them. Shirts were piled on the table. Shirts hung, dripping, from ropes across the low ceiling—everywhere the odour of wet flannel.

The fire had gone out to look for some coals, thought Belinda. She sought some matches in vain, so sat in the darkness, thinking of No Man's Land—and Reggie, Reggie who had not written her for over a week yet had sent Lucy three letters. Her thought went more kindly towards Pink-tache. He was like her—he had nobody, really.

Belinda heard footsteps and brightened up. She heard a pretty voice swear. The wicket gate, set up as a barrier against cocks and hens, had fallen down.

"And she wonders why I don't come ofter," muttered Anne Peters, hurling the barrier aside.

Belinda thought it better to make her presence known.

"Hello!"

The young woman gave a cry.

"Robert," she said, eagerly.

"It's only me—the skivvy," said Belinda.

"Oh," disappointedly.

Anne lighted the miserable gas. The mantle was broken and all on one side. She looked at the clock.

"But I can't stop," she said. "I've an appointment."

Belinda would have bet on that. She was as pretty as Lucy Gardener, and there was that about her which said she was no daisy. Both were about the same age, with the same cloudiness of hair, brightness of dark eyes, and pale, clear complexion. But how unalike.

"She'll happen not be so long," said Anne. "I'm off."

Belinda sat another hour before Mrs. Peters came in, sighing heavily.

"Where's *he*?" she asked, flopping on a chair, after sweeping the bundles off.

Belinda had only barely had time to introduce herself.

Mrs. Peters lit the gas-jet, calling Mr. Peters a damned old "whilk," and tossed the burnt-out match on the dirty floor. The floor was covered with burnt matches.

"There's been a young woman in," said Belinda.

"Oh, it would be Anne—my daughter," said Mrs. Peters.

She looked too old and too plain to have a girl so young and pretty as Anne.

Anne bounded in just as they were at supper. She warned Belinda with a look. Her appointment with Robert Greenacres was against her parents' wishes.

"I don't know if this 'servant do' will pay or not," said Mrs. Peters, who still had on her head an old black hat, all on one side, like the gas mantle.

"Anne, throw out the tea-pot. He'll be in any time now. Night brings crows home," she sighed.

"The what?" said Anne, pettishly.

"You know what I mean," said her mother, sighing again.

Anne went out.

"But *she's* got a servant," said Mrs. Peters, "and I says to him, ' Well, if *she* can run it, I can'—her across there, I mean. She's a bad woman, a right bad woman. But she's no luck with it, for she's a lass with St. Vitus' Dance, and bad health herself. I'll swear to my dying day she stole my little white hen."

Belinda, feeling that something was expected of her, kept nodding her head.

"Oh, the same old gag," said Anne, impatiently, coming in with the tea-pot. She went out soon afterwards.

"And no talking to them soldiers," shouted her mother.

Belinda could not hear what Anne said in return.

"Nothing but cheek and impudence you get these days," said Mrs. Peters, sighing still. She looked across at Belinda.

"But this village isn't no place for Anne," she said, in a softer, changed voice. "You wouldn't think her father was ever such a big swell, would you?" Her voice changed again. "But it's far back and nearly forgotten, now."

"You don't mean Mr. Peters?" said Belinda.

"She's not his!"

Mrs. Peters smiled at the idea of Anne being Peters' girl.

"No. She's not his. It was before his day. But he's as fond of Anne as if she was his own. Fonder, happen, for if I get a bit hard on her with all this washing and what not, Peters, he says, 'You can't judge Anne, Esther, her with blue blood in her veins. She's up another street.'"

Belinda was nearly asleep.

Hearing Mr. Peters, she made an excuse to go to bed. Mrs. Peters handed her a half-burnt candle, stuck in its own wax, on a broken saucer.

It was a little room with walls that had once been white. There was a flat-looking bed with a little girl in it. Her face, even in slumber, had an old and harassed look that made Belinda sad. She got into bed without disturbing the child.

In the darkness, she lay awake, wondering where her moving tent would next be pitched. In her travels she had learned a lot about human nature, but what good was it? If only she could write like her father! She fell asleep at last, but a flea awakened her. She could not go to sleep again, the wind was howling so, crying around the place, reminding her of the night Reggie went to the war. She had had only two hours' sleep when the alarm went at seven o'clock.

"I didn't know you'd a little girl," said Belinda, as she gave Geraldine her breakfast. What an odd name it was for the tousle-headed bairn! It reminded Belinda of Coleridge's "Christabel." Geraldine was rickety, and always crying.

"She's my sister's girl. Had a misfortune," said Mrs. Peters, sadly. "She's in service. So we took her."

They were a queer mixture of selfishness and generosity, these people.

Weeks ticked on. Shirts and yet more shirts poured in, now that the soldiers found they could get them sooner. The "servant do" was paying.

It was just after Christmas that Anne came into a room Belinda was turning out.

She had seen Belinda's French books.

"Can you tell me what this means?"

Anne held a letter, with two words uncovered, for Belinda to read.

"I think it means "Dear Chicken," said Belinda. "Is he an officer?"

Anne glanced over her shoulder to where her mother was ironing.

She nodded.

"He'll never marry you," said Belinda.

Anne laughed.

"He's told me so," she said.

"Little fool," said Belinda, gently.

Anne's face was calm as wax.

"I love him," she said, tenderly, as if it were a relief to tell someone.

"I wouldn't make myself cheap," Belinda reproached her.

"I'm fond of him," said Anne. "I could work for him, slave for him, for threepence a day and a kind word a year. But he wouldn't marry me—to save my life. I expect you can't understand that."

"I've read about it. But it's beyond me," said Belinda. "Anyhow, it never lasts."

"Who thought it could?"—scornfully.

Anne went out, leaving Belinda in deep thought. She recalled the woman who ran away with the policeman.

"No. Give me a safe investment," she said to herself.

She saw Anne's lover several times. He came once alone. Only Belinda was in the house. She could not help having a smack at him.

"If you'd call that girl a fool instead of a chicken, you'd do her a good turn, and I'd think the better of you," she said.

It was as useless as arguing with the sea.

"She might marry someone in Sparsell," said Belinda. "But all the Sparsell lads is away."

"She can have one when they come back," laughed Greenacres.

"Just because you fancy her—to make her your plaything," reproached Belinda.

"She has me for her plaything," he said. "She'll forget me."

Belinda did not dare to tell the spruce officer what Anne had said. She could not have said it as Anne had. She knew that Anne had not revealed that side of herself to him. He was playing with her, and Anne had given him the idea that she was playing with him. It was one sort of pride.

"Anyhow, we're going out soon," said Greenacres. "So don't worry."

There was many a night when Belinda went out for a breather, and tumbled across Anne and Robert —blind to the world, as Belinda termed it. Anne Peters would walk out with other soldiers, would probably marry one. But all her life, what had been an amusement to the young officer would be to her a haunting memory of bliss forever gone.

Early in the New Year, Greenacres went out.

"Ey, he'll come back," said Belinda to Anne.

"Not to Sparsell. Not to me. We agreed on that. It was the bargain."

Anne had got an hour or two off, and went to see the last of the laughing young officer.

"It's ended now," she told Belinda on her return.

Belinda had never seen such a look on anyone's face.

"There," she said, patting her, "happen he'll think different about it—when he gets out yonder."

Anne shook her head. She saw the tragedy of the life that lay before her—all makeshift, even to the husband she would have.

"His folk are swells," said Anne. "Even if he had cared as I care, he would not have wed me. But he didn't care as I do, so that's the end of it."

When she came down, next morning, Belinda saw that Anne had closed the door on her affair with Greenacres, and had not only closed it, but locked it.

Two months later, a fat, red-faced Corporal, a little sweet on Anne, came for some shirts.

He had known something of Anne's fancy for Greenacres—but not all.

Anne was sitting at the sewing machine, making a new blouse.

"Greenacres has gone under," he said.

Belinda dared not look at Anne, who went on sewing.

When the Corporal had gone, Anne went into the scullery, drew a cup of water, remained some little time, then came back to the machine. That was the last of it.

A week later, she was walking out with a private soldier, a soft-looking lad, who worshipped her.

"I thought it would be the Corporal," said Belinda.

But Anne had taken an unreasoning dislike to him from the moment he told her that Greenacres had gone under.

Reggie's letters, and glimpses of Reggie's sweetheart, were the bright spots in Belinda's life. Then Spring came. Her fears for Reggie grew in intensity as that dreaded date of her dream came near. She would tell herself that it was only a dream—that awful vision she had had of Reggie and mud and blood. But a letter came bearing that date, and Belinda grew hopeful again.

The slight jealousy she had had of Lucy had gone in the fight she had made on their account. Jonathan had asked who this girl was that Reggie wanted them to know, and to love—for his sake. The parents were wild when Belinda explained that Lucy, like herself, was a skivvy, and they reproached her for backing Reggie in such nonsense.

The Great Retreat began.

Letters ceased to come from both Reggie and Pinktache.

Belinda waited. Then she heard from James. But no word came from Reggie. She went to see Lucy, whose pallid look told plainly that she, too, had heard nothing. Weeks went by. Then, one morning, the postman came. He had seen her up at the window, and had waved a letter. She thought he meant it was from France, and ran down to the gate.

It was from Jonathan.

She changed colour as she read.

"He's missing," she murmured.

She leaned against the gate for support.

The old postman looked as sorrowful as if he had been the cause.

"Cheer up," he said, at length.

Belinda went into the house.

"What's up?"

Mrs. Peters ran to Belinda.

"Missing," said Belinda. "It's official."

"Happen he's a prisoner," said Mrs. Peters and offered Belinda a pot of tea.

"They've crossed 'prisoner' out," said Belinda.

"Some is three months before they hear they're prisoners," said Mrs. Peters.

Belinda went on washing shirts.

Little Geraldine could not understand. The child was abnormally dull. But one day she went out and gathered Belinda a few flowers, tied the posy with thread, and brought it to her. That touched Belinda.

Belinda lived for the post.

Every morning, as the old man went by, shaking his head, she began to live for the night post. She kept vigils by that window.

And the news came when she was out, after all.

She was dragging along in the heat of the sun, with a big basket of shirts from the camp, when she saw the old postman waving something and hurrying.

"I've brought it at last," he said, sweat running down his face. "I read it when I saw what it was. He's a prisoner of war in Germany."

Belinda emerged from her nightmare. At least Reggie was alive.

She could have kissed the old postman.

"I like to bring them sort," he said. "Didn't I tell her?"—beaming at Mrs. Peters.

Belinda took full advantage of the panic Reggie's parents had been in, and asked them to let Reggie have the girl of his heart, when he came back to them safe and sound. Other folk, she reminded them, had lads who would not come back.

They replied. Belinda and Lucy went over to Syke Gate, and Annie admitted that Lucy was a nice girl.

Meanwhile, Reggie, behind the German lines, was one of an army of ghost-like, famishing men—rummaging refuse-heaps for scraps of food, almost too weak to stand, chaotic fancies in his brain, hatred seething for the first time in his young heart. One picture and one picture alone, stood out to sustain him. A rigid figure, a face wearing the mask of a brave smile—Aunt Belinda, on the platform, waving her old nose-rag, and shouting, "Keep your hearts up, lads!" Whilst every day, some bullied and famished prisoner, unable to keep his heart up any longer—died.

CHAPTER XIX

"Peace"

BELINDA decided to leave Sparsell, when she saw the first may-blossom out in the lanes. She had stayed much longer than she could have thought possible, for the whole atmosphere of the House of Shirts had dragged her down, mentally and physically. Only the feeling that she was doing something for the comfort of the Tommies had kept her up so long. But when she had to rest six times on the way to the camp with the basket of shirts, Belinda realized that she would have either to go or become really ill. She could not afford the luxury of an illness, so decided to quit. Mrs. Peters seemed a little disturbed at that, but it was only because she thought the woman across would crow about it.

Belinda had been used to a hand-to-mouth existence. But the House of Shirts, in her own language, took the cake. Everybody in that house thought only of themselves. Anne, dodging and deceiving, thought only of her own ends. Mr. Peters, consistent and insistent in his appeal for sixpences, was the same. Mrs. Peters, keeping apart, spoke of "her money," and allowed her husband no share in her shirt-washing prosperity. Even little Geraldine partook of the same spirit, from example. Belinda caught herself, at times, doing the same.

Yet, sordid and selfish as the spirit of the place had been, she had learned that one cannot judge the hearts of people from the outward seeming of their lives. Mrs.

Peters, weeping tears of joy at a rumour that the war was over, was not the Mrs. Peters that refused the old man the price of a drink. Anne, weeping in secret when she heard that Greenacres had been killed, was an Anne with possibilities.

Belinda packed up, got out the old familiar labels. She had ennobling memories to take away with her, besides the cargo of depression that had made her feel so unlike herself. When she had got away, she knew that she would recall only the pleasant things about the place, or recall the unpleasant with an indulgent smile. She would recall Mrs. Peters, ironing in her hat; the way the sun came in on the red tiles of the floor making a shadow of the window frames; the cupboard-love of little Geraldine; and the beauty of the orchard at all hours, despite the shirts that hung there.

So Belinda gave Mr. Peters the "last" shilling. He stood to watch her go, with genuine regret—by the rain tub, the place where they had first met.

Belinda went to Syke Gate and stayed with Jonathan, at his request, until she had found an easier place. It was now the middle of June. Reggie had been a prisoner of war since the second of April. Belinda, despite all advice, continued to write letters to Limburg a/d Lahn, though Reggie never mentioned receiving them.

Belinda heard things that fed her anxiety.

"After all, they can't feed him well, when we're blockading them," said Jonathan, a little morosely. "We're starving them, and they'll have to starve Reggie."'

"They could let him have the parcels that's been sent," whimpered Annie, who looked ill.

It was all bewildering to Belinda, but she thought Reggie might only be going a little short.

How they would feed him up when he came home!

"This sounds a nice place, Belinda," said Annie, one morning. Then, quickly, "But don't think we want to get rid of you."

It was over the morning paper.

"Read it out," said Belinda.

"Wanted, elderly woman, for light housework."

"Elderly!" exclaimed Belinda, with a grimace.

"Well, what do you call yourself?" asked Annie, smiling.

"Not a day more than twenty-one—if the War was over," Belinda said. "But go on."

"No washing—"

"Hooray!"

Like a certain brand of cleanser, Belinda would not, if she could help it, wash clothes. She felt that she had washed enough for a lifetime, during the last six months.

"Charwoman on Fridays—" continued Annie. "Now, you'd get a rest there. And, really, Belinda, you look tired."

"I am, a bit," confessed Belinda, grudgingly. "But then, we haven't to be weary of well-doing. And them shirts needed washing."

"Good reader preferred—" said Annie.

That did it.

"You'll have a daisy of a life," Jonathan told his sister. But Belinda recalled Mrs. Bairns.

Stanley House, Merton, nr. Branswo rth.

Belinda wondered, as she set out, if ever she would be able to get to the meetings of the Poets. But Merton might be ten miles away. She turned down the warm hope.

It was a very small place, and Belinda had trouble in finding the house, the words *Stanley House* being in dark paint over the fanlight.

When she found it, a man of about thirty answered her knock.

"Are you Miss Higgins?" he asked.

"That's me," said Belinda, smiling.

"Mother," he called.

A woman of some sixty years came out of a front room. The young man went off upstairs, whistling, and left the two women together. Mrs. Bevale was a woman who must have been very pretty in her youth. She asked Belinda a few questions, glanced at the two testimonials, and said, "We are just two of a family at present, myself and son. The wages are thirty pounds a year. Perhaps you will find it a little dull in Merton. But the town is only two miles away."

"That'll do me," said Belinda, warmed at the very thought of being so near Bransworth.

It was a very homely, unpretentious house into which Belinda had come, so far as its outward appearance went. It was furnished quietly, too.

"You'll find the bathroom on the left of the big window on the landing," said Mrs. Bevale, that evening.

Belinda received a shock.

She recalled the wash-house in which herself and another maid used to keep guard on each other, whilst having a dip, neither bolt nor bar being on the door.

"Where do I feed?" inquired Belinda, fancying that she had been treated merely as a visitor, getting her whereabouts.

"You will dine with us," said Mrs. Bevale, surprised. "But, perhaps, you would prefer your own kitchen?"

"Not me!" said Belinda.

She had dined with the Freebootles down in the basement of that London boarding-house. But the Freebootles had appeared little more than menials themselves. It had not counted the same. Here were people of evident refinement, who took it for granted that the domestic dine as one of the family!

"May I ask where your other son is, ma'am?"

Belinda asked this, with respectful friendliness. George Bevale was upstairs reading. Belinda had seen him take a book up.

"I have two sons besides George," said Mrs. Bevale. "Albert is in France. He enlisted the first year."

"And he's never been hurt?"

Belinda put the question with wide eyes.

"He has had several narrow escapes," said Mrs. Bevale, busy at her knitting. "But his body escaped injury."

Belinda noticed the peculiarity of the remark.

"Oh—I dare say they see a lot as hurts their minds," she said.

"He went from the highest of motives."

It seemed to Belinda that her new mistress found it a comfort to talk to someone.

"Yes," she said, surveying her work. "He went because he felt it to be his duty. Even Allan could see the splendour of it—though they look at things from entirely different planes."

"Is that your other son?"

Mrs. Bevale nodded.

Belinda, fresh from her bath, was kneeling on the fender, shaking her hair by the fire. Her eyes shone as she looked at Mrs. Bevale, through the tangled hair. Belinda made it easy for the mother to open her heart.

"And where's Allan?" asked Belinda, innocently.

Mrs. Bevale spoke with pride.

"Allan is in prison."

The hair brush clattered as it fell from Belinda's hand.

"In prison?"

"He is a conscientious objector, though, being an unpaid preacher, he could have escaped military service. But he would not appeal on those grounds."

Belinda was certainly taken aback.

She had not a good opinion of "Conchies" or what she knew of them, through the Press.

"I thought it better to tell you. Our last domestic could not bear the sneering she had to put up with, because she lived with us."

"Oh!"

Belinda picked up the hair brush and brushed her hair meditatively.

"If they sneer at me," she said, after a pause, "I'll pull their hair out."

Which rather took Mrs. Bevale back.

Belinda was certainly no pacifist.

She showed Belinda a picture of her son who was in prison. He had a broad, fleshy forehead, dark, soft, earnest-looking eyes, a mouth as fine as any woman's. Nothing weak nor fanatical about him. Despite the impression of gentleness, the photograph showed a man who would die rather than become a mush of concession.

"I consider," said Mrs. Bevale, "that both my sons are soldiers. Some say they are fighting against each other. But both are doing their duty, as they see it. It is enough."

She had a rare serenity and human warmth. In the days that followed, Belinda found that Mrs. Bevale's Christ was He who walked with poor fishermen of Galilee and frequented lazar-houses, and taught by parable. The Bevales were poor. They could not be otherwise, being Christians, trying to live in Merton according to the Sermon on the Mount. Around them tossed a sea of calumny, malice, hatred—they had a son who would not kill. They persisted in patronizing the store of a naturalized German woman, married to an Englishman thirty-odd years ago—a woman who, long before war was thought of, had been the good Samaritan to the poor of Merton. But she was a German. It was enough.

Belinda soon became conscious that women were eyeing her askance.

She was at the greengrocer's cart.

"There's some in this street ought to have to go," said a woman, glancing at Belinda. That was George.

Belinda took up the gauntlet. She was not going to have other folks' opinions tacked on to her.

"Mean me?" queried Belinda, pleasantly.

The neighbour was puzzled.

"I've just been looking at them arms o' thine," said Belinda, "and thinking thee and me wouldn't look amiss in a bayonet charge. Anyhow, them as shouts so hard for other folk to have to go, ought to have a lick at it themselves. Why don't you go?"

Belinda held the woman's eye glued fast to hers. The woman turned livid.

"They wouldn't have me," she said.

"Them Russian women managed to get there," said Belinda. "I can admire them. But it gets my hump up to hear a lot o' women screaming for all the chaps to go, and sheltering at the back of a lot o' little lads. Go an' join the W.A.A.C's.

Even the greengrocer laughed, and that cost him a customer. The woman left, boiling with rage.

"All *hers* are lasses," one whispered.

"Ten pound o' potatoes," Belinda ordered.

"But for all that, there is some in this street as fit to go as mine," said a nice little woman.

"Do you mean George Bevale?" asked Belinda.

"Well, we can't help but think—" said another.

"He'd have gone long since, but he's only one lung," said Belinda. "They wouldn't have him. He's tried both army and navy."

Evidently that was a bomb.

"And anyhow," went on Belinda. "Do you think you'll put a fire out with chucking coals on?"

She then whizzed into the house.

"Yon's a cough-drop," said the greengrocer.

Belinda got a letter from the man with the pink moustache. He was to be invalided home. He would write again. There was something about him that touched Belinda. She was glad he was out of it.

Allan fell ill, and Mrs. Bevale went away for two or three days to visit him. George went away, too, on a walking tour, having, on account of his health, been spared from his work as a clerk. So Belinda was alone in the little house.

She was reading in the dusk and felt lonely. It was so long since she had been in a house alone. The reading-spell broke. People she had met began to wander through her mind.

How was Bill Greenwood going on? She had been very fond of Bill, she admitted, reluctantly. And Rupert and Eddie, the Scarborough lads— where were they? She sat thinking and brooding on the War until midnight, then crept upstairs, almost nervously. The house seemed so empty. She wondered if she should say "Yes" should Pink-tache propose to her. Then she laughed, though she felt that the companionship of a human being was a very precious thing.

Belinda awoke late in the morning. She was out of bed at once, and downstairs into the passage, and back again to bed with her letters. There was one for Mrs. Bevale. O.H.M.S. That hit Belinda in the eye. Whatever could it be! Belinda could not wire, having no address to wire to. It would have to wait. It worried her. Perhaps Albert Bevale—

There was one from Jonathan saying that the address she was sending Reggie's parcels to was no good. Belinda's heart sank.

That morning, she set out for Bransworth, having recalled that the Poets met on the first Tuesday in the month. She bought a book she thought would make Pink-tache laugh.

Evening found her hurrying to the room where the Poets held their meetings. She bumped into a perambulator. The impact made her almost sick. She stared into the face of a young woman in black.

"Why—Mrs. Greenwood!"

It was Bill's wife.

"How is he?" asked Belinda at once.

"Killed," said Dorothy.

"Not—Bill —" protested Belinda.

"It's true," said the other. "In that retreat. Oh, it's true. Official. They are going to change the allowance to pension money. So they must be sure."

Belinda could not believe it.

There's been lots turned up," she said, hopefully. "And the kid," she added.

"He's never seen him," sadly.

"What are you doing here?" asked Belinda.

She was still dazed. Yes. She knew now she had been very fond of Bill.

"I'm back with my parents. It's cheaper."

"And Mrs. Greenwood?" asked Belinda.

"She's alone."

Belinda guessed that Dorothy and Bill's mother had not got on well.

"Here—take this for the child," said Belinda. "Go on—buy him something to wear. Ey, all my family's under my hat. Take it."

It was a crown.

Dorothy took it. Belinda kissed Bill's child, and walked away a little unsteadily. She did not go to the meeting of the Poets after all, but took a car-ride, then walked on to their old street in the old town. It was a long walk and late when she got to Mrs. Greenwood's. A light was burning, so Belinda knocked. Slow steps came, and the old woman opened the door. The light from the kitchen streamed on Belinda, with her understanding, sorrowful look.

"Ey, Belinda, Belinda!" said Mrs. Greenwood, and fell a-sobbing. "Come in, come in."

"I'll have to stay the night," said Belinda.

"Tha mun," said the old woman.

They sat up talking until two o'clock, talking of Bill most of the time, of Bill in all the stages of his life, from babyhood to the days when he played the tin-whistle, and of when he had fallen in love with Belinda.

"I found that out because he never grumbled at the noises you made—music, I mean," said Mrs. Greenwood. "Ey, tha should have had our Bill!"

Belinda praised the baby, said how like Bill it was. Mrs. Greenwood had not seen the baby.

"She went right into black, as soon as she knew," complained the old woman. "No. I haven't gone into black. I believe our Bill 'll happen come back yet—I do—Belinda. I can't give him up."

Belinda took the work-worn hands and pressed them.

"It's harder for you than for anybody else to do that. But if he doesn't—he'd like you to be right with Dorothy, you know, and see his little child."

"If she'd only give it to me!" sobbed the old woman.

"But you couldn't expect her to do that," said Belinda. "Could you have given Bill away when he was a baby?"

"No," sobbed the old woman.

Walking back, next morning, Belinda saw the first wild roses of the year—the red for Lancashire, the white for York. She took hope. War between nations would cease as war between Houses had ceased. Some day the banners would all be furled, the spears drop to dust, and the blossoms of Peace litter the ways of the whole world. But that did not alter the fact that Bill was dead. The man who had killed him might never have seen him.

It had been raining in the night. A light wind stirred the leaves above her head, and shook raindrops on Belinda's face. They were like tears. A deep sorrow was in her heart, not the wild grief of passion, but a deeper hurt. The earth was poorer for Bill's loss. Belinda was poorer. She pictured the German firing—the beast, she thought, but faltered, recalling that Bill must have killed Germans, that away in the German country a mother was perhaps clinging to the piteous hope that her lad would turn up.

At Stanley House, Belinda found a letter from Reggie, and opened it eagerly. Reggie had been ill. He asked for some little puppy biscuits to be put in his parcels. That gave Belinda a shock. Dog biscuits!

Mrs. Bevale bore it like a Spartan when she returned to learn that her son, Corporal Bevale, was wounded and missing. She had two great comforts. Her son had gone out, quite prepared to die, if necessary. And Mrs. Bevale held that this life is only the ante-room to the next.

"And Allan?" asked Belinda.

"They have moved him to a hospital. He has been out once before, in a camp, but he went speaking to the men, still fighting for what he believed —and—they sent him back to jail." There was a short silence, then Mrs. Bevale, wiping a tear that would come in spite of her, said: "This will be a sore blow to George."

It was.

When George heard, he sat down and cried like a little child, and Belinda had to sneak into the scullery to wipe her own eyes.

For weeks did Mrs. Bevale wait for news of her missing son. Then she got a letter from a man who said he had seen Allan—dead. Himself wounded, he had not been able to write to her before.

The War Office letter "Presumed Dead" would follow in due course, concluded Mrs. Bevale. She let go of hope at once. Willing to accept the best if it should come, she faced the worst. But Belinda, at the greengrocer's cart, heard the woman whose children were all girls say something about “conchies “ one day. Belinda knew that Allan Bevale might be killed by inches, but would not himself kill. Belinda resented the implication that a conscientious objector was a coward.

“I can stand conscientious objectors,” said Belinda. “What I can’t stand is them unconscientious objectors. What is your soapy husband doing? Driving anybody there—to save his own skin! Bits o’ lads, like two laths put together, can go and defend him—and him wi’ a armlet on, too, an’ appealing, every time up.”

“I don’t believe you’ve anybody there,” said the woman.

Belinda smiled.

“You ought to be there yourself!” cried the infuriated woman.

“Don’t worry!” said Belinda. “I know it. All us that can tolerate it for them, ought to be there. Never mind our sex. I’m as good as a fellow any day in the week. It makes me sick to think o’ sheltering at the back of a lot o’ chaps.”

“It can’t last long, now,” said the little woman who had lads there.

“I hope I didn’t hurt your feelings,” Belinda said.

The little woman smiled.

“No. She wants telling off. He helped to drive mine there,” she said.

Sunday morning it was, when Belinda heard another rumour that the war was over. She almost ran from Merton to Bransworth to learn the real truth.

She walked back—shaking her head on seeing Mrs. Bevale.

“False alarm,” said Belinda. Her voice gave way.

But the glorious truth came at last. The Armistice had been signed. Belinda had said at Sparsell that she would dance on the table when peace was declared. But it did not take her that way, now. Her heart grew lighter, easier. The sunlight seemed cleaner. She saw the paint removed from the street lamps. Reggie would now come home. But many would not. Belinda felt, too humbly grateful to dance.

Then came a letter.

Reggie had been one of the first to reach the British lines. Many had perished on the march. He wrote from a hospital in London, and poured out the thoughts of his young soul—telling Belinda all he had not dared to put into those letters sent from the prison-camps. He had been thrashed for darting out for bread thrown to them by the Belgians. He had seen wounded Tommies driven mad by the vermin in their wounds. He gave a picture of a hell where famished and verminous men had degenerated into beasts, tearing at each other for scraps of food. Belinda saw it all —through Reggie's eyes—that tattered army of ghostlike men, too weak and demoralized even to retaliate against the brutal guards.

Belinda went nearly crazy as she sat over that letter. She wanted a sword, though Peace was declared. Her judgment was gone. All that she knew was that men who could thrash hungry-eyed ghosts, sick men, were not fit to live, and Belinda wanted to kill them with her own hands. She could have forgiven them putting Reggie against a wall and shooting him outright. But this torture—

She held the letter with shaking hands.

"I have lain awake in the dark, shaking with hate and rage, wishing I was back in the firing line, to mow them down like grass."

Jonathan wrote asking Belinda if she could go to see Reggie, as Annie was ill. The excitement had overcome her.

It was a savage that went up to London to see Reggie. Belinda spoke to no one in the train. She sat brooding over Reggie's letter—her heart a live coal of hatred.

She reached the great hospital, climbed mountains of steps, saw blue-garbed soldiers walking about, cheerful, back in Blighty, hating no one. Then she remembered that she had left the special parcel in the train.

A nurse sat at a little table, in Reggie's ward.

"Reginald Higgins—oh, I'm sorry —-"

"Is he dead?" asked Belinda, paling.

The nurse smiled and shook her head.

"No. You should have got a wire that he was being moved."

Belinda took the next train North—to Warrington, after being assured that Reggie was not consumptive, as had been thought when he came in.

Belinda travelled all night. Her rage was gone—her strength had gone. The darkness and the booming of fog signals depressed her unutterably. It was a world in which there was more cruelty than ever she had dreamed of. Her own bloodthirsty longings had been a revelation. The fire of her wrath had gone out, leaving the dull smoke of disillusionment—terror, fear. There was nothing to rebuild on, when human beings could treat each other so—when folk could feel as she had felt. It seemed to her that she had now blood on her hands. Chaotic pictures jumbled and jostled in Belinda's mind—live men snatching food from dying men; famished ghosts of men prowling ceaselessly for refuse, putrid, raw, stinking; lucky men, with the accumulated parcels of months, lugging them around, so terrified of going hungry again that they would not part with a crumb, even to a comrade in misery, decivilized, bestialized.

Daylight came at length. Belinda had found a companion, a young girl of seventeen, going North to see a shell-shocked uncle, her mother's brother. They were going to the same hospital.

"We'll have a wash and a cup of tea before we go to the hospital," said Belinda.

The girl reddened.

"I've no money. Mother didn't know how far Warrington was. She can't read nor write."

"We don't even know our geography," mused Belinda. "No wonder we have wars."

After breakfast they went to the hospital and Belinda did not see her new friend again.

With a beating heart, Belinda went along the aisles in Reggie's ward. She heard bravely suppressed groans, a sudden scream now and then, that made her tremble. Most of the men looked cheerful. But here was the agony that had cried aloud on the battlefields.

A pretty nurse came to Belinda.

"That will be your nephew," she said.

Reggie was not in bed, but sitting by the side of another man, who was laughing heartily.

When he saw Belinda, he got up and went to meet her. He took her into another room. Neither spoke for a time. Reggie broke the silence. "How long are you staying?"

"As long as tha wants me to stop," said Belinda.

He coughed sometimes. She would not have known him. He had changed. He stared on the floor. The nurses told her, afterwards, that, when he came in at first, he jumped if anyone spoke to him. He could not quite realize that he was back, where there was nothing to fear, nothing to hate.

Belinda found lodging at a farmhouse, down a twisting, rutted lane. Reggie got permission to go out with her, for an hour, just one hour, that evening. He walked with her down to the farm. Everything was black with night, save the water-gleam in the ruts.

Reggie stopped suddenly beside a gate. Belinda stopped too.

“I can’t feel anything, yet,” he said, apologetically.

“I know,” said Belinda, recalling her own numbness of unbelief.

“Good-night, lad,” she said, at length.

She kissed him, and walked a dozen steps. Then she ran back to him again, splashing through a pool.

“I don’t like leaving thee,” she said.

Reggie laughed.

The next morning, Belinda took piles of sweets to the hospital. They disappeared like magic.

“Tha’ll be sick, Reggie,” said Belinda, scared.

“We just eat and eat and eat,” explained Reggie.

Belinda understood why they did not let prisoners come home at once.

They often sat on a little bench in one of the red-carpeted corridors—Belinda stayed three days— and she got Reggie to tell her all about his life over there. He was reluctant at first. But when he began, it became like an actual experience—Belinda also walked, a ghost amongst ghosts; lay trembling, nightly, on cold damp flags, packed with hundreds of others, reeking of dysentery. Her heart softened, warmed, when she heard of the brave Belgian women who flung bread to the tattered Tommies—she laughed shakily to hear of the woman, the tiny hunchback woman, who stuck out her tongue at the guard as she banged the door in his face. Her eyes filled with tears as she heard of the Belgian women standing weeping as the ghosts dragged past.

“They couldn’t be all alike—all them guards, Reggie?” she asked.

Reggie’s face was hard.

“All I met—but one,” said he.

“Bless him!” cried Belinda.

Her own hate was gone. Never would she forget its fire. But the smoke of it, the sad, dreary sense of having been as cruel as the cruellest Prussian, though only for twenty-four hours, lingered a long time.

Reggie was home for Christmas Day. Mrs. Bevale gave Belinda a holiday. She had heard nothing more of her son. George had asked Belinda not to tell his mother of what Reggie had said about the wounded.

Lucy arrived for Christmas, too.

During the Christmas Eve, Belinda was out shopping. A man in khaki tapped her on the shoulder.

"I've been to your house," he said.

"Pink-tache!" exclaimed Belinda. "Turned up—like a bad shilling."

"H-m!"

Pink-tache said it in a new sort of way.

Belinda stared at him.

"Too many folk about here. We can't talk," he asserted.

"What's to stop us?" she asked.

She gave a half-startled cry. He could not tell if she had blushed. She had on a hat which someone had given her, and it shadowed her face, which was thinner, older—the war-look battling with the old valiant, cheerful smile.

"Turned up—like a bad shilling," was Belinda's greeting.

"Ay."

They talked a little while.

Belinda stamped her feet to demonstrate that her feet were cold.

"Come on. Let's walk a bit."

"Here, don't get hold o' my arm—"

"But I'm hold!" Pink-tache told her.

"You can't shake me off—in the main street," he added.

There was a new note in his voice.

It had lost its hesitancy.

"Tha wants to get them rags off," Belinda told him, making the best of it—and walking on. "It makes me feel I'm walking out wi' a soldier."

“Are we walking out?” asked Pink-tache, quietly. “Are we—Belinda?”

“Hanover! I did not mean that,” she said. He saw the blush now—by a window which has cast its dark blinds.

“No—*but are we*?”

“How do I know?” fenced Belinda.

“Under all the bunkum, Belinda, tha'rt just the same old—*Eve*,” Pink-tache told her.

“Happen. Made to match some old Adam!”

“It's a starry night for a ramble among the bush and bramble,” sang Pink-tache.

“But there's some pork-pies in this bag—and they're waiting for 'em,” Belinda told him.

“Let 'em wait!” Pink-tache told her. “I've been waitin' longer nor they'll wait. Just till we can see the fields, Belinda—then I'll say Good-neet.”

So they walked on.

They reached the stile he had noticed some hours before. Belinda was passing through—when he checked her.

“Did ta ever think about me, Belinda—out yonder?” He held her—and his hand pointed somewhere—towards a dark mass of piled clouds, which looked like fighting men—plunging horses—and titanic demons—and chaos all at once.

“Sometimes,” Belinda told him. Then, “Let go my hand.”

“But—I'm hold!” he told her. “Tha doesn't want me to let go, Belinda!”

“It kept me up—all the time. But I don't want to be taken—out o' pity. She's dead.”

“I heard,” Belinda murmured.

“Not—for pity,” he continued. “Out yonder, we learned to do without it. It's killed a lot o' men, Belinda. It's made devils of a lot that's come back. But, it made a man o' *me.* I've learned to fight, Belinda—and—I'd like to think I could fight for thee, here, at home, same as I thought at first—I were fighting for thee—out yonder."

Belinda peered at him.

"I know it. There'll be as much to fight here, now it's over, as there were there—out yonder."

"Till all the wars is over," he told her, out of the silence. "Till everybody's happy, Belinda. Till there isn't one lot allus trampling t'others down under their heels. Till there's real peace, Belinda. So—what is it to be?"

He kept his hold of her hand—the work-grained hand that trembled a litte now.

"Did ta like me a little bit, Belinda?"

"Happen."

"How much?"

"These pies'll be frozen," she told him.

He took his courage in both arms.

Belinda gave a little cry, then she gave him a push.

"Tha great noodle!" she told him.

The noodle laughed.

He knew he had won.

She handed him the bag and the pork-pies to carry, and from the heights above them they heard voices singing, with that ethereal beauty which comes from the many distances, "How beautiful upon the mountains are the feet."

"There'll be no peace in our time," said the man with the bag. "But happen—if we fight hard —in somebody's time. Tha'll make a good General —Belinda."

She thought he was suffering from war-shock. But now she understands. And they fight side by side—but in the quiet hours, they still "follow the poets" —and wonder that the world is so far removed from the dreams of the bards, even whilst they do "their bit" to make it nearer to *Their Hearts' Desire.*

Printed in April 2022
by Rotomail Italia S.p.A., Vignate (MI) - Italy